A
DUKE FOR
Adela

MEARA
PLATT

CHAPTER 1

London, England
May 1824

AMBROSE THORNE, SEVENTH Duke of Huntsford, had been brazenly approached by young women all of his life. In fact, everywhere he turned, young hopefuls would pop up in front of him, sometimes dropping a handkerchief to gain his attention, other times swooning at his feet, or on occasion dispensing with such ruses and openly propositioning him. But until this moment, he had never – not ever in his entire life – been bodily tackled and brought down flat on his back amid bleached skulls and ancient bones on public display.

His head was reeling and shoulder ached from the tumble he had just taken in the Huntsford Academy's newly opened exhibition hall. It was located across the street from the British Museum and ought to have attracted an elegantly academic crowd.

But the mad young woman with dazzling eyes and kissable lips now sitting atop him was no such thing.

Whatever possessed her to fling herself at him?

"Botheration!" she cried, her knee missing his privates by a hair's breadth as she attempted to scramble to her feet and dart away.

"Oh, no you don't." He grabbed the girl's ankle to hold her

fast. He'd had quite enough of these brazen debutantes making free with him.

"Let go of me, you idiot! Can you not see that despicable toad is getting away?" She tried to jerk her leg free of his grip. But she had just called him an idiot and he was not about to let her get away with that. "What are you doing? I am not the culprit, you nitwit!"

After a moment, she emitted a soft cry of frustration and stopped struggling. Instead, she cupped her hands to her mouth and shouted across the hall, "Thomas Runyon, you sneaky thief! I'll report you to the Duke of Huntsford! You won't get away with it!"

Ambrose, who happened to be the duke in question, rolled to his feet and now exchanged his grasp on her surprisingly shapely ankle for a grip of her hand. "Come with me," he said with a low growl, his voice laced with as much authority as he could muster after she had flattened him in front of a throng of startled onlookers who were still gawking at them.

Without giving her the chance to protest, he dragged her out of the exhibition hall and up the stairs into the chairman's private office. Her pretty lips did not stop moving the entire time. "You nitwit," she called him again, obviously having a fondness for that insult. In addition, she repeated her conviction that he was the biggest idiot alive.

After slamming the door shut behind them, he plunked her down in one of the soft leather chairs. "Now," he said, his voice laced not only with authority but with barely leashed fury as he placed his hands on the armrests to keep her trapped between his arms. "Who are you? And what were you doing charging down the exhibit halls like a rampaging bull? Do you not realize you might have destroyed valuable artifacts?"

"I never would! No one appreciates these relics more than I!" Her slate blue eyes blazed magnificently and her equally magnificent dark curls were on the verge of coming undone. He tried not to compare her hair to dark silk, but he could not ignore the fact that her mane appeared surprisingly soft and lush.

If he weren't on the verge of throttling the impudent girl, he might enjoy running his fingers through that massive pile. It was precariously perched and threatened to tumble in gorgeous waves if he blew on it with a single breath.

"Who are *you*?" she shot back, looking angry enough to pound her fist into his midsection. To his good fortune, she was not quite as bloodthirsty as first appeared. Perhaps she was afraid of him and not about to rile him further, especially since she was trapped in his office alone with him. "How did *you* appear out of nowhere like a block of granite?"

No, this young lady was no shrinking violet.

Indeed, although she was small and shapely, she was also full of determination. The sort who could knock him over while running at full tilt despite her diminutive size. Well, she was of average height and rather slender except in her bosom. Yes, her chest was another magnificent attribute of hers, especially as it was now heaving. "Thanks to you," she said with marvelous indignation, "that no-good, plagiarist lizard, Thomas Runyon, has just stolen my latest research findings. Months of work lost! Now he will claim it for his own...and it is all your fault."

"In what way, shape, or form is it my fault? I've never heard of either of you until this moment. And since you seem to know the identity of this so-called thief, he is hardly likely to get away with whatever it is he took from you. What's your name?"

"What's yours?"

"Huntsford."

She stared at him a long moment, and then swallowed hard as understanding dawned. "As in His Grace? The Duke of Huntsford?"

He nodded. "One and the same. Must I ask for yours again?"

She held out her hand as though he was supposed to shake it...or kiss it...or, it struck him that he would rather kiss her lips.

Lord, they were pretty.

She would probably bite him if he tried.

"My name is Miss Adela Swift." She dropped her hand to her side when he did not reach for it. "Obviously, thanks to your meddling, I was not *swift* enough to catch that crook."

He shook his head as though not hearing right. Was she still berating him? Even now that she knew he was the Duke of Huntsford? He ought to have been outraged. Instead, he threw his head back and laughed.

The girl was priceless.

Completely clueless and befogged.

It pleased him that she cared not a whit for his status.

"You've called me meddlesome, an idiot, a nitwit, and countless other insults. You do realize I could have you banned from this exhibition hall for the rest of your life." He wasn't going to do it, of course. People who spoke honestly to him were rare and not to be lightly dismissed.

She appeared shocked. "But I am a scientist! Well, more of an amateur archeologist, to be precise. I know my ancient bones and the significance they represent. In fact, I have made some important finds and–"

He groaned.

Dear heaven, spare me.

A bluestocking.

She had the look of one, too. Atrocious clothes. Upswept curls that were more likely to have pencils stuck in them than pretty hair clips. Intelligent eyes.

Yes, he quite liked her eyes that were rather a remarkable shade of blue softened by swirls of gray that added a beautiful depth to them.

Her scent was that of chestnuts warmed on an open fire, rich and sweet when licked off the tongue, soft and delicious to the bite.

Not that he intended to bite into this bluestocking, but he would not mind nuzzling the slender curve of her neck.

"You would ban me from your exhibit hall for chasing a thief?" she asked in utter disbelief. "Where is the justice in that? Um…you do not strike me as an unreasonable fellow, Your Grace. Quite the opposite, your museum has been designed not only with great care and thought, but with obvious love of science. Particularly that of archeology. Your research library is far better than the public one in the Royal Society, and more than equal to their secret private library."

He sighed and eased away, now settling his large frame in the chair beside hers. "It cannot be much of a secret if you are openly talking about it. Have you seen their private library?"

She nodded.

"Did you break into that, as well?"

She inhaled sharply. "I beg your pardon? I am not the thief here."

"Is that so? The Royal Society Fellows never allow women inside their inner chambers. How did you get in?"

"The Duke of Lotheil gave me a private tour. He and I are kindred spirits when it comes to fossilized bones."

He laughed again, for there was more to the remarkable Miss Adela Swift than met the eye. "You know Lotheil?"

She nodded. "I am very good friends with the Farthingale sisters. Lily Farthingale is married to the duke's grandson. But I am closest to Laurel and Daisy, who are Lily's sisters, and I am also well acquainted with Daisy's sister-in-law, the former Miss Viola Ruskin. She recently married Viscount Ardley. It is through Viola that I met them all. Do you know their husbands?"

"Quite well. We fought together on the Continent against Napoleon's forces."

"You do have the look of a warrior," she remarked. "You are awfully big for a duke."

"I did not realize we came in regulated sizes."

"I only meant that you do not look like a vain and pampered popinjay. Forgive me for knocking you over. I must have caught you completely unaware or else I would have bounced off you and gone flying. Please do not ban me from the Huntsford Academy. I shall be bereft if you do."

He could have given the girl a hard time, but did not have the heart to do it. Her big eyes were shimmering and he feared she might start to cry. "You are not banned," he said with a resigned sigh. "Do you wish for my help in bringing this Runyon fellow to task?"

"You would help me?" She stared at him in an obvious confusion mixed with a good dose of hopefulness. "Thank you. Yes, I would. Not only for my sake, but for yours. He also ran off with one of the Huntsford Academy's rare books, although he will probably return it once he realizes what it is he has accidentally purloined. He is too much of a coward to ever dare take you on. But I am merely a woman and not likely to be believed or listened to, so he will walk all over me."

"No, he won't. I will not let him." If this girl was telling him the truth – and there was something in her demeanor that made him believe her – this Runyon character was the sort of fellow who deserved a comeuppance. He felt this way not only for the man's disregard of scientific truth, but also for his pettiness in treating the weaker sex with such arrogant disdain. Not that this girl appeared weak at all, but the odds were stacked against her since men made up the rules of play.

Miss Swift cast him a dazzling smile. "I think I am going to like you, Your Grace. I am sorry we got off to such a bad start. But you really are a good egg."

He was going to laugh again.

He had never received such an odd compliment. Women did not describe him as a good egg. Big. Fearsome. Handsome. But never an egg. "Where do you reside, Miss Swift? I'll need to contact you once I retrieve your research papers."

"I am presently staying with Lady Eloise Dayne at Number 5 Chipping Way in Mayfair. I will happily show you any of my other work. I have a trunk full of notes and sketches of my findings on cave drawings my friends and I discovered in Devonshire. They are similar to the drawings found in the Lyme Regis caves in Dorset and those discovered in France."

Her eyes lit up as she took in a light breath and continued. "I also think I have figured out what those mysterious dots and lines found alongside all of those drawings represent. The realization only struck me today, moments before Runyon – that lizard – stole my notes. Fortunately, I had not written down my hypothesis or he would have stolen it, too. Do you wish to hear it?"

"Perhaps another time, Miss Swift."

"But surely, you must realize how important those symbols are."

Oh, Lord.

Was she going to lecture him now?

"Another time, Miss Swift."

"Oh, I see. You also believe I am just a foolish amateur. This is why no scientific journal will publish my monographs on the cave drawings. They are demanding proof the extinct animals depicted on the cave walls my friends and I discovered ever existed."

"Any reputable journal would require such proof from someone lacking credentials in the field," he said with a nod.

"I understand their concern that it might all be a hoax. This is why I hope to find bones in these caves to prove these drawings are real. But I have turned up nothing so far beyond a few shards of pottery. It is quite frustrating because I think I am very close to discovery. I am certain the proof is buried deep, I just have to hit the right spot. However, my family will not allow me to return to Devonshire. I am not permitted to leave London for the foreseeable future."

"Why not?"

She cast him a wry smile. "Lady Dayne and her friend, Lady Withnall, are sponsoring my second Season. It is exceedingly generous of them, and my parents will disown me if I muck it up. They insist I put all thought of ancient bones aside and find myself a living prospect to marry."

He chuckled, knowing it was quite perverse of him to like the fact this young woman admired dead things more than the unremarkable prospects one often found on the marriage mart. "You do not appear thrilled."

"Would you be?" She shook her head. "It is humiliating to be paraded in front of all those gentlemen, most of whom consider me a country cow."

Ambrose drew in a breath. "Has anyone called you that?"

She nodded. "Several people, in fact. I have a tiny dowry, lack social polish or significant family connections, and am too clumsy and bookish to be considered elegant. I am also no frail, thin creature, as I'm sure you noticed when I landed flat atop you."

He cleared his throat.

Lord in heaven, he certainly had felt that lush bosom of hers mold to his chest and her slender hips grind against his thighs.

"No, I had not noticed. I hit the ground hard and had the wind knocked out of me."

Her eyes widened once again, for she was obviously dismayed. "Dear me, how thoughtless. Did I hurt you? Do you wish to see a doctor? George Farthingale is one of the best in London."

He held up a hand to still her fretting. "I am fine. No harm done."

He rose to signal their meeting was at an end and held out a hand to assist her to her feet. "Until we meet again, Miss Swift."

He drew her hand to his lips and kissed it.

Botheration.

Why did he do that?

She was not wearing gloves and his lips had directly touched her surprisingly soft skin.

He could have just bowed over her hand.

But there was something inexplicably appealing about the girl. As she'd said, she was no wispy, waif of a thing, but neither was she built like an ox. In truth, she was nicely formed and her features pleased him. He could not figure out what it was about her just yet. Certainly not her clothes, for they looked like they had been borrowed from a dotty maiden aunt. Nor the style of her hair, which had no style to speak of, although the hair itself was quite spectacular.

She was full in the bosom…he liked that immensely.

And she had a beautiful smile, one that reached into her rather lovely eyes.

There was no way this young woman resembled a cow.

She cleared her throat.

He followed the direction of her gaze and realized he had yet to release her hand.

He did so now.

She was still smiling as she backed out of his office, smacking her shoulder against the door jamb on her way out. She made it no more than two steps into his antechamber before tripping over the carpet because she still had her eyes on him and not on where she was walking. Fortunately, it was just a small misstep and she recovered quickly.

The girl was not exaggerating when she said she was clumsy. "A moment, Miss Swift."

He reached her side and offered his arm. "Let me walk you out of the building. Wouldn't want you to fall atop any of our patrons."

She groaned. "Now you think I am an utter peahen."

"No, Miss Swift. To tell you the truth, I find you surprisingly charming."

"You do?" She eyed him warily, as though waiting for him to spring his cruel jest. His heart gave a little tug, for this girl had enthusiasm and intelligence along with decent good looks, and yet no one seemed to view her as a prize.

He would have to do something about that.

Now that the Huntsford Academy was built and open to the public, he was looking for a new endeavor to occupy his attention.

Why could it not be Miss Adela Swift?

CHAPTER 2

ADELA'S HEART WAS pounding as the Duke of Huntsford led her out of the Huntsford Academy's exhibition hall onto the busy London street. The day was crisp, for the breeze off the Thames brought cool air swirling around her. But the sky above was a deep and vivid blue typical of the skies in May. Soft, white clouds billowed harmlessly overhead, passing quickly under the force of the wind.

"How did you get here, Miss Swift?" the duke asked, the waves of his dark hair falling back into perfect place after each wind gust, while hers would not stay put even if she glued her tresses to her head.

"I walked, and now I shall walk back." The irritating strands whipped her cheeks, so she used both hands to brush them off her face, while the duke – ugh! – remained before her in utter perfection.

"To Chipping Way?" He frowned, his silvery eyes reflecting his concern.

Well, he did look like the protective sort, as many of these former soldiers were. She could often tell if a man had served in the military just by these little courtesies. It went against his code of honor to leave an unescorted woman to fend for herself, especially one as incompetent as he believed her to be.

"I shall have my carriage brought around and deliver you home myself." He nodded to one of the footmen standing at the entrance of his exhibition hall, obviously a signal for the man to summon his conveyance.

"You?" The wind was still blowing her hair in her face, making an utter mess of her coiffure. That is, if one could call it a coiffure. Before leaving home this morning she had haphazardly piled her hair atop her head and stuck as many pins as could be found in her bureau drawer around that pile to hold it in place as best as could be managed. "Surely, you have more important things to do than ensure my safe return to Lady Dayne's home."

"Yes, I do." He gave no further explanation, which was quite irritating to Adela because she did not understand why this duke was determined to stick to her side if he had other pressing matters requiring his attention.

He did not like her.

Oh, he probably did not trust her, either.

Was he keeping close to her because he was determined to find out if she was a liar?

Of all the gall!

She was about to berate him when his carriage came around the corner and the driver drew it to a halt in front of them. "Dear heaven," she muttered, having never seen such a magnificent conveyance in her entire life. It was brightly polished and shining black, obviously made with every travel comfort in mind.

His ducal crest was emblazoned on the door, a fierce, horned stag with crossed swords in front of it and the background was a field of red. Blood red, to be precise. "Impressive, isn't it?" the duke remarked, no doubt expecting her to fawn over it and him.

He quirked an eyebrow in expectation of her compliment.

She shrugged and put her hand to her mouth in an obviously faked yawn. "It appears adequate."

He chuckled. "Just adequate?"

She smiled at him. "All right, perhaps better than adequate. I am surprised you would deign to allow a commoner like myself to ride in it."

His horses were equally magnificent, a team of four matched bays, each one more exquisite than the next.

"You are correct, Miss Swift. I usually permit only sun gods and other deities to ride with me, but I shall make an exception for you since you are in no way common. In truth, I find you extraordinarily uncommon. Climb in."

He did not give her the chance to object, but took her hand in his and then circled an arm around her waist to guide her up. He gave his driver her direction, and then climbed in after her, chuckling again when she bounced twice on the padded bench and remarked favorably on its comfort.

He settled diagonally across from her, his silver eyes boring into her and his long, powerful legs stretched out before him.

She blushed and cleared her throat as the carriage took off for Chipping Way. "I suppose it is too late to comment on the scandal of my riding alone with you."

"Do you care?"

She shook her head. "No, but Lady Dayne might. However, I think we are safe enough since no one would ever believe you have a romantic interest in me."

"Why do you put yourself down, Miss Swift? Have I said anything to make you believe I find you inferior to the other debutantes in this year's marriage crop?"

"You haven't," she acknowledged. "I thank you for it."

"No need."

She turned her face to the spotless window to peer out of it. "This is actually quite wonderful. Dare I admit it? I am enjoying the ride, and your company, of course."

He gave a chivalrous nod of his head. "As I am enjoying yours."

She emitted a soft trill of laughter. "What a kind and gentlemanly thing to say. I am sure it is utter hogwash, but I think I must thank you again."

He frowned. "Has the *ton* beat you up that badly?"

"I wouldn't really care what any of them think except that I am forced to be in their company constantly. Museums and bookshops are my element, not a ballroom. I know I ought to better ingratiate myself, but it is hard to do when most of the gentlemen I meet are shallow, vain, and boring. The ladies are often just cruel, although I do not see why they should pay me any mind since I am no competition for them."

"You are a very pretty girl, Miss Swift."

She grinned. "Are all dukes this polite and tactful? I think I could be passable enough if I worked harder on my appearance. But then everyone's expectations would be raised and I might actually receive a gentleman caller."

"Is that not the entire point of having a Season?"

"Yes, I suppose. But I would soon bore him and he would bore me because we would have nothing of interest in common. I do feel badly about disappointing Lady Dayne and Lady Withnall, however. They have been exceedingly kind and patient with me."

"Why are you so resistant to finding a husband for yourself?"

She pursed her lips and gave her answer some thought. "I am not resistant to it. I do hope to marry, just not yet."

"Because you are determined to find your ancient bones first?"

She nodded. "Yes, exactly. I fear that once I marry, that dream will have to be set aside forever. I am not ready to give up on my dreams yet. Would you be?"

"I don't know. As a man and also a duke, I am pretty much allowed anything."

"And we women are allowed so little. Is it so awful for me to want to make something of myself before I accept to marry? I know I am not like most women, nor am I suggesting they ought to be unhappy with their choices. However, I cannot bear the thought of passing from this earth like a wisp of smoke, nothing to indicate I was ever here. Even if I am merely a footnote in some forgotten book, at least that would be something. *Miss Adela Swift discovers mysterious bones belonging to terrifying, mammoth creatures in Devonshire cave.* Is this such a terrible ambition?"

He studied her in silence for a long moment. "The right husband might support you in fulfilling your dreams."

"That would be remarkable. I would adore such a man, but he will not be found on the marriage mart or anywhere in London, for that matter. No Fellow in the Royal Society will ever allow me to pursue my search, yet they are the very ones who should understand my passion for discovery better than anyone else. Instead, they shun and revile me because I am a woman. Runyon is not the only callow knave among them."

They were not far from Chipping Way now and Adela was not certain she would ever see the duke again. Well, she probably would see him at various social events, but he was not likely to engage her in conversation or even acknowledge her presence.

He traveled in the most elite circles.

Diamonds of the first water swooned over him.

How was she ever to get near him again?

She also doubted he would make a personal visit to return her stolen material once Runyon turned those papers over to him. Why should he waste his time when sending a messenger to deliver them would do?

"Ah, here we are," he said as his carriage turned down Chipping Way, one of the prettiest streets in Mayfair.

A footman jumped down to open the door as soon as it rolled to a stop.

The duke hopped down and held out his hand to assist her.

She gladly took it and managed to step down effortlessly, but was grateful for the support because with the horrid way her day was going, she feared to miss a step and end up sprawled on the ground. "Well, I do apologize for running you over earlier. But thank you for delivering me home and offering to go after that odious lizard, Runyon. Please let me know if I can be of any assistance in that regard."

He shook his head. "I'll alert Lotheil to what has happened. He will assist me in having your research notes returned to you if that *odious lizard* dares refuse to turn them over to me."

Once again, she noted he had not released her hand.

Not that she minded, for his touch was warm and pleasant. "Well...good afternoon, Your Grace."

Instead of letting go of her and leaving, he tucked her arm in the crook of his own. "I shall walk you to the door."

She sighed. "It really is not necessary. It is only ten steps from here to there and I am wholly capable of managing it on my own."

"I know."

"Then why–"

"My family has been on friendly terms with Lady Dayne for years. It would be rude of me to simply let you out and be on my way."

She eyed him warily. "Oh, you are a smooth fellow, aren't you?"

He quirked an eyebrow. "What are you talking about?"

"You don't believe I presently reside with her, do you? You think I have made all of it up."

"Miss Swift, I can assure you that if I did not believe you, I would have delivered you straight to the magistrate's office instead of Chipping Way."

She stared at him open-mouthed. "You would have had me arrested?"

"The point is," he said with a smile that melted her heart, "I have already assessed your character and decided against having you clapped in irons."

The front door opened and Lady Dayne's butler appeared. "Your Grace, it is good to see you." He cast a dubious glance at Adela, regarding her as though she were a stray cat being delivered back to its home. "Miss Adela?"

"His Grace and I just happened to bump into each other," she said with a nervous titter, although Watling was the kindest man and there was no reason for her to be uncomfortable in his presence in the least.

He showed the duke into Lady Dayne's private parlor, an elegant room decorated in cheerful blue and yellow silks, and then hurried off to alert the dowager. Adela remained with the intriguing man since it would have been rude to leave him standing there on his own. "Will you stay for refreshments?" she asked, knowing Lady Dayne would expect her to attend him until she arrived.

"Why, yes. I believe I shall." He settled on the blue silk settee, taking over most of it with his broad-shouldered torso.

Her eyes widened. "You will?"

He nodded.

"But aren't you a busy man?"

His lips broadened into another of his devastating smiles. "Adela, are you trying to be rid of me?"

"Not at all, but…" She sighed and sank onto the chair beside him. "You are an odd fellow."

It was not long before Lady Dayne hurried in. "Watling, tea for us, please."

"At once, my lady." The elderly butler scurried off.

"Huntsford, this is a pleasant surprise. What brings you here?" She glanced at Adela as they both rose. The duke, ever the gentleman, bowed over Lady Dayne's hand. "Oh, um…I see you have met Miss Swift. Has she told you? Lady Withnall and I are sponsoring her for the Season."

"Yes, she let me know." He waited for the ladies to seat themselves before resuming his seat on the settee. "It is quite admirable of you to take her on."

Adela shot him a glance.

Did he mean 'admirable' in the sense she was proving to be a trial for these elderly ladies?

"Did the two of you arrive together? Watling mentioned it. Dare I ask how you came to know my charge?"

The duke related the incident at the Huntsford Academy with surprising accuracy. Adela was relieved he saw the incident exactly as she had seen it, which was rather generous of him because the two of them were strangers until an hour ago, and he had no reason to believe a word of what she had said.

But he was marvelous in the recounting and did not accuse her of wayward behavior at all.

She cast him her warmest smile before turning to address Lady Dayne. "And now His Grace has kindly offered to retrieve the stolen notes on my behalf."

By this time, the tea had been served and they were all enjoying a cup along with some cakes. The kindly dowager took a sip of her tea and then set her cup aside. "I shall have a word with Lotheil as well. I know how hard Adela has worked on her research. What a low thing for this scoundrel to do."

The duke agreed. "Along with insight and creativity, there must be integrity and honor. Who will ever trust our findings if we are deemed no better than cutthroat pirates?"

Adela listened to him, rapt. "Well said, Your Grace."

He grinned at her. "I am relieved my opinions have met with

your approval."

She blushed. "I am of no importance, but I do appreciate your words."

Lady Dayne cleared her throat. "Huntsford, will you be at Lady Marbury's party this evening?"

He nodded. "I was planning on it."

A tingle shot up Adela's spine.

She would see him again and very soon, although she expected he would make his grand entrance, take a turn around the room to gather all the swoons and accolades, then take himself off to his club where his real evening would begin.

Lady Dayne eyed him speculatively. "We shall be there as well."

He turned to Adela and cast her a rakish smile. Not that he was trying to be rakish, but there was just something appealingly naughty in his look. Perhaps it was those silvery eyes framed by dark lashes and a head of wavy, almost raven black hair that he wore just the slightest bit too long so that the ends curled at his neck. "Then I shall make it a point to seek you out."

Dear heaven, even his neck was sinfully attractive.

Adela held back a groan.

Why on earth would the Duke of Huntsford care to see her again? Especially in a social setting. He might find her ineptitude acceptable within the confines of the exhibition hall since many men of science were eccentric and socially inept, so she fit in quite well. But in a glittering London ballroom? He would soon see her as everyone else did, as that country cow.

"Please do not feel obligated," Adela said, clasping her hands to the edge of her elegant chair. "I am sure far more important personages will be vying for your attention."

He nodded. "Toadies, mostly. Why do you look pained, Adela? Am I not permitted to spend time with someone who is a refreshing change from all the rest? May I not be in the company of someone I know will speak intelligently and always tell me the truth?"

Lady Dayne chuckled. "Oh, you will get plenty of truth from Adela."

His laughter was deep and resonant as he shook his head. "I have no doubt of it."

After another moment of polite conversation, he rose to leave. "Alas, I had better get home and attend to the work amassed on my desk. A pleasure to see you again, Lady Dayne." He bowed over her hand and kissed it lightly.

He then turned to Adela. "Miss Swift."

She was surprised when he took her hand and raised it to his lips. "Until tonight."

Botheration.

What was this duke doing?

She wanted as little attention as possible foisted on herself. "Oh. Yes…um, Your Grace. I am agog with anticipation."

He might have believed her if she had put a scintilla of enthusiasm behind that obvious lie.

Fear.

Dread.

But never anticipation.

He cast her yet another of his heart-melting smiles. "It was a pleasure *bumping* into you."

She shook her head and laughed. "All right, I give up. It was a pleasure to meet you, too. I shall try to leave you standing next time we meet."

With him gone, she and Lady Dayne breathed a sigh.

But what was Lady Dayne sighing about?

"I cannot believe it," the kindly dowager said, ringing for Watling to bring her cape and reticule. "Have my carriage brought around immediately."

"At once, my lady."

Adela stared at her. "Where are you going?"

"I must tell Phoebe all that has happened. This cannot wait."

Adela regarded her with marked surprise. "Do you think she will care that my research papers were stolen? I cannot believe it happened to me, either. The brazenness of that despicable lizard, and he a Fellow in the Royal Society. I hope he is driven out in shame."

"Adela, what are you going on about? I am talking about

Huntsford bringing you home. Do you have any idea how significant that is?"

"No, not a clue. Oh, please do not make more of it than it is. Eloise, you know I adore you both, but Phoebe is a notorious gossip. The duke and I are not an item and never will be. Dear heaven, he is the most magnificent man I have ever met. I am nothing but a clumsy bluestocking. I do not need the entire *ton* laughing at me if rumors were ever to spread. They already consider me a halfwit."

"Adela, why do you refuse to see the obvious?"

"Because it is not obvious at all. I knocked him over. He brought me home. He is convinced I am a clumsy clot. We all had tea together."

Eloise sighed again. "For a smart girl, you can be awfully dim sometimes. You have just received a visit from your first suitor."

"My..." She burst out laughing. "Him? That Greek god? I cannot tell you how irritating it was to see his perfection even amid the gusts of wind that made a mess of everyone else. Nothing diminished his exquisite looks. And who is born with silver eyes like his? Or a strong, patrician nose? Or those muscles straining beneath those impeccably tailored clothes? And you think that paragon is interested in me?"

Still laughing, she excused herself and went upstairs to ready herself for tonight's party. Eloise, obviously unmoved by her comments, took off for the home of her partner in crime, Lady Phoebe Withnall.

Once alone in her bedchamber, Adela stared at herself in the mirror. "You had better shape up," she told herself.

If the duke meant what he said, then she would have to be ready for him. It wasn't for herself, for she really did not care if she showed up looking as though she had been lost in a library for a week. But her two dowager sponsors cared, and she would not disappoint them for the world. "Betsy, I will need your help preparing for tonight's party," she said when the young maid assigned to assist her walked in.

"Of course, Miss Adela. Lady Dayne sent me to you for just this purpose. Let's see what we can do to have you steal the Duke of Huntsford's heart."

Did the entire household know he had brought her home?

And now believe he was interested in her?

Utter nonsense.

But she had to set matters straight before their one encounter was blown completely out of proportion and turned into a social disaster.

She relaxed in the tub while Betsy washed her hair and scrubbed her back. She even added scented oils to the water as though Adela were some exalted Egyptian queen. A slightly aching queen, truth be told, but a long soak in the bath did wonders for her bruises.

When her hair dried, Betsy styled her unruly curls into a surprisingly flattering upsweep.

Not that she was hoping to entice the duke.

How could she possible entice such a man?

But if he were to approach her, she did not want to embarrass the two lovely elders who had taken her under their wing. After all, should she not look her best when he snubbed her? He would not do it to be rude, but everyone of more noteworthy consequence would be clamoring for his attention.

It was well past eight o'clock in the evening by the time she and Lady Dayne made their way along the reception line. Adela smiled politely and greeted their hostess, Lady Marbury, warmly. She received a cold look in response.

What had she done to offend the woman?

She pondered the reason while she and Eloise strolled into the ballroom to await the start of the dancing. "Eloise, did I imagine it or was Lady Marbury angry with me?"

"Indeed, my dear. She was quite put out."

"But why?" Adela really hated these affairs.

"Because you look beautiful tonight and will outshine all the diamonds, including her daughter." Eloise patted her hand. "I think the young men are going to start taking notice of you."

She rolled her eyes. "Lord, I hope not."

"Adela, there are plenty of fine men here. You must stop scaring them away. You look exceptionally pretty tonight, which only proves how attractive you could be if you ever bothered to take interest in your appearance. I am glad you wore the blue silk gown. I have been trying to get you to wear Madame de Bressard's magnificent designs for weeks now."

"I know. I still do not feel comfortable in something so elegant, but I agree that it is now necessary because–" She was about to explain her reasoning when a buzz suddenly swept through the crowd.

All eyes turned to the entrance.

Huntsford had arrived.

Young ladies all around her were suddenly fluttering their fans. Well, she could not blame them since the heat level in the room had just soared.

Despite his cool demeanor, this duke was hot enough to set the room ablaze. He looked magnificent in black tie and tails that enhanced the black of his hair, the silver of his eyes, and the broadness of his shoulders.

He made his way slowly through the crowd and...was he coming toward her?

Drat.

She tried to back away, but Eloise now held her wrist in an iron grip. Phoebe, who had joined them several minutes earlier, now grabbed her other wrist. "Don't you dare run," Eloise whispered. "The dancing is about to start and he is going to claim one from you."

"How do you know? Dear heaven, I hope not."

Phoebe, the little dowager, frowned up at her. "Adela, what is wrong with you? Every young lady here would kill to be asked by him."

"Well, every young lady here has practiced her dancing. I haven't so much as tapped a toe in time to the music since last year's debut fiasco."

Eloise cast her an encouraging smile. "Then just tell him. He will take extra care to guide you. He knows how to hold a woman in his arms."

"Of course, he does," she muttered under her breath as he was now upon them.

Up close, he was even more magnificent than at a distance.

Was there anything he could not do to perfection?

He even knew how to stand there in perfect nonchalance.

He arched his eyebrow as she stood there gawking at him, then glanced at the two elderly ladies. Upon noting the grip each had on her arms, he grinned. "Good evening, Miss Swift."

His deep, glorious rumble simply melted her.

"Good evening," she replied, breathless as she struggled to get out the words.

"Don't you look lovely tonight?"

"Thank you, Your Grace." Her face was in flames as she bobbed a curtsy. She felt the insufferable heat rush up her cheeks and along her neck.

"The third dance is to be a waltz." His voice remained deliciously deep and husky, pouring over her like a smooth, aged brandy. Of course, she always choked on those hard spirits. "Would you do me the honor? May I claim you for it?"

"Yes, you may," Phoebe responded before she could beg off. "She is looking forward to it. Aren't you, Adela?"

"A veritable dream come true for me," Adela muttered, not bothering to hide her sarcasm as she resigned herself to the humiliation certain to occur within the hour.

"I look forward to it as well," he said with a sparkle of amusement in his eyes.

As the two dowagers released her wrists, he took hold of one of her gloved hands and placed a light kiss on it. "Adela," he said in a whisper. "It shall be a dream come true for me, too."

"What is wrong with that man?" she grumbled when he strode away.

Of course, the crowd parted as though he were Moses at the Red Sea. Honestly, did they all have to grovel because he was a handsome, wealthy, eligible duke?

She had to get out of dancing with him.

But how?

She could not possibly hold her own, and soon everyone would be watching them. All those eyes on her, laughing at her every misstep.

There was no help for it, she had to get away.

Two dances came before the dreaded waltz.

Each was about twenty minutes in duration, which gave her a good forty minutes to plot her escape.

Too bad, really.

She liked the duke and could not imagine anything more enchanting than dancing with him. But not amid this crush. It would have to be somewhere out of the way, out of everyone's sight where no one would mock her if she stumbled. He would never pass an unkind remark, for kindness and concern seemed to be his manner around inept souls who crossed his path.

Unfortunately, the two dowagers outwitted her at every turn.

They trailed her like bloodhounds, making it clear there would be no fleeing this impending debacle.

She drank a glass of champagne, and then downed several more. She must have gulped down at least three glasses of champagne, but who kept count? By the time he approached to claim her for the waltz, she was undeniably foxed.

Everyone was gawking at her, most of them in disbelief.

She thought drinking herself numb might help calm her nerves, but it only made her lightheaded and clumsier than she already was. "Your Grace," she whispered as he took hold of her hand and led her onto the dance floor. "This is a horrendous mistake. Won't you reconsider?"

"No. I wish to dance with you. Just let me guide your steps. Trust me, Adela. Do you trust me?"

She nodded.

"Good. We'll take it slow. I won't let you stumble."

There was nothing she could do but believe in his words of assurance and pray hard for the best outcome. Her stomach churned as he swept her into their first turn, and churned again as they spun into their second.

She was not going to make it through their waltz without casting up her accounts.

Well, this was one way to scare off every man within a hundred miles of London.

"Your Grace..."

"Blast it, Adela. How much did you drink?"

"I'm not sure. Even one would have been too much since I rarely have anything stronger than lemonade."

He slowed their pace and took wider turns, no doubt hoping to get her safely through their dance. "I know you are feeling ill, but it might help if you close your eyes and concentrate on the feel of my hand at the small of your back." He was talking to her in that gloriously husky murmur again. As for feeling his hand? Dear heaven, it burned through the silk of her gown with scorching heat.

Everything about him overwhelmed her.

His musk scent.

The strength of his muscled arms.

"Do you think you can manage to talk to me, Adela?"

She shook her head. "No."

"All right. This really frightens you, doesn't it?"

"Yes, but it isn't you. It is dancing in general, made worse because it is you."

"Now you are worried everyone is looking at us?"

She nodded. "They never take their eyes off you. How can you stand it?"

"One gets used to the attention. This adulation has been happening to me for years. But my parents taught me early on never to be swept up by it."

"You do come across as a very intelligent and sensible man. I do not wish to suggest you are not worthy of everyone's notice. In fact, you are probably one of the few men deserving of the admiration of others."

"And your admiration?"

"You will likely gain that, as well. I am a bit slower than most to form opinions, especially about character. But I am quite favorably impressed by you, so far."

"This is what I like about you, Adela. You think for yourself."

She looked up at him and laughed softly. "Sounds much nicer than calling me stubborn and too independent for any man's liking. How much longer before this agonizing dance ends?"

"Agonizing?" He burst out laughing, earning quizzical looks

from those around them. "Not long now. Oh, this is priceless."

"What is?"

"You are dancing with a duke, Adela. London's prize catch, in fact. Yet, you do not give a fig about it."

"Oh, I do apologize."

"No, don't. I like that you see me for the man I am and not as an object to be snared. You make me work to gain your approval. It is an odd and wonderful feeling. You have me smiling, Adela. Smiling, laughing. Everyone believes I am enchanted with you." His smile faded and his expression turned serious once again, stoic and stone-faced. But there was a lingering warmth to his eyes as he regarded her thoughtfully. "Perhaps I have indeed fallen under your spell of enchantment."

"My spell? And you caught up in it?" She laughed in disbelief. "That is quite a jest. I am sure I will do something to break the enchantment. You needn't worry."

"I am not worried. In truth, I hope it lasts."

She looked up at him in horror. "It will break, I can assure you. I do not hold anyone's interest for very long."

"You are an odd girl. I am trying to be charming and give you compliments."

"Please don't. It will only make my stomach churn worse than it already is."

"All right. I'll keep my mouth shut." He cast her a tender smile.

The rest of their waltz proceeded in silence.

She closed her eyes through most of it, although that was not very clever of her because she *felt* him, her heart melting a little at the gentleness of his touch and the powerfully protective way he held her.

When the music stopped, she opened her eyes to find him looking at her with an unreadable expression. "What are you thinking, Your Grace?"

"That I would like to dance with you again."

Was he serious?

He could not be.

She looked up at him in dismay. "You would subject yourself

to this ordeal again?"

How many times had she stepped on his foot?

She had lost count after three.

"Ordeal?" he muttered, his smile breathtaking in its warmth.

She laughed lightly because she liked this man and the gentle way he was treating her. "Are you merely a glutton for punishment or completely insane?"

CHAPTER 3

ADELA WAS SURPRISED to find bouquets of flowers littering Lady Dayne's elegant entry hall when she came down to breakfast the following morning. "Watling, is there a flower fair going on that we are not aware of?"

"They are all for you, Miss Adela," he said with a kindly smile.

"All of them? Do you know who sent them?"

"Various suitors, I expect. Shall I have them put in vases now or do you wish to read through the cards sent with them first?"

"What do you think Lady Dayne would do?" she asked him since the dowager was still in her bedchamber and not likely to come downstairs for another few hours yet.

"She would read through the cards and make a note of who sent which flowers. There is also an art to the meaning of each flower, but I suppose you are aware of this."

She laughed softly. "One would think I should be, but I never gave it a moment's thought. If it isn't skulls or bones, then it does not hold my interest. Does Lady Dayne have a book on flowers in her library?"

"I am certain she must have several. It is the sort of thing she would find of interest."

"Thank you, Watling. You have been most helpful." Adela went into the library and searched through the rows of books until she came upon some that appeared to be on the topic. She took a few into the dining room and also had the bouquets brought in along with quill pen, ink, and notepaper.

First, she had the footmen lay a protective padding over the table so as not to accidentally damage it or the table linens while the flowers and writing supplies were laid out upon it and she scribbled her notes. There was an abundance of honeysuckle and red roses in the bouquets, so she decided to look up the significance of those blooms first. The honeysuckle, she read in one of the reference books, represented ardent devotion and the abundant red roses represented love.

What a jest!

If her so-called beaus were trying to impress her, they had failed. How could she ever trust the very gentlemen who had considered her a country cow all of last Season and into this one? Were they all suddenly struck dumb by her beauty at the same time? Love was not a disease that infected everyone at once. The truth was obvious, for these men were merely aping the Duke of Huntsford's supposed interest in her.

If the duke liked her, then surely they ought to like her, too.

She went through all the bouquets with a diligence usually reserved for her research on bones and took precise notes regarding each.

Yellow tulips symbolized happiness.

A gentleman by the name of Lord Faun had sent her those, but she had no idea who he was.

Red tulips meant mates of the soul. Ha! Which dolt had sent her that bouquet? No doubt, it was one of the men who had openly snubbed her last year. And now she was expected to forget his callous behavior and consider him as her true love?

Never.

Lavender signified purity, grace, and devotion.

A viscount had sent her those.

Dahlias also signified devotion.

A 'Right Honorable' had sent those.

There were a lot of lilies, too.

Those blooms represented purity and fertility.

Adela shook her head and laughed.

The lords who had sent her those were never going to get their itchy hands on her. They had to be among the vain peacocks who had dismissed her last year.

She had just finished her breakfast and made her list when Lady Dayne came downstairs. "Adela, what is all this? Not that I am surprised you received flowers this morning. I just had not expected quite this many. You are most deserving of the attention, of course."

"All of these gentlemen are the same hounds who ignored me last Season and the start of this one, Eloise. I did nothing to change their opinion of me. It is all Huntsford's doing. We shared a dance, and suddenly everyone is convinced there is something worthy about me, something deeply hidden that only the duke, in his infinite wisdom, discerned."

"He merely helped them see the beauty in you."

Adela shook her head and sighed. "But they don't *see* me. They are merely aping the duke and will drop me as soon as he does. What am I to do with these? The men are dolts, but the flowers are quite lovely."

"We shall put them in vases around the house. You had better run upstairs and put on a suitable gown. Have Betsy fix your hair, as well. She did a lovely job of it last night. You must look your best. We'll be having quite a few callers today."

"But I was hoping to—"

"Do not dare say you were hoping to go out today. You must be home to receive these gentlemen when they call on you."

"But there is an important lecture at the British Museum this afternoon on the ancient practice of brain surgery. Were you aware the ancients knew how to pierce a man's skull, successfully drilling straight through bone, and—"

"Dear heaven!"

"The point is, I have been looking forward to Dr. Nordberg's talk all month long. And we both know these gentlemen are not sincere. Everyone is making too much of the duke's interest in me. We have only shared one dance. He will forget my name by next week at the latest, and so will all of those hounds. Why must I forfeit a fascinating lecture just to be in their company when we all know it is going nowhere?"

"You will simply have to grin and bear it. Truly, Adela. The duke has opened up a world of opportunity for you and you must take full advantage."

"All right," she grumbled. "But if they hold this lecture again, I am going. I do not care if I have been granted an audience with the king. The lecture takes precedence."

"I shall worry about it if and when the king requests to see you," Eloise retorted jovially. "Did the duke send you flowers?"

"No, none of these are his."

"Hmm."

Adela eyed her curiously. "What is so surprising about that? He is not courting me, no matter what anyone believes. In fact, I am certain he is amusing himself at my expense. I'm sure he will howl with laughter when he hears of all the gentlemen he has bamboozled into thinking I am a diamond."

"You are a diamond."

She gave Eloise's hand a light squeeze. "You are genuinely wonderful. I know I am no *ton* diamond and never will be. I would much rather be known as a bluestocking. This is truly who I am. I will not give up the essence of myself just to please some pompous lord."

"I wonder if Huntsford will join us today," Eloise mused.

"Oh, I doubt it. He might come by once he has my stolen research papers in hand in order to deliver them to me, but that is all. He does not strike me as the sort of man who would get in line to court anyone, much less me."

"I suppose you are right."

Adela gave their discussion no more thought as she reluctantly prepared herself for the visitors they were to have this afternoon. The British Museum lecture was scheduled to start at three o'clock.

They were scheduled to be home to visitors starting at two o'clock.

The timing was atrocious.

Was there any chance she could be rid of all her callers in under one hour and rush off to the museum? Even if she missed the first half hour, at least she would catch most of the two-hour lecture.

Betsy had worked wonders on her hairstyle again and chosen a lovely gown the pink and red hues of a raspberry for her to wear.

Adela had to admit, the gowns Eloise and Phoebe had ordered for her were exquisite and very much to her liking. She felt quite womanly in them, for they were softer and more attractive than her usual afternoon garb which consisted of durable, dark fabrics that were mostly practical for hiding ink stains.

Seeing herself in this gown made her wish the duke would stop by, if only to have a glimpse of her in it. She was curious to know whether he would find her attractive.

Perhaps, even delectable?

She laughed at herself.

By five minutes past two, Eloise's salon was filled with callers.

Phoebe was there, of course, her nose twitching like a little ferret's as she attempted to glean some juicy gossip.

Adela was truly fond of the woman, but she was an incorrigible snoop.

She smiled at John and Sophie Farthingale, their neighbors who resided at Number 3 Chipping Way. They had stopped by with two of their daughters, Daisy and Daffodil, and a newly arrived relation of theirs by the name of Marigold Farthingale who was remarkably poised for a girl of only seventeen. Marigold was still a few years away from entering the marriage mart, but Adela expected this amiable girl would steal hearts when her turn came.

All the Farthingales were warm and friendly, and Adela had become quite close with the family now that she was living with Eloise, who was the dowager Countess of Trent. Daisy Farthingale had married Eloise's youngest grandson, Lord Gabriel Dayne. Daffodil was married to the Duke of Edgeware, but one would never know she was a duchess because of her charmingly unassuming manner. She had insisted early on in their acquaintance that Adela not hold to formality. "My parents named me Daffodil," she had remarked, "but all my friends and family call me Dillie. You must do the same. Perhaps when I turn fifty, I shall demand to be addressed as Your Grace. It feels quite odd to require my family and close friends to do this now."

These Farthingale sisters were nice as can be.

Adela had taken to them immediately.

She loved how deeply caring and protective they were of each other, especially of their newly arrived cousin, Marigold.

Adela was also fascinated by how much in love they were with their husbands, a feeling reciprocated in full by these strong, rugged, and affectionately doting men.

This is what Adela wished for herself.

But how did one go about finding one's perfect match? The marriage mart was not the place to do it. Of all the gentlemen now present in Eloise's salon, not a one had ever spoken to her before today. They had no idea what her interests were, what she enjoyed, or what she disliked.

Yet, these were the very men who had sent her flowers representing eternal and abiding love. How could she believe any of them?

She was lost in her thoughts as she sipped her tea and endured another of her supposed suitors waxing poetic about her eyes, when all chatter came to an abrupt halt.

Watling appeared at the portal. "His Grace, the Duke of Huntsford."

Adela set down her cup with a clatter and looked up hopefully.

Had he already retrieved her stolen work?

But he strode in empty-handed.

Well, perhaps he had turned over the stack of papers to Watling for safe storage since he could not very well hand them over to her in the midst of this throng.

He took one look at her and smiled in understanding of the entire trail of her thoughts.

He greeted Eloise first, then moved on to greet Dillie who took precedence because of her rank as duchess, then Phoebe, Daisy and the senior Farthingales, and finally turned his attention to her. "Miss Swift, an infinite pleasure."

She blushed as he took her hand, not merely bowing over it but planting a kiss on it, something he had not done with any of the other ladies.

Of course, everyone noticed.

She suspected this was entirely the point. "To what do we owe the pleasure of your visit?"

His insistence on singling her out for notice was quite irritating. Did he believe he was doing her a favor? She had been quite happy *not* being noticed by all these gentlemen with whom she had nothing in common.

"No reason other than the joy of your company." He kept hold of her hand for a moment longer than was warranted before finally releasing it.

"No other reason?"

"None, Miss Swift." He gave an almost imperceptible shake of his head to indicate this was not about her stolen work.

She could not hide her disappointment. "Oh, I see."

Her less than enthusiastic response at his arriving empty-handed appeared to amuse him, for he smiled once again.

Good thing he found her frankness charming, but she knew the novelty of it would soon wear thin for him.

She sighed. "I am happy to see you, even if it is for no reason at all."

The seat beside her magically cleared, no doubt the fawning dolt who had been droning on about her eyes had given up and moved away. The duke took it over, indeed taking command of the entire salon merely by the force of his presence.

"Has Runyon at least returned your book to you?" she asked in a whisper as she poured him a cup of tea. "Surely, he would not be so stupid as to hold onto it."

"No, he hasn't. I stopped by the Huntsford Academy to inquire, but he hasn't shown his face there yet. I will check again later. There's a lecture at the British Museum that I–"

She almost leaped out of her seat. "Dr. Nordberg's lecture?"

He chuckled. "You know of it? Of course, you must have been in raptures when it was announced. Skulls, bones. Ancient rites. The very one."

"Lady Dayne will not permit me to abandon our visitors," she said, casting him a look of utter misery. "It is frustrating beyond belief. I would be forever in your debt if you could contrive to take me with you. I cannot believe I am forced to miss it because today, of all days, these gentlemen have come around."

She glanced around the room and was relieved to see everyone now occupied in other discussions. "Both she and Lady Withnall watch me like bloodhounds. They insist I play out this marriage mart farce even though we all know these men are not interested in me."

He frowned. "Stop putting yourself down, Adela. It is quite an impressive turnout."

"I am not belittling myself. Truly. I am comfortable in my own skin, but have no illusions about these bachelors on the marriage hunt. They are not looking to marry a bluestocking, especially one as opinionated as myself and with little dowry. They are only here because *you* noticed me last night. Gossip will be rampant since *you* appeared by my side again today. They are here for *you*, not me. I ought to give *you* the piles of flowers delivered today since they are really meant for *you*."

"That is ridiculous."

She set down the pot of tea and offered him a slice of poppy cake which he politely declined. "Your Grace, you know it is the truth. If you have not recovered my stolen papers, then why did you really come here today?"

"To see you. Must there be another reason?"

"Yes, there must. You are not the sort who goes along with whatever others do. Nor do you strike me as the sort who takes time out of his busy schedule to take tea with a young lady and her court of admirers. If you liked a young lady, I think you would seek her out when you knew she was alone. Do you know what else I think?"

"Pray, tell me." He took a sip of his tea, the delicate cup looking tiny in his big hands. "I am always eager to hear what you have to say."

His eyes once again glittered with mirth.

"I think you are a bored, little boy who is amusing himself by behaving as everyone's puppet master. You enjoyed shocking everyone last night by dancing with me and are here today to see the effects of the havoc you wreaked. You must be quite pleased by the results. Of course, you are purposely adding to the hysteria by visiting me today."

"Hysteria? That is a harsh assessment, Adela. Do you find it impossible for me to like you?"

"In a romantic way? Yes, frankly. Not that I find fault with myself. I have already told you I am happy with who I am. You and I might even become good friends in time, for our scholarly pursuits are similar. Your Huntsford Academy is a marvel and I could listen to you talk about every aspect of this project from conception to ultimate design for hours on end."

He quirked an eyebrow. "Perhaps we shall do this someday."

"I hope so. Truly, it would be the high point of my Season. I am in raptures over everything you have done with it. I would live in your magnificent library if I could. But the possibility of my stealing your heart? Highly improbable. What appeal could I possibly hold for you?"

He made a sound of what sounded like exasperation. "You are diminishing yourself again."

"Truly, I am not. I know I am clever, probably more so than most men or women. I am no diamond, but still pretty enough. However, you are a duke. A wealthy, stunningly handsome one, at that. You can have the most extraordinarily beautiful, sophisticated, and accomplished ladies in all of England at your beck and call. So, forgive me if I am dubious about your fascination with me, Miss No Name from Devonshire, whose parents are equally insignificant."

"Adela—"

"Did you really have to kiss my hand upon your arrival? You could have bowed over it just as you did with the other ladies. There was no reason for the gesture other than to stir more gossip. Have you finished amusing yourself?"

"I see." He set down his cup and rose. "So this is all you think I am? A thoughtless manipulator."

This is what he got out of her response?

She put a hand to her heart, too late realizing how offensive her words must have sounded to him. "No, you are nothing of the sort. Well, perhaps not intentionally. But you must admit, you are playing with all of us right now. Even if you were not and were sincerely interested in me, how could it last? You are so far above me, I can hardly see you for the sun blinding my eyes."

"Good grief. Now you are sounding like all the others." He shook his head and emitted a soft grunt to go along with the disappointment clearly etched on his face. "I must be off. Forgive the brevity of my visit."

She rose with him. "Oh, but...I do wish you would stay longer."

"Why? My coming here was clearly a mistake."

"Not at all. Oh, me and my big mouth. Please give me the chance to apologize to you. I spoke out of turn."

"Unfortunately, I cannot stay." He gave a curt bow. "Another time, Miss Swift."

"I hope so, Your Grace." But she had insulted him thoroughly. Well, their exceedingly brief *amour* was better ended now before anyone – meaning her – was hurt. "Enjoy the lecture. I don't suppose..."

"What, Miss Swift?"

"If you ever decide to speak to me again, would you tell me what Dr. Nordberg said in his lecture?"

He tossed her an impatient scowl. "I shall take copious notes for you. Is this all you think of me, worthy only to be your scribe?"

Everyone was looking at them now and trying to listen in on what seemed to be a lover's spat. She shot him a pleading look not to humiliate her. "That is unfair," she said in an urgent whisper, hoping no one would overhear them. But was this not the irony of the situation? The more privacy she hoped to have, the more curious everyone was to listen in.

She ushered him out of the parlor and into the entry hall. "You started this, made everyone think I was a diamond when clearly I am not. Do I not prove it every time I open my mouth? And now I have insulted you who deserved it least. You are the most incredible man I have ever met."

"Blast it, Adela," he muttered under his breath, his eyes no longer blazing with anger. "Until tomorrow, Miss Swift."

He took hold of her hand and kissed it.

Would he attend her tomorrow?

She doubted it.

Once the afternoon visits were over, she settled in with their remaining company, all of them now relaxing in Eloise's parlor. Their neighbor, Sophie Farthingale, and her daughters, Daisy and Dillie, remained. So did Marigold, who was staring at her wide-eyed. Also present were Eloise and Phoebe who appeared eager to give their opinions on the events of this afternoon.

"I knew Huntsford would show up," Phoebe remarked, nodding her head in satisfaction.

"I had hoped he would," Eloise agreed.

Sophie pursed her lips. "He did not stay very long and did not look happy when he left. Do you think he was jealous of his competition?"

"No," Adela insisted. "I'm sure he dismissed them all at first glance."

Dillie nodded. "I agree. I saw no serious prospects for you in that group. Still, it cannot be overlooked that he was not in good humor when he left. It may not signify anything. Ian was the most difficult duke imaginable, yet he is a wonderful husband."

"Men like that have a lot to sort through," Daisy mused, "especially when it comes to losing their hearts. Gabriel did his best to push me away, but love always triumphs in the end."

Adela tried not to look pained. "Oh, he does not love me. How could he when we only met yesterday? Besides, how can a man like that ever lose his heart to me? If ever there was hope of it, I've quite dashed it with my stupid remarks."

They all looked at her with some surprise.

"What did you say to him?" Eloise asked.

"Terrible things." She put her hands to her face and mumbled into her palms. "I suggested this was all a grand hoax for him, that he was amusing himself at my expense because he was bored and thought it would be fun to set tongues wagging. I told him he enjoyed being a puppet master and pulling everyone's strings to see their reactions."

She now looked up to gauge their reactions.

They were all staring at her, saying nothing until Phoebe finally broke the intolerable silence. "No wonder he sprang up as though he'd sat on a nest of thistles." But she began to laugh.

"Well done, Adela."

"What? It was not well done of me at all. He has been kind to me. In return, I slapped him in the face with my insulting comments."

Phoebe shook her head. "No, my dear. You called him out on his game. Although, I truly do not think he considers you a game. You intrigue him."

She shrugged. "I slammed that door shut pretty fast, didn't I? I'm sure he thinks of me as an ingrate now."

"No, you spoke the truth," Phoebe insisted. "Once he calms down, he will realize you were right. Yes, he thinks most members of the *ton* are nothing more than simpletons and puppets. So do I, truth be told. But in amusing himself, he never considered that you are the one likely to be hurt. If he is angry, it is with himself."

"I hope you are right. I felt the only reason he danced with me last night was to see the response he would rouse in others. He knew I dreaded it, but drew me onto the dance floor anyway."

"Oh, that sounds frightening," Marigold said, venturing a remark after avidly following their conversation. "One can keep silent if unsure in conversation, or watch others if unsure of which fork to pick up in the midst of a formal dinner. But there is no escaping a dance. You either know it or you will stumble and bump into others. There is no hiding from a dance."

Adela nodded. "Yes, this is precisely why it terrified me."

"I am glad he chose a waltz," Eloise said. "He was never going to let you fall. Perhaps he was using you in order to create a stir, but he also sees you more clearly than you see yourself, Adela."

The notion surprised her.

How could he know her so well on a single day's acquaintance? "What do you mean?"

"You have strengths that you are not using because you are quite comfortable in your bluestocking ways. You blame the men for not appreciating your intelligence, but what have you done to show yourself to best advantage? Why did it take until last night for you to do something lovely with your hair or put on one of your prettiest gowns?"

Eloise was right.

Adela groaned. "I owe you and Phoebe an apology. You put your hearts into helping me this Season and all I have done is resist. Then, when the perfect opportunity presented itself in the form of the Duke of Huntsford, what did I do? I trampled it. Stomped on it. Crushed it beneath my boots. Now, it is too late for me to make amends. He will never speak to me again."

Sophie glanced at her daughters. "If raising five daughters has taught me anything, it is that men who are truly in love do not go away. They stand their ground stubbornly and fight for what they want."

"But this is entirely the point. The Duke of Huntsford does not love me. A deliberate man like him? How could he fall in love with me in the span of less than a day? He might have grown fond of me had I given him the chance. But he will never do it now."

She buried her head in her hands once more. "I've chased him away and missed out on Dr. Nordberg's lecture, too. Could this day possibly get any worse?"

CHAPTER 4

"GOOD EVENING, HUNTSFORD," said his friend, Thomas Halford, the Earl of Wycke, finding him later that evening sitting alone in a corner of White's, the gentlemen's club to which they both belonged. "Why the glum look? It wouldn't be trouble over a certain young lady you danced with last night, would it? The *only* young lady you asked to dance at Lady Marbury's ball, a gesture noticed by everyone, I might add."

Ambrose groaned, for Wycke's wife was a Farthingale...Honey Farthingale, which meant she had heard everything of what went on, not only last night but during his disastrous visit to Lady Dayne's residence this afternoon.

He was curious to know precisely what gossip was being circulated. After all, he had a right to know what heinous deeds he was accused of committing. "What have you heard?"

"You know I never give credence to gossip." He settled into the plump leather chair beside Ambrose's and called for one of the club stewards to bring him a brandy. "Care for a drink, Huntsford?"

"No, I'm nursing one already." He held up his own glass that shone half full in the amber glow of firelight. "Why are you here, really? Merely a coincidental chat? I know your wife sent you, so let's skip the polite dancing around and just tell me what you know."

His friend grinned. "I've only heard bits and pieces second hand, and we all know how things get distorted in the retelling.

Whatever happened, it is obvious you are not happy about it. Why not seek out the young lady and talk to her privately about whatever it is that is bothering you?"

"She does not wish to speak to me."

"Has she said so? Because I got the impression she does wish to see you. What she does not wish is to be used as a doll for your amusement."

Ambrose snorted. "I thought you said you did not know anything?"

Wycke shrugged. "I don't. However, having been through the agony of falling in love, I know what your glum look signifies."

"I am not in love with the girl. I only met her yesterday. In that short time, she has managed to knock me flat on my back, almost cause a riot in my exhibition hall, and thoroughly insult me."

"Well, at least you cannot call her dull. Did you deserve to be insulted?"

"No, I was kindness itself." However, he shifted uncomfortably because there was the slightest bit of truth in his using her as a diversion.

But it was harmless.

He was not taking her on as his mistress, although she certainly had the pleasing body and good looks for it. He was not looking to Adela for that sort of diversion.

Not that he would rule it out completely.

In truth, she had a spectacular body. However, she took great pains to hide it under those hideous, bluestocking gowns she chose to wear.

Her wardrobe was bound to improve now that Phoebe and Eloise had taken her into the fold. The gown Adela had worn last night fit her to perfection, and she looked soft as a kitten in the one she had worn this afternoon when home to visitors, a little raspberry confection that made him want to pop her right into his mouth.

Well, he could not repeat what he wanted to do to the girl with his mouth.

Wycke laughed as he accepted his brandy from the steward and nodded in thanks before returning his attention to Ambrose.

"Kindness itself, you say? Then I am sure you were not in the least at fault. What wallflower who is terrified of dancing would mind being dragged onto the dance floor with the likes of you? It isn't as though anyone would notice her."

"Wycke, stop kicking my arse. Did your wife instruct you to scold me as well as pry information out of me?"

"No, they all expect Lady Withnall will haul you over the burning embers when she sees you later tonight. Will you be at the Granville's supper party?"

"Yes, it is expected of me. I accepted the invitation and cannot back out now. I suppose Lady Withnall and Miss Swift will be there, too?"

Wycke nodded. "Honey and I will not, unfortunately. We are going to the theater tonight, although I think the show you are going to put on will be far more entertaining."

"Gad, stop. I am not going to do anything foolish."

Wycke set aside his brandy. "I hope you do. I knew the moment I met Honey that I would make a monumental fool of myself if this is what it took to win her heart."

Ambrose sighed. "You needn't concern yourself. No hearts are involved here. Right, I had better be on my way if I am to get to Granville's on time. I have never made a fool of myself over any female and am not about to start now with the likes of Miss Adela Swift."

Blessed saints.

One would think he had known Adela all of his life and been pining over her for years, the way everyone was talking about her.

He was no fool.

No one fell in love in the span of a day.

If he was eager to see her again, it was only because they had parted on bad terms. Perhaps he *had* been amusing himself at her expense, but what was so unpardonable about claiming her for a harmless dance? What about all the good things he was doing for her? First and foremost, getting her research papers back from that Runyon character. He would attend to it tomorrow, for he hadn't had the chance to look into it today.

Lord and Lady Granville's residence was a lovely townhouse

in Belgravia not far from his own elegant home. Most of their guests had arrived and were already in the parlor waiting for the dinner bell to sound by the time he strode in.

Eighty people were shoulder to shoulder, everyone chattering until the moment he appeared at the threshold.

As usual, all talk came to a halt when he strolled in.

Could he never slip in unnoticed anywhere?

He marched in wearing his usual stoic facade.

The toadies immediately surrounded him, as did this year's crop of diamonds and their eager mothers. One young beauty introduced to him as Lady Felicity Rose was particularly persistent.

He ignored her as best he could and scanned the room for Adela.

He thought he would have trouble finding her in the crowd because she was not very big and tended to blend into walls, but it took him no more than a few seconds to notice her.

It was as though his gaze was instinctively drawn to her.

She looked as lovely tonight as she had last night.

These lighter colors obviously suited her complexion, the soft pink of tonight's gown enhancing the pink of her lips and the sweet, rosy blush of her cheeks. It also brought out more of the blue in her eyes and lessened the gray swirls in them.

He tried to look away, but quickly saw she was distressed and knew he had to be the one to make the first move and speak to her. This was one of the advantages of being a duke. No one got in your way or dared interrupt you when you strode off toward your purpose.

Adela cast him a hesitant smile as he approached her.

"Will you forgive me for being a lout to you earlier?" He took her hand in his and raised it to his lips, knowing it was going to cause a stir again. But it was more important to send a message to Adela that he was not angry with her.

Her hand trembled in his. "I was the lout. Can you ever forgive me?"

"For speaking the truth? I never considered your feelings, just assumed you would be honored by my attention. But you are shy in social situations and uncertain of your dancing skills."

"Uncertain?" She arched her eyebrows and cast him a soft smile. "I am quite certain I have no dancing skills whatsoever."

"You were fine. However, I completely ignored your concerns and dragged you in front of everyone who had previously subjected you to scorn. That was most unfair of me."

"I was frightened out of my wits," she admitted. "But you were not to blame. I have been hiding away and making no effort to come out of my shell. I needed someone like you to kick me out of my hiding hole."

"Well, it is done. Fortunately, we have both survived. You look lovely tonight."

"Thank you." She glanced down at herself. "Lady Dayne and Lady Withnall have outfitted me in the loveliest clothes. Their modiste is a miracle worker, somehow managing to bring out my better qualities and hide my flaws."

"You have no flaws, Adela."

She laughed and shook her head. "No, Your Grace. *You* have no flaws. I have many. But we need not argue over that. How was Dr. Nordberg's lecture? Did you sit through all of it?"

"Yes, and took copious notes for you," he teased. "Well, I did not jot anything down. But I hope I did something better. I engaged him to speak at the Huntsford Academy next week."

Her eyes widened in obvious delight.

"Will you be my guest, Adela? I hope you will attend."

She nodded. "I would love to! This is the best news I could possibly receive. Did you do this for me? It is extraordinarily generous. How can I ever thank you?"

"Your smile is all the gratitude I need." Indeed, her smile was as radiant as the sun and pleased him immensely. "Excellent. It is to be next Monday afternoon. I'll have my driver pick you up at eleven o'clock. The lecture starts at two, but I'll be hosting a private luncheon for Dr. Nordberg beforehand. Your two watchdogs are also invited, of course. I will send out formal invitations tomorrow."

"Oh, Lady Dayne and Lady Withnall will find reasons to politely decline. Skulls and bones are not to their liking, but I shall be there. No one is going to stop me from attending this time. Do you suppose I will require a chaperone since I am not merely sneaking off on my own to work on my research? That is of no consequence. Lady Dayne will arrange for someone to accompany me if she believes I must be protected from you. My maid will be more than happy to take on that role."

He doubted either of those dowagers would put their trust in a maid to guard her. Those two were too shrewd to be lax about this, especially since Adela was to be in his company and he had a reputation for seducing ladies.

In truth, it was the other way around. Women constantly threw themselves at him. Sometimes he resisted and sometimes he did not.

No, the girl would likely be accompanied by someone as formidable as either of them.

Nor could he insist their fears were groundless.

While he did not intend to bed Adela, he sorely ached to kiss her. It was no stretch of the imagination where those kisses might lead.

Well, nothing was going to happen tonight since there were too many people around and everyone had their eyes on him.

They said no more to each other as the dinner bell rang.

One of the consequences of being a duke was that dukes were always placed in positions of honor beside their hosts. This meant he would not be seated anywhere near Adela or ever have the chance to speak to her until supper was over and card tables set out for the guests who wished to engage in card games.

As Lord and Lady Granville's guests began to saunter into the dining room, Ambrose held Adela back a moment. "Do you play cards?"

She nodded. "Yes. In fact, I am quite good."

"Partner me. For the entire night. Refuse anyone else who attempts to claim you."

She laughed lightly. "All right. I shall fight off all of my ardent suitors with mace and sword. Honestly, no one else is going to ask me. But I look forward to being your partner."

He cast her a soft smile. "So do I."

"Have we made up now? Are we friends once more?"

"Yes, Adela. However, we never stopped being friends."

She accepted his remark with a gentle breath of relief. "I'm glad."

His thoughts about her were anything but gentle.

He could not finish his meal fast enough. It was odd how much he looked forward to being with Adela again, how much he yearned to be alone with her. But that would not happen tonight while all eyes remained on them amidst this party.

He wished they could have been seated closer, for he missed having her by his side throughout the meal.

Well, how did one miss something one never had before?

He hardly knew the girl and should not have been so caught up in thoughts of her.

But she had the ability to hold intelligent conversations, unlike the peahens who were seated beside him. When they weren't passing snide comments about others within their social circle, they chattered incessantly about the dullest topics. The parties they were to attend, the frightful lack of a good modiste these days, or the latest debutante ruined by scandal.

While polishing off dessert, an excellent *blancmange*, he endured listening to the intricacies of curling one's hair. The frustrations of engaging the best dance instructors. And was it not shocking that Lady Cartwright ran off to Italy with one of her husband's footmen?

"Why did she have to run away?" his dining companion, Lady Felicity Rose, the *ton* diamond who had earlier accosted him, muttered between bites. "It isn't as though he ever cared what she did with her time since he now spends all of his in London with his latest mistress. I believe she is an actress and was formerly Lord Hough's mistress."

"There was no need for her to run off," the young lady seated across the table from him agreed. "They could have led their separate lives without fuss. Now, he will cut her off and possibly divorce her."

"I would not have made a fuss," Lady Felicity Rose said, as though speaking directly to him. "If I had the title, a fine London home, and a suitable allowance, why would I care what my husband chose to do?"

She stared at him, awaiting his response.

Ambrose chose to give none.

Did these women truly believe this is all he wanted? A wife who was a showpiece and would not shed a tear when he died?

When the meal ended, the ladies sauntered into the parlor while the men remained behind to have their drinks and smokes. The talk turned to politics and horses, topics he found slightly less tedious than those the women had raised.

Perhaps he was being too harsh on everyone, for he did enjoy horses and had several scheduled to race at Newmarket. Politics was also an important matter and he had been working hard to introduce bills to address the vital issues of the day.

But it irked him that not a soul had asked about the newly opened Huntsford Academy, a project into which he had poured his heart and soul. He had not done it to gain their approval, but for himself and his brothers to honor their father's memory.

Still, it genuinely surprised him that not a soul other than Adela had passed a remark. Her excitement over his labor of love was the greatest compliment she could have paid him, and she had no idea how much it had touched his heart.

He had created a serious center for learning and stocked its library with the finest scientific resource materials. Scholars from around the world had already written to him in the hope of visiting this new exhibition hall and the forensic laboratory he intended to build next to it. The exhibits were of top quality, and only Adela was interested in hearing about those.

Indeed, Adela's eyes lit up whenever they spoke of his labor of love.

As for the others, the marriage mart was all they cared about. The social whirl of dinner parties, balls, picnics, and musicales were battles to be won by young ladies as determined as Felicity Rose.

Every dance and every conversation was a tactic to be used in snaring a spouse.

Finally, the men joined the ladies in the music room that had been converted into a gaming parlor. He strode directly to Adela, not surprised to find her standing alone against the wall. He stifled a grin, for she was a very pretty wallflower. "What's our game to be, Miss Swift? Whist? Piquet? Or would you like to try your hand at gambling?"

Her eyes widened. "I have never gambled before. Would you mind if we tried that first?"

"It shall be my pleasure to corrupt your morals." He gave a smooth bow. "I am at your service."

Smiling, she placed her arm in his when he held it out to her. "Where should we start, Your Grace?"

"You might enjoy *vingt-et-un* which is sometimes referred to as pontoon. Have you ever played it?"

"No."

"It is a simple game that requires a little bit of mathematical skill. You play against the dealer and must beat his hand but not go over twenty-one points. Each card is equal to its value. So a nine would be worth nine points and a four would be worth four points, for example. Face cards are worth ten points each. Aces are valued as one point or eleven points."

"Why are they the only cards to be assigned different values?"

"That's just how the game is played. So, if I dealt you a ten and an ace, you would have twenty-one points and be a winner. If I dealt you a ten and a five, leaving you with only fifteen points, you might ask for another card, especially if you knew I, as the dealer, held cards worth sixteen or more points. If you drew an ace, you would then have sixteen points because if you treated it as an eleven, you would be over twenty-one and immediately lose."

She nodded. "Sounds easy enough."

"It is. There are a few more intricacies, but I'll show you what to do if those arise. All you need to do right now is pay attention to the cards dealt and the probability of your receiving a card that will *not* take you over that magical twenty-one points." He fished into his pocket and withdrew several coins. "Here, I'll stake you."

"All right. This is quite exciting." She had such a sweet, open-hearted look as she took a seat beside the other ladies and gentlemen playing at her table.

Her delight at this new endeavor was quite refreshing and gave Ambrose reason to smile.

He hoped she would be as enthusiastic about the other things he intended to teach her.

Starting with kisses.

He watched her lose the first two hands before she fully picked up on the tactics. Although he did not play, he drew up a chair beside her and watched her nibble her fleshy lower lip as she concentrated on the cards.

It was not long before Adela was winning most of her hands.

After winning her final hand, she beamed with pride and held out her pile of coins to him. "Will you have a turn now or shall we give way to others who may wish to play?"

"Let's give the space over to others." Ambrose shook his head when she tried to place the coins in his hand. "These are your winnings."

"But you gave me the funds to get started, so should they not be yours?"

He tucked the coins in her reticule. "Use your winnings to purchase more research books for yourself."

"No, I think I will donate them to the Huntsford Academy so *you* may purchase more books for your library. Or apply it to giving free admission for children. After all, they are the young minds who should be inspired and encouraged."

He arched an eyebrow as he briefly pondered the notion. "I like that idea."

"You do? Would you be open to another idea?" She was nibbling her lip again, so she obviously doubted he would go for her next suggestion.

"Of course." If it came from her, then he was eager to hear it.

"I have been so impressed by the Huntsford Academy and it got me to thinking...most museums concentrate on attracting scholars, the Upper Crust, and the wealthier in the middle classes. But I do not know of any museums in England that design exhibits specifically for their children. Of course, you would want to locate such exhibits away from the library or other sensitive exhibits not meant for rambunctious hands. But would it not be something special to introduce children, any and all children, to various areas of scientific learning?"

He thought back to his childhood when his father had been alive. They had spent summers turning over every stone, twig, and seashell on their Devonshire estate near Thurlestone. They explored caves, some abandoned and some not, climbed up to nesting grounds for migratory birds on seaside cliffs, found a sunken pirate ship, and all manner of other wonders his father had seen fit to show him and his younger brothers.

"Oh, you are saying nothing to me," Adela remarked. "Do you find the notion foolish?"

Those summers had been some of the happiest times in his life. Perhaps this is why he had felt an attraction to Adela when they first met. He knew she had to be someone special the moment she spoke of her cave findings in the area of her Devonshire home.

Had their paths ever crossed?

They could not have been exploring far from each other, for Thurlestone was not all that distant from her Dartmouth home. "Not foolish at all. Would you care to give me a proposal on it? The Hall of Planets seems a perfect place to start. Can you give me some ideas on making it more appealing to children?"

She eyes brightened as she nodded. "Yes, I would love to. Will you give my suggestions serious consideration?"

"Absolutely, Adela. I am eager to hear what you propose. I mean it, truly."

"Thank you," she said with a quiver to her voice. "I must admit, you are surprising me."

"Because I want to hear all of your ideas? It is no indulgence on my part. I'll explain in greater detail next time I see you. Do you know that your eyes turn to starlight whenever you speak of research and learning? It is a genuine relief to be looking into your beautiful eyes instead of enduring the vapid gazes of most of the women I encounter at these *ton* affairs."

"Are you not being harsh on the others?"

"No, actually I am showing great restraint." He tucked her arm in his and led her to the whist tables.

They had just taken seats across from each other and expected to be playing opposite Eloise and Phoebe, when instead, two others hurried forward to sit beside them.

Ambrose groaned inwardly, having had his fill of Lady Felicity Rose and her snide remarks at the dinner table earlier. She was beautiful, had impeccable bloodlines, and her dowry was impressive.

None of it mattered to him because she was a vain creature and her instincts were heartless. She would never stoop to help someone unless there was profit in it for herself. Of course, she would likely go on to catch some poor sod with a vaunted title and make his life a misery.

But he would never be that poor sod.

"Good evening, Your Grace," she said, fluttering her eyelashes at him.

"Good evening, Lady Felicity Rose," he responded with a curt nod.

The wretched girl did not bother to acknowledge Adela.

So typical.

However, Adela appeared more amused by the snub than hurt over it.

The gentleman partnering Felicity Rose more than made up for any lack of attention on Adela. Lord Brynmore, a wastrel and someone never to be trusted, began fawning over her, taking hold of her hand while he referred to her as divine, a goddess, and so many over the top remarks that Ambrose was tempted to smash his fist into the man's face to shut him up.

It did not take a great intellect to understand what this pair intended. No doubt, Lady Felicity Rose wanted his undivided attention and had connived that lackey, Brynmore, into occupying Adela while she made a play for him.

Did this girl not get the message when he ignored her earlier advances?

Women like her had been coming on to him all of his life.

The overtures were always the same, and always included a willingness to offer their bodies, as though this alone was enough to entice him into marriage. First of all, he was not so stupid as to take any of these debutantes into his bed, no matter that most were not virgins. Some were probably as adept at the sexual arts as he was.

But the end game was to get him into a compromising position by any means possible. If he lowered his guard for even a moment, that parson's trap would be sprung on him so fast, his head would spin.

Resisting this young woman's wiles was no hardship for him. "Are we ready to play?"

"I am always ready to play with you, Your Grace," Felicity Rose replied in a breathy voice, slipping her hand under the table and resting it on his thigh.

He scowled at her, one of those fierce, ducal scowls designed to intimidate and convey displeasure.

She removed her hand.

Adela noticed his expression. "Is something wrong?"

"No." He dealt the cards.

London was full of convenient places where a man might seek his physical pleasures. What he had yet to find was the woman who could offer him both the physical delights and the intelligence to match him. Not only intelligence, but she also had to have a caring nature and a quick wit.

Someone like Adela who instinctively understood his likes and dislikes, his interests and passions, and wanted to learn and grow along with him.

Yes, Adela...she was different from the others.

"Trump suit is hearts," he said, turning over the last card.

But it wasn't long before Adela kept ducking her head under the table to search for something. "What is the matter, Miss Swift?" he asked when she did it a third time, her gaze as perplexed as the first two instances.

"I think Lady Granville's lapdog must be...but no, he's there on her lap. Perhaps it is a rodent skittering around. Oh, dear. I would not think so. But something keeps brushing against my ankles, and I–"

She stopped suddenly and her cheeks caught fire. "Lord Brynmore, kindly keep your feet from straying."

"Stop encouraging him," Lady Felicity Rose shot back. "He would not dare flirt with you unless you were shamelessly flirting with him."

Adela gaped at her. "Oh, yes. You have found me out. It is my goal to seduce every man in the room."

Ambrose growled softly and set down his cards. "Miss Swift, join me on the terrace."

He knew he sounded severe, but Adela had to realize his irritation was not with her. The others obviously mistook his expression as one of anger at her remark, for they smirked behind their cards.

Adela had not helped the situation with her sarcastic retort.

He had to warn her to always watch her words.

That sort of caution had been ingrained in him since childhood.

Obviously, Adela's parents had taught her no such thing.

He held out his arm.

Adela placed hers in his as they made their way through the room and onto the terrace. Other guests were outside, so they were not alone. Not that Ambrose cared anymore. He almost wished he and Adela would be caught in a compromising position. His hand would then be forced. He would have to do the honorable thing and marry her.

Chore concluded.

Duke married.

Adela would suit him just fine.

"Goodness, I am so dense sometimes," she muttered as they stood together beside the balustrade. "Three glances at my feet before I realized it was that clunch, Brynmore, tickling my ankles. Does this ever happen to you?"

"All the time. It is not only my legs they rub up against."

"What else do they–" She gazed into his eyes and silently mouthed an 'oh' as she continued to stare up at him, realizing he was referring to his manly parts.

He nodded.

"Dear heaven, are they that brazen?"

"Yes, and far worse." He had given up on house parties because of the women he would find waiting naked for him in his bed. It happened in carriages, stables, at his less elite clubs. His own home was maintained as a veritable fortress, no one entering his sanctuary unless permitted inside by his head butler who was built like an ox.

It was a ridiculous way to live.

"I am so sorry, but it is your own fault for being so handsome, wealthy, titled, and still unmarried."

He leaned back and rested his elbows upon the balustrade, coming to know Adela would give him no quarter. "My fault? For the constant barrage of unwanted attention?"

"You enjoy much of it, especially the power you have over everyone."

"Are you going to accuse me of being a puppet master again?"

"No, but you know your woes are minor compared to the daily struggle for survival faced by most of the population. It cannot be overlooked that you have also done much good with your power. The Huntsford Academy is an obvious labor of love. I am eager to learn how the idea for it came about. Did your love of history and science begin as a child? It did for me."

"Yes, for me as well."

"You look stiff and stern on the outside, but I think you have a very good heart. I would not be surprised to learn you have also quietly taken on charitable projects. Sponsoring hospitals, orphanages, schools, societies to feed and clothe the hungry."

"Ah, now I am redeemed in your eyes."

"You were never in need of redemption. I sensed you were someone special the moment I met you. Of course, I also worried you might have me tossed into prison," she said with a light laugh. "Then you offered to help me retrieve my stolen research papers and I knew you were a man of honor. There will always be hierarchies of power in our society, and I am glad you are one of those at the top. You do enjoy your power, but you also create much good out of it. I am glad control is in your hands and not in those of someone like that idiot Brynmore."

"About that. Adela, you have to watch what you say around that pair. They will look for any way to misconstrue your words."

"Are you suggesting I keep my mouth shut and say nothing?"

"Yes, this is what I do. They cannot make fodder out of nothing." He took off his jacket and wrapped it around her shoulders when she began to shiver. Her gown was light and the silk wrap matching it was no defense against the cool, night breeze. "Here, Adela. This will keep you warm."

"Goodness, you have set tongues wagging again. We could have just walked back inside."

"I wasn't ready to go back in. Besides, I don't care what anyone thinks. I have made an important decision tonight."

"You have?" She regarded him dubiously. "What decision might that be?"

I am going to marry you.

But he was not ready to say anything to her yet.

The cool breeze swirled around them, whipping her gown flat against her body so that the silk molded to her curves.

She was too busy trying to hold onto his jacket and at the same time keep her curls from tumbling out of place to notice his avid gaze. "Are you not going to tell me your decision?"

"I will, in time. Not yet."

Yes, he could be happy with someone like Adela as his wife.

But should they not know each other at least a week or share at least one kiss before he took that leap and offered for her hand in marriage?

CHAPTER 5

AMBROSE ORDERED HIS carriage driver to take him to the Royal Society the following morning. He knew their board of directors was to meet today at the noon hour. The Duke of Lotheil was their chairman and in charge of conducting the meeting.

Ambrose merely wished to catch him before the session began.

He strolled upstairs and asked a clerk to summon the crusty, old duke. Within moments, Lotheil bustled forward to greet him. "Huntsford! Good to see you. What brings you here today?"

"I was hoping for a private word with you. It won't take long." They entered Lotheil's spacious office which was filled with exquisite pieces of furniture one could barely see because they were buried beneath piles of books and relics. "I believe you are acquainted with Miss Adela Swift."

Lotheil settled in the massive, tufted leather chair behind his desk. "Yes, a delightful girl. I understand you also find her delightful."

Ambrose took a seat across from him. "I hardly know her. I have yet to decide whether I want to court her or throttle her. Perhaps a little of both. But I am here on a serious matter concerning her research materials."

He proceeded to relate what had happened at the Huntsford Academy the other day.

"Runyon, you say?"

Ambrose nodded. "He grabbed her papers and one of the Academy's rare books. Adela thought he might return the book because she believes he took it by accident, but it has not turned up yet. I checked with my clerks before coming over here to see you."

"Are you certain he ran off with it?"

He sank back in his chair. "No, I only have Adela's word for it. However, the book is definitely missing. Adela had signed it out earlier that day and my clerks assured me she had not left the reading room in all that time. So, she could not have walked out with it. Nor was it among her belongings. And my clerks also confirmed she had come in with a pile of notes and had been scribbling in them for several hours. Again, those notes could not be found."

"I had my doubts about Mr. Runyon," Lotheil said, pursing his lips. "It pains me to think we admitted a shady fellow such as he into the Royal Society. What idiots men can be. We would not offer the same courtesy to a far more qualified candidate such as Adela. Not to mention my own grandson's wife, Lily."

He knew of Lily Farthingale.

Everyone in the Royal Society knew of her.

If ever anyone deserved to be inducted as a Fellow, it was that brilliant girl.

"Not even I, despite all the power I wield, can change the minds of our very stubborn membership," Lotheil said with a disgruntled sigh.

"I am aware. It is one of the reasons I decided to establish the Huntsford Academy, a center of research and learning that is open to *all* academicians."

"I knew your father, lad. He and I were good friends. I think he would have been so proud of you had he lived to see the work you have done." Lotheil raked a hand through his thick mane of white hair. "But about this Runyon chap and how to expose him for the thief he is, it cannot be difficult to prove his perfidy. Those notes are all going to be in Adela's handwriting. I cannot imagine how he will explain that away."

"My concern is that he will argue she was serving as his clerk and transcribing his notes."

"If that were so, then what reason would he have to steal them from her? It would be the same as stealing from himself. And if so, let him produce the notes he had supposedly given her to transcribe."

"Oh, he'll level some accusation about why his are missing." Ambrose nodded. "You and I would never believe his story, but what of the other board members? They are thick-headed, which is why I have had run-ins with them before. I fear they might believe him only because it provides them convenient ammunition against allowing women as members in the Royal Society."

"Ah, I understand your concern now. Perhaps this will be more difficult than I first imagined. Bringing him up before our board of directors might not work if the directors view this dispute as a battle of the sexes instead of rightly regarding this as a matter of theft. Perhaps you and I will do better to handle this situation privately."

"You needn't get involved then. I will confront him on my own. No sense putting you at odds with the board and membership if matters turn ugly."

Lotheil grunted in disgust. "I'm glad you came to me. I will support you if the need arises. The board members need to be kicked in the arse from time to time. And why should they not be made to address our concerns? You and I are Fellows here, too. I must remain a member, to my regret. I believe in the Royal Society's goals and vision, and as chairman, I am doing my best to see those goals fulfilled. It is important that we both stay on and keep arguing our positions. The old stodges might eventually come around one day soon and admit those of the fairer sex into our membership."

"I doubt we will see it happen in either of our lifetimes." Ambrose rose to leave. "Let me know if that book he stole turns up here."

Lotheil escorted him out. "I will. Good to see you, Huntsford. I'm sorry I do not have anything better to offer. But I can assure you, I will have my eye on Runyon and intend to have him booted out the moment I catch him doing anything untoward."

Ambrose next stopped at one of the local antiquarian bookshops called Gresham's. If Runyon thought to turn a tidy profit and sell the rare book, he would likely approach Gresham himself since the old codger was the foremost dealer in antique manuscripts.

The bell above the door clanged noisily as he walked into the musty shop.

The shelves were as stuffed as ever with books of every shape and size, and on every topic imaginable. Those unable to fit on the shelves were piled high beside them. The shop was tiny and walking through it was like walking through a maze.

"Your Grace, it is a pleasure to see you," Gresham said, popping his head out from behind a stack of old books. "How may I assist you?"

He told the man of his concerns about Runyon. "If he approaches you about selling that book, I want you to agree to purchase it."

His eyes widened. "Your Grace! I would never–"

"I do not doubt your honesty, Mr. Gresham. Just play along with him and offer him a tempting price for it should he try to sell it to you. Tell him you need a little time to gather the funds to pay him, then ask him to meet you here the following day. Send word to me immediately and I shall have one of my Bow Street runners on hand to reclaim the book and turn him over to the magistrate."

"What if he demands immediate payment or else he'll go elsewhere?"

"Then pay him whatever you can. I shall reimburse you. You do not need to do anything in particular other than be willing to purchase the book."

Ambrose had already put a Bow Street man onto trailing Runyon, a very good runner by the name of Homer Barrow who was well respected and known as honest by judges and constables alike. Between Gresham's testimony and that of Mr. Barrow, that thief, Runyon, was going to prison if he did anything other than return the book to the Huntsford Academy.

Having dealt with that chore, Ambrose then headed to his club for a quick bite to eat.

Seeing none of his friends around, he picked up one of the newspapers lying about and took it to his table in order to peruse it while he ate. It was one of the gossip sheets, not something he would normally choose to read, but he wanted to be sure there was nothing scandalous written about Adela.

Not that he expected there would be anything beyond speculation about his interest in her. But his heart shot into his throat as he began to read. "By all that is holy!"

He stormed out, mad enough to crack skulls.

Instead of heading back to the Huntsford Academy, he instructed his driver to take him straight to Chipping Way.

Eloise's household was in an uproar as he strode in.

One look at Eloise's face and he knew this was going to be bad. "Oh, hell," he muttered with a groan. "Of course, you've read that story."

She nodded. "It is Adela's worst fears come true."

He groaned. "Where is she?"

"In the garden, trying to walk off her anger. She is quite overset. Is this why you are here? Have you read the full story in The Tattler?"

"Yes." He nodded to the ladies assembled in her parlor. Phoebe and several Farthingales were seated with Eloise and not looking happy at all. Fortunately, their young charge, Marigold, was not with them, although this sad turn of affairs could be a lesson for her. Learning when to open one's mouth to reveal what was on one's mind and knowing when to keep it firmly shut were just as important as lessons in dance and etiquette. "I had better go to her."

He knew he had to take full responsibility for this debacle.

Singling Adela out for his attention had been foolish. Wrapping his jacket around Adela's shoulders last night had compounded his mistake. He knew it and had done it anyway, not caring that it would add to the already rampant speculation about his intentions toward her. He also knew she was unhappy with his obvious displays.

Still, he had ignored her wishes and continued the game.

Puppet master, she had called him.

Yes, he had to accept full blame.

But his biggest mistake – and he could kick himself ten times over for his folly – was in not immediately pulling Adela away from the card table when Felicity Rose and Brynmore had connived to sit with them for a game of whist.

He knew they would be up to no good.

Once again, he was smug and thought he could handle that sneaky pair.

He could have, but Adela could not.

"This is big trouble, Huntsford," Phoebe said.

He raked a hand through his hair. "I know."

He strode outside and saw Adela standing near the rose arbor. "Adela, I am so very sorry I let this happen to you."

She turned to him, her anger quickly dissipating as she regarded him in surprise. "You? Why are you shouldering any of the blame?"

"Is it not obvious?"

Adela shook her head. "This scandal is of my own creation. How could I have been so stupid? It was my big mouth that provided the fodder for this article, just as you warned."

"But it was my paying attention to you that started this disaster. I must take full responsibility for the consequences." He led her to a bench against the stone wall that divided Eloise's home from that of her neighbor. "Sit down. We need to talk."

When she did so, he sank onto the bench beside her.

Next, he took the newspaper Adela had been holding in a death grip from her hands and set it aside. "You weren't stupid."

"Have you read this horrid tripe? Seems I am having an affair with you *and* Lord Brynmore, not to mention leering after every other man at that party."

"Should I be jealous?"

"Do not tease me about this. He is such a revolting toad. How can anyone believe I would ever look at him? They are calling me wanton. Indecent. Lacking in morals. I cannot even take them to task because they are repeating my exact words."

"Words spoken sarcastically, Adela."

"I know, but they do not care. I said the words. *You have found me out. It is my goal to seduce every man in the room.*" She shook her head and groaned. "Just gag me next time I think to open my mouth. I knew that hideous Lady Felicity Rose was trouble. I played straight into her hands."

"You did not." He wanted to grab that diamond and her toady, Brynmore, and feed their entrails to the dogs.

Adela clasped her hands. "Do you think there is a chance it will be old news by tomorrow?"

He shrugged. "There is always the possibility some hot-headed clot will do something incredibly stupid and draw everyone's attention away from us."

"It would have to be something rather spectacular in its idiocy, I should think. Your Grace, what shall I do? I am at a loss when it comes to these *ton* games. I think even Eloise and Phoebe are at a loss as to how to respond. The worst part is that I have blemished Eloise's sterling reputation. I can never forgive myself for that."

"She will survive the temporary setback."

"And what of Phoebe? I have besmirched her reputation, as well."

He laughed lightly. "She is viewed as a witch, a bat, a feared avenger. You have only enhanced her reputation and she is delighted."

Adela shook her head. "It is so galling to be bested by that horrid girl. Phoebe and Eloise have now called in the Farthingale ladies to help. They are trying to plan battle tactics. Fortunately, our next engagement is not until Friday. Lord and Lady Knightly's ball. Will you be there?"

"Yes, I'll escort you and Eloise."

"Assuming I go. The Farthingales insist I must attend."

"I agree."

"I don't. I just want to hide. But they think I have to show my face or the repercussions will be worse. Did you see them when you entered? Daisy, Dillie, and their mother, Sophie? They have kindly promised to support me. Not only them, but they have assured me a horde of Farthingale cousins will come to my assistance. I am so grateful for that family. They are wonderful, don't you think?"

He nodded.

She emitted a sigh and continued. "As for our

situation…although, it is mostly *my* situation and *my* problem, not yours. Did they send you out here to calm me down?"

"I came of my own accord, but I expect they are hoping I can do something to fix this ridiculous scandal."

"What can you do? I doubt there is anything to be done other than ride out this mess of my own creation. I am such a coward. I cannot face that crowd. I just want to hide away. Do you know the worst part?"

"Another worst part? Besides besmirching Eloise's sterling reputation?" He took her hand in his and shifted closer. "Tell me, Adela."

"I am probably the only one among this year's crop of debutantes who has never even been kissed. Yet, here I am ruined when I have never once taken a step out of line."

He glanced toward Eloise's parlor and saw all eyes on him.

Well, he knew what needed to be done.

Had he not come here specifically for this purpose?

"Would you mind if I kissed you?" Ambrose said.

She stared at him in confusion. "You? Why would you want to kiss me? Especially now? I did not mention it to give you ideas. I was merely stating my lack of experience as fact. Ugh, what if every *ton* wastrel, scoundrel, lecher, and dissolute now thinks I am available and starts making advances? I much preferred it when they treated me like wallpaper."

"No one is going to touch you."

"Who is to stop them? Lady Felicity Rose is going to whisper in their ears to goad them." She grunted in dismay. "And I handed her the opportunity on a silver platter."

"All the more reason why you must kiss me now."

"Why are we still talking about kisses?"

"Why do you think?"

"Here? Now?" She glanced at the faces peering back at them from inside the parlor. "While everyone is looking at us."

"Yes, that is entirely the point."

"But will I not be ruined? I mean, worse than the gossip rags already imply that I am? And will that not put you in a compromising position?"

"It is generally the young lady who is considered compromised, and then the gentleman is required to do the honorable thing."

She frowned at him. "Precisely my point. Eloise and Phoebe might demand that you marry me."

"I fully expect they will whether I kiss you or not. So what's it to be? A proposal with a kiss or without?"

Her eyes popped wide. "Are you suggesting you will bow to their demand?"

"Yes, although it is not merely a suggestion because I am stating it as fact."

She shook her head and sighed. "You are not making any sense."

"I am making perfect sense. I would much rather kiss you. And yes, it will be a thoroughly compromising one. I am going to ravish you until your body melts."

"Oh." Her gaze shot to his.

"Are you ready for it?" He cast her a tender smile. "I promise you will like it."

"What happens if I do not like the kiss?"

"That could be a problem, because I am going to marry you whatever the outcome."

She coughed. "Your Grace–"

"I am going to kiss you and then I am going to marry you. Stop fretting, Adela. You will adore the kiss."

"I have no doubt. I am sure it is something you do rather well."

He shrugged. "I like to think so, although someone in my position can never be too certain. People lie to me all the time in order to gain my favor."

"I will tell you the truth."

He cast her a wry smile. "I know. This is one of the reasons why I am determined to marry you. Would it be such a terrible thing if we were husband and wife?"

"No, certainly not for me. I expect it will be a dream come true. My heart is already beating rapidly in anticipation of our first kiss. If I am to go down in flames, I may as well enjoy it by kissing a breathtakingly handsome duke."

His smile turned affectionate.

"But I am not certain about this marriage idea of yours. Is this your highhandedly honorable way of absolving me of all responsibility? Your Grace, do not be a fool." She tried to stand and leave, but he kept hold of her hand and nudged her back down beside him. "What are you doing?"

"We are not through talking," he said.

She frowned at him. "There is no turning back once you kiss me in front of these ladies. I can ride out a few months of scandal, but you cannot ride out a lifetime of an unhappy marriage."

"Why do you think our marriage would be an unhappy one?"

"Oh, so many reasons." She was now gaping at him. "Why can I not simply go into hiding? It is not such a bad idea. In fact, I could hide out at the Huntsford Academy library every day from morning till night. It is a magnificent place. Without these irritating social entertainments, I can be left in peace to reconstruct the work I have lost."

"You can do that and be married to me, as well."

"Why are you being so generous? And stubborn, I might add. I am trying to think of a way out of this predicament that doesn't burden you."

"And I am telling you that you are not a burden and I do not want a way out."

She stared at him, looking utterly confused.

As for him, he was viewing their circumstances with more clarity than he had ever viewed any problem in his life. "There is only one way to make Lady Felicity Rose's cruel jest blow up in her face and that is for us to marry. She will spend the rest of her life knowing her spiteful actions put me forever out of her reach. Quite the opposite effect she hoped."

"So, you are willing to chain yourself to me for life just to get back at her? This is about your taking revenge?"

"Not really. I could care less about her. I am doing this for you."

"I do not want you to sacrifice yourself for me."

"Then I am doing it for me. I will never forgive myself for the misery brought down upon you because of my foolish actions."

He startled her by drawing her onto his lap.

She clasped onto his shoulders for support. "What are you doing?"

"Following through on the best decision I have made in my entire life." He circled an arm around her waist to draw her closely up against him. "Are we agreed?"

Her hands slid down his chest to clutch the lapels of his jacket. "No, we are not agreed. I'll need more convincing before I–"

"This might convince you." He plunged his hand into the magnificently unruly coils of her hair, holding her still while he brought his mouth down on hers with crushing heat.

CHAPTER 6

ADELA SLID HER hands up the Duke of Huntsford's broad chest and clutched his muscled shoulders, holding on for dear life as he kissed her with breathless abandon. What was the stubborn clot thinking?

His lips were warm and marvelously pressed against hers in an obvious attempt to melt her resistance.

She ought to have been incensed.

But she was melting, completely captivated, and hoping his kiss would never end. How could she be at all outraged when this was the most wonderful thing ever to happen to her in her exceedingly dull life?

Even the day was beautiful, the sun shining brightly against the bluest sky. Birds twittered in the blossoming trees and the gentle scent of lilac filled the air. It mingled with his delicious, musk scent and the raw heat of their kiss.

She would deal with the consequences later.

Right now, she was on fire.

This plan of his to persuade her to marry him was working.

Dear heaven.

Was he offering this to her for a lifetime?

Why would he allow himself to be shackled to her because of a moment's mistake which was not even his own?

She meant to protest, but her feeble attempts did not sound convincing. Nor did the way her body instinctively molded to his give him any reason to doubt her attraction to him. Why should it? She loved how he felt, the hard length of him and his muscled arms holding her up against him so that her bosom pressed softly against his solid chest.

He deepened the kiss...her very first.

If nothing else marvelous happened in her life, she would have the memory of this moment and a perfect first kiss to warm her cold and empty nights.

Assuming she rejected his proposal, which seemed an incredibly stupid thing for her to do.

But she could not allow his kisses to sway her.

Was it possible he truly wished to marry her?

He certainly kissed her as though he meant it.

Or was it merely his manner to kiss all ladies this way, with passion, power, and possessive hunger?

No wonder women swooned over him.

"What is that scent you're wearing?" he asked, moving his lips off hers and beginning to drop soft kisses along her neck.

"Um...orange blossoms. It's...um...oh, that feels nice. The Farthingale soap. It is one of my favorite scents. I have several and use them depending on whether I'm feeling fruity or...um...what was the question?"

"Your scent," he said in a husky rumble, now suckling her neck.

"What?" She sighed.

Her body was like a volcano, hot and about to erupt.

"Convinced yet?" He nibbled her earlobe.

She moaned and tried to squirm out of his grasp, but he wasn't letting her up and she wasn't trying very hard anyway. Hardly trying at all, for she could not get enough of him. "You are not playing fair."

"Adela, I am going to explode if you keep rubbing your body against me."

"I cannot help it. You are purposely setting me on fire."

"Is it working?"

She closed her eyes and sighed. "Yes. You are a fiend."

"I know," he said and closed his mouth over hers in a second kiss obviously meant to leave her scorched and yearning for more.

He meant to conquer her resistance.

Claim her for his own and show her the promise of what could be between them.

He kissed her with heat and a raw intensity, even though this was her first romantic encounter and she had never experienced passion like this before.

Were the others watching?

Could they see the duke kiss her in this alarmingly splendid way?

They must, she realized, for he did not permit his hands to roam as freely as she sensed he wished, and she could feel the tension in his arms.

A scorching first kiss and swallowed up in the duke's embrace.

Could this day get any better?

His arms formed a protective circle around her body.

"Adela." He sank his mouth deep onto hers once again.

Her lips felt as though they were perfect pillows against his mouth, soft, plump, and surrendering.

He kissed her as though he wanted to lose himself inside her.

"This is sheer madness," she whispered, taking a breath as their lips momentarily drew apart.

"Not mad at all. Inevitable. I knew it the moment you landed atop me when chasing after Runyon. The scent you wore that day reminded me of chestnuts and I wanted to eat you up."

"It was vanilla...but it is easily confused with–"

He chuckled and kissed her once again on the lips, then began kissing her throat. "Marry me, Adela."

She hugged him fiercely. "What will happen if I accept?"

"Happiness for both of us."

"Are you sure?"

He eased back so that their gazes met. "I am not doing this for purposes of revenge or atonement. Nor am I doing this for you."

"You're not?"

"All right, it is for you as well. But mostly, I am doing this for me. Or better said, for the two of us. Why are you so resistant to the idea of marrying me?"

"I'm not at all. My concern is for you. How are you helped in all this? You must think this through more seriously than you are doing now. What is the advantage to you?"

"Marrying a woman with beauty, brains, and who will never lie to me...I think that is quite a good advantage."

"You think I am beautiful?"

His lips curved in a rakish smile. "Yes, Adela. You are."

He studied her, appearing to be done with kissing her for the moment. Well, these kisses had served their purpose.

She was convinced.

She had to marry him.

Who else could ever kiss her this way?

"I think you are the handsomest man in all of England. Will you be angry with me if I think on it overnight and give you my answer in the morning?"

Her reluctance was for his sake, not hers.

"No, Adela. I will not be angry. You would not be *you* if you leaped at my proposal merely because I am a duke."

Her arms were still circled around his neck, and she now rested her head against his shoulder. "I liked our first kiss. And our second. Well, I liked our entire string of kisses."

"So did I."

"Do you mean it?"

"Yes, Adela."

"Did these count for passionate kisses?"

"They were a very good start. It may take a little while to turn you into an insatiable nymph."

"Oh," she groaned. "This is what that horrid rag implied I was."

He tightened his protective hold on her. "Adela, all will be fine once you are my wife. And I do not mind if you are hot and wanton in my bed. I would be happy to have a wife who desired my touch. You are worried that I am making too big a sacrifice for you, but I assure you, it is no sacrifice for me at all."

He kissed her lightly on the forehead. "What do you think my life would be like if I were married to a *ton* diamond like Felicity Rose? Hellish, for certain. As for you, it is not merely about our suitability in bed. I know we will enjoy each other. But you would bring far more into our marriage. Intelligence. Honesty. Friendship. Trust. Support. Loyalty, for I know you will never break your marriage vows."

She inhaled sharply and looked up at him, distress clouding her eyes. "What about you? Will you be faithful to me?"

"Yes."

"Are you certain?" Her heart was in an uproar, for she had not considered this distressing possibility before. "This is important and I need you to answer truthfully."

"Yes, Adela. I give you my word of honor. It is no chore for me to give up the supposed freedom of a bachelor life. I know what is out there, probably sampled more than I should have. I am not going to stray. But I have a question in turn for you. Would you be willing to share my bed?"

"Do you want me to?"

He nodded. "Yes, I will enjoy falling asleep with you in my arms."

"Dear heaven, I must be dreaming. I would like that, too." He was addling her senses, and she was more certain than ever she needed to think things through before giving him an answer. Of course, she wanted him desperately, but she never expected him to jump into this marriage idea so eagerly or agree to fidelity and truly living as husband and wife without a moment's hesitation.

"Adela, you are fretting again." He tipped her chin up and kissed her on the lips once more, this time softly. "Do you still wish to sleep on it before giving me your answer?"

She nodded.

"Then I'll stop by tomorrow morning."

He rose, keeping an arm around her as she got up along with him.

"Will you stay for tea?" she asked.

"No, I have other business that requires my attention."

"Your Grace…" She held him back when he gave her a final kiss before leaving her side.

"The name is Ambrose. You have my permission to call me that whenever we are alone."

"Ambrose." She smiled up at him. "Ambrose. *Ambrose*. Sounds nice."

He arched an eyebrow and chuckled lightly, obviously glad things appeared to be settling as he hoped even if she was slow to go about it. "Did you wish to ask me something? Or simply keep chanting my name?"

"This is serious. If this other business pertains to Mr. Runyon, then be careful when you go after him. He is no pure academician working archeological digs for intellectual pleasure. He is a relic hunter, in it only for fame and profit. Such men are an unsavory lot. Their profession is cutthroat and they will not think twice before stealing precious work from others. Indeed, you ought to be careful because men such as Runyon are desperate. They are not above hurting high-ranking noblemen such as yourself."

"I will keep your warning in mind. But I am not scared of Runyon. He ought to be cowering in fear from me. To set a hand on me would mean a life of imprisonment for him. Do not worry, Adela. I will not proceed recklessly and ignite a new scandal."

"It is your life I am worried about, not some stupid scandal. Do not take his wicked motives for granted. As for scandal, that is the least of your worries. As you said, dukes are impervious to such things."

He caressed her cheek. "As my duchess, you will be impervious, too."

All Adela needed to do was accept his proposal.

She could see the advantages in being his duchess.

No one would dare touch her.

Every door would be open to her.

As for Runyon, she imagined Huntsford would tear the man apart limb from limb if he dared come near her once she was his wife.

Goodness, when had anyone ever protected her like this wonderful man intended to do? All the more reason she had to think things through quite seriously. There would be no turning back once she accepted his proposal.

He arched an eyebrow. "Are you still worried about scandal following you?"

She nodded.

"You needn't be, Adela. I mean it when I say becoming my duchess will cure all ills. Our betrothal alone will shut most people up. No one wants to get on the bad side of the future Duchess of Huntsford."

She cast him a hesitant smile. "Oh, Ambrose. I hope you are right."

CHAPTER 7

AMBROSE RETURNED TO Number 5 Chipping Way the following morning, eager for Adela's decision. The sky was overcast, but he hoped it was not an omen of the news to come. He shook out of the thought, for Adela would eventually make the right decision. He would not give up on asking her until she did.

In truth, he had no doubt what today's answer *should* be. A joyful and unhesitating yes. But Adela was not the usual sort of girl and he could not be completely certain of the outcome.

Of course, neither Eloise nor Phoebe would allow her to refuse him.

But he wanted Adela to accept him willingly.

It would not feel right if she were forced.

He stepped down from his carriage which was getting to be a recognized sight on this elegant street, and strode toward Eloise's front door.

"Good morning, Your Grace," Adela said, standing beside Watling as he approached, her eyes sparkling and her smile radiant. She bustled him into the parlor and surprised him by shutting the doors behind them. "May I kiss you on the cheek? Or is it too presumptuous of me?"

He arched an eyebrow. "That depends. Are we betrothed?"

He awaited her nod, for it had to be an acceptance or she would not have donned another of her lovely gowns or done her hair up in that attractive style if she meant to refuse him. She looked very pretty, as luscious as a future duchess ought to look. The apricot muslin enhanced the shapely form of her body as well as brought out the vividness of her eyes and creaminess of her complexion.

Her hair was styled elegantly atop her head in soft, sweeping waves that followed the natural arc of her curls and suited her heart-shaped face. Of course, he wanted to remove all those pins and bury his hands in that luscious tumble of hair as it fell down her back in a delicate cascade.

She sighed. "Is there any doubt of my answer after the way you kissed me yesterday? Besides, I think my parents will disown me if I refuse you. Not to mention, Eloise will kick me onto the streets."

"Adela..." He took her hands in his. "Don't give me everyone else's reasons. What do you want?"

A delicate blush rose in her cheeks. "I want you. Truly, I have never met a more impressive man in all respects. You leave me breathless. But I must ask you the same question. What do *you* want? Do you think ours could ever be a love match?"

He nodded. "I hope it will, in time. We know so little of each other just yet."

"Yes, precisely. We don't know each other at all. How can we risk a lifetime together? This is my greatest worry."

"This rush is for the best because you and I are both creatures of logic who are always going to think too hard about these questions of love and marriage. It is better that we are pushed to a decision, made to think with our instinctive hearts instead of coming up with all the sensibly cautious reasons not to make the leap. Adela, marrying you is what I want to do. Truly, there is nothing on heaven or earth that could move me to offer for you if I did not wish to do so."

"Dear me, I suppose this means we are betrothed." She cast him a radiant smile that eased his heart. "I am officially accepting your proposal of marriage. I do so with joy and heartfelt gratitude. What happens next?"

He chuckled. "I'll write to my brothers and have them return to London for the wedding."

She gasped, obviously surprised. "Oh, goodness. You have brothers? Yes, of course. You've spoken fondly of your family a time or two. This is something I should have known, and would have had I bothered to give my *Debrett's* proper attention. I'm sure Lady Felicity Rose can recite it by heart. What will your brothers think of me?"

"They will adore you once they see that I adore you. I have two, by the way. Octavian and Julius."

"Will you tell me more about them?"

"Yes, but another time. There is much we need to get through today."

She nodded. "We? That sounds nice. I am an only child, by the way. My parents thought one of me was more than enough for them to manage. In truth, they never intended to have children and had no idea what to do with me when I came along. Once I was old enough to walk and talk they did warm up to me because then they could treat me like a little adult."

He frowned. "You are their daughter, not a passing neighbor. Did they show you any affection?"

"Oh...yes. They are not bad people at all." She appeared to struggle for a moment in forming an answer obviously meant to reassure him. "They are not effusive by nature, but they were never cruel to me. I never lacked for food or comforts. I just think they were helpless to deal with a child they never expected to have. As I said, we got along very well when I grew older. My father and I became particularly close because we shared a love of cave exploration. What about you and your brothers?"

"We are very close and always have been. I'll write to them and explain what is going on. You ought to do the same for your parents. But first, we had better announce the news to Eloise. I'll talk to her about the planning involved in our wedding."

"Yes, please do. My mother and I will make a mess of it if left up to us. She will have no interest whatsoever, for it will distract her attention from her bird studies. Um, I hope Eloise will allow my parents to stay here for the wedding. I wouldn't know where else to put them. Perhaps Mrs. Farthingale will be amenable to putting them up if Eloise cannot."

She began to fret.

"Adela, the details can be worked out later. I'll take them into my home, if necessary."

"Your Grace–"

"Ambrose."

She nodded. "Ambrose, we are not a family of means. My father is a knight and we are comfortable enough, but we cannot come close to matching your opulence. I hate to be blunt about such matters, but we can only afford a modest wedding. By modest, I mean very small and with no extravagance involved."

"No, that will not do. I am a duke. We are in London in the midst of the Season. This cannot be a small wedding. It is bad enough it will be rushed. But I do not expect your family to take on any of this cost. In fact, I will not allow it. I am not marrying you for financial advantage."

"I bring no advantage at all to this union," she said, sounding distraught. "Are we making a mistake?"

"No, Adela. Do not ever think it." He wrapped his arms around her. "You may not bring wealth or a prestigious title, but those are not important to me. I already have those. What you bring is something far more precious...a chance at happiness. It is something I despaired of ever finding in marriage until you barreled over me the other day."

She circled her arms around his neck and laughed softly. "You are impossible to resist when you say such nice things to me. Ambrose, I dare not let my heart soar. I am so worried something will go wrong. But I feel the same about you. It scares me that I should feel so comfortable around you when we hardly know each other, or that I should trust you so completely. But I do. It has nothing to do with your rank or wealth, I hope you know this."

"I do. You would not have gotten an offer out of me if I did not believe this about you." He eased away a moment to reach into the breast pocket of his jacket and withdraw a small box. "My father gave this ring to my mother as a token of his love on the day of their betrothal. I now give it to you."

He opened the box to reveal a star sapphire encircled by tiny diamonds. "Will you wear it for me?"

Adela gasped. "Do you dare trust me with anything so fine? Well, I know you must, but I can be so clumsy sometimes."

She allowed him to slip it onto her finger, her eyes wide as he did so. "It is a little too large for your finger," he murmured.

"Yes, perhaps we ought to set it back in the box for now. What if I lose it?"

"You won't. I'd like you to wear it from now on. We will have it properly sized. In fact, we can attend to it today. Do you have any plans?"

"Other than to sit in Eloise's garden and dream about you?" She emitted a soft, lilting laugh. "No, I am completely at leisure."

"Good. We have a bit of running around to do besides getting that ring fitted."

"Such as? And should we not tell Eloise what we've done before we begin traipsing around London? Phoebe ought to be told, as well. Oh, and you will need my father's consent because I am still shy of my twenty-first birthday. I only turned twenty last month. How old are you, by the way? Or is this an impertinent question?"

"I am just shy of thirty, Adela."

"And you held off marrying for this long? Women must have been pursuing you since you were sixteen."

"Even earlier than that. You would be appalled to know how young I was when women first began propositioning me."

"That is awful. But did none of them steal your heart?"

"No, not a one. Not even close." He sighed. "You are fretting again. What is troubling you now?"

"I had hoped for a love marriage. But if you have never once been in love in all this time, then how will you ever fall in love with me?"

"Who is to say I won't?"

"No one, but you must consider the odds. They are worse than I thought."

He was not going to get into a discussion about love. It was pointless. He wasn't in love with her nor could she possibly be in love with him in less than a week's time. But she obviously had a strong streak of the romantic in her and wanted theirs to be a love match.

He liked that she had a logical mind that could sort out the most complex puzzles of the ancients and at the same time had a soft heart that yearned for romance.

In truth, he could fall in love with someone just like her.

Time would tell.

She certainly affected him.

Was this not a good starting point?

Eloise entered, putting an end to his and Adela's private conversation.

She shrieked when she saw the ring on Adela's finger. "I am delighted! We must tell Phoebe at once. When is the wedding to be? Dear me, I must write to your parents at once. They must be told the good news immediately. Your father will consent to the marriage, of course. I will insist upon it."

"I have no doubt he will agree. He and my mother will dance a jig when they hear the news. They'll want to know of our plans as they are firmed." She emitted a breathless laugh. "We haven't set a date yet. But is there a rush? We are betrothed and this ought to suffice for now."

Ambrose had no intention of waiting.

Having made his decision, he wanted the matter done fast. "We'll marry within a month's time, Adela. I am not going to allow for an extended betrothal. I know what you are thinking."

She tipped her pert chin in the air. "What am I thinking?"

"That if we wait long enough, the scandal will pass and I can quietly back out of marrying you. It is not going to happen. Stop thinking of me and worry about yourself a little, will you? My backing out, even if I am quiet as a mouse about it, will only create a fresh scandal for you."

She sighed. "Are all dukes this persistent?"

"This one is. I cannot speak for others."

A short while later, he escorted Eloise and Adela into his coach to make their way to Phoebe's home. Her butler, an ancient relic as old as Eloise's trusted Watling, took forever to dodder to the door. He recognized them immediately and escorted them into the parlor. "Lady Withnall shall be right down, Your Grace."

They heard the telltale *thuck, thuck, thuck* of her cane upon the marble floor of her entry hall. The little termagant hurried in moments later, her nose twitching in expectation of their news. "Well, Huntsford?"

He grinned. "Adela and I are betrothed."

She clapped her hands. "Well done, dear boy. I always knew you were the cleverest of the lot. You have secured the hand of this Season's true diamond."

He glanced at Adela and winked. "I am in complete agreement."

Adela smiled up at him. "I am the one who found the pot of gold at the end of the rainbow. Oh, but I do not mean your wealth. I hope you know I am only referring to *you* and not those other trappings."

"I know," he said softly, for this was the greatest treasure to him, to be admired for his true self and not the false allure of his fortune and title.

They did not stay long at Phoebe's home, for he was eager to be on his way. He and Adela left the two dowagers to themselves to do what they did best...spread gossip and organize wedding plans. He expected word of his and Adela's engagement would race like wildfire throughout the *ton*. All of London would hear of it within the hour.

He assisted Adela into his carriage and settled in the seat opposite hers. This not only gave him the space he needed to stretch out comfortably, but also had him facing Adela as they spoke.

She had the prettiest face and he would never tire of looking into her lovely, intelligent eyes.

He enjoyed looking at every bit of her.

The first stop he intended to make was the jeweler's to have the ring properly fitted. She would spend the day in dread fear of losing it if the matter were not attended to immediately.

Afterward, he wanted to stop by the Huntsford Academy to see if the missing book had been returned. He had met his Bow Street runner earlier this morning before riding over to Chipping Way, and was not pleased to learn Runyon had slipped out of town.

Ambrose was now worried the wastrel had taken the book and Adela's notes with him. However, Mr. Barrow indicated Runyon had merely taken a small, overnight pouch that was not big enough to fit the book and a change of clothes. "If he's gone off, it cannot be for more than a day or two, Your Grace," Mr. Barrow had assured him. "His rent has been paid in advance for the next month and he does not strike me as the sort to let a ha'penny go to waste. He'll be back for the rest of his belongings."

And what of the book?

Had he gone off for the purpose of selling it outside of London?

Mr. Barrow assured him again there was no book inside the man's pouch, but how could he know for certain? Not that he doubted the Bow Street runner's ingenuity or extensive contacts. The man knew everyone and seemed to have connections with those from every walk of life. This probably included the mail coach driver who must have been paid to take a peek inside Runyon's travel pouch as it was loaded atop the roof of the coach headed for Oxford and report what was inside.

Perhaps Mr. Barrow had climbed up there himself to have a look.

Well, he had no choice but to rely on his man.

Still, it troubled him that the book and Adela's notes were nowhere to be found.

Ambrose's carriage traveled slowly through the crowded streets of London, but he did not mind since he was alone with Adela. He took advantage of their time together to relate the earlier conversation he'd had with Mr. Barrow. Indeed, traffic was unusually heavy and it would take them a while to reach the jeweler's shop.

She listened attentively and then added her thoughts. "Mr. Runyon often works with an archeologist by the name of Roman Hollingsworth who resides in Oxford. He is also an untrustworthy knave, if you ask me. I am not concerned about my notes, for they contain nothing that is not fresh in my thoughts and easily reconstructed. Much is already in the public knowledge. It is the loss of your book that worries me most. What if Mr. Barrow is wrong and he did take it with him? He could not have had more than a minute or two in which to open the man's pouch and search inside, assuming he and not the mail coach driver was the one who searched."

"Adela, I have no choice but to trust Mr. Barrow's report. The man is very good at what he does."

"Perhaps Runyon did not have it with him this time, but what about next time? What if he intends to hand it over to Hollingsworth and that fiend attempts to sell it on the Continent? How will you ever get it back?"

"The wonderful thing about thieves is that they do not trust each other. By your description of Runyon's character, I do not think he will ever tell his confederate about that book. But do you think Runyon himself will leave England?"

"No," Adela said with a purse of her lips. "Not for another few weeks, for certain. He is trying to gain funding from the Royal Society for a new expedition. He submitted a proposal last month and will lose out if he suddenly disappears in order to sell your book. Besides, I think he is afraid to sell something that unique and will likely return it to you if he gains his funding."

"I hope so."

"I know how this man thinks. He is too close to obtaining his funding to risk getting caught by you. However, if he is denied, then I would not put it past him to sell the book and run off with his profits. Still, it worries me that he ran off to Oxford in the first place. He and Hollingsworth must be up to something, even if it is not about your book. But what if we are wrong and he is now setting Hollingsworth up as a go-between to sell it?"

Ambrose shook his head. "If Mr. Barrow is right and Runyon did not take it with him, then he is not yet ready to share the information with his cohort. But it is possible he has his own shady sources in Oxford that he plans to approach. Greed is greed. If there is profit to be had, Runyon will keep it all for himself."

"He will act quickly if his proposal is rejected by the Royal Society. We ought to ask the Duke of Lotheil to give you fair warning before Runyon is told of their decision. If he loses that source of income, he won't waste a moment before rushing off to sell your book."

"I will take care of it, Adela. Don't worry."

"But I do worry. How can I not? I think your Bow Street man ought to search Runyon's residence again. He would not leave that book lying out in the open. But with Runyon gone, this is the best chance your man will have to conduct a thorough search. Perhaps the wretched fellow has it hidden under a floorboard."

"Mr. Barrow is most capable. He would not overlook something that obvious, but I will ask him to search again. He may even be doing so as we speak."

She nodded. "It is also possible Runyon squirreled it away in the Royal Society building. We ought to stop there after the jeweler's and ask to search the place. I have a few other ideas where it might be. I know Runyon's habits. He and this Hollingsworth fellow have a favorite tavern they usually go to for a drink not far from the Royal Society. It is called The Red Drake, and–"

"How do you know this?"

She cast him a guilty look. "They are not discreet about anything they do. It is not the first time Runyon has attempted to steal my notes. After he tried the first time, I thought I had better learn a little more about him, so I followed him to the tavern one afternoon after a lecture."

Ambrose did not want her doing this again. This Runyon fellow was not a good character and he did not want his future wife following wretches like him into any seedy drinking establishments. "You are betrothed to me now, Adela. Promise me you will not run off on your own again."

She frowned. "Will I never be permitted to leave Eloise's house? Or yours after we are married?"

"You may come and go as you please, so long as you have two footmen to accompany you at all times. I am serious about this. You are to be my duchess. You are no longer Miss Adela Swift, penniless bluestocking."

She gasped in indignation. "My family is not penniless."

"I do not mean…" He groaned. "What I wish to convey is that

you are now a potential ransom prize. A desperate fool might think it is a good idea to abduct a duchess. *My* duchess. Do you understand this? Keep a sharp eye out, that is all I am saying."

"Ransom? Abduction? All right. I had not thought about that part of becoming associated with you."

"More than associated, I should hope. We are to be husband and wife." He sighed. "All I am saying is that you must take extra care in what you do."

"And also watch what I say, for certain." She pursed her lips and nodded. "I was also thinking about the teas, charities, and ladies societies that might require my time once we married. My thoughts were on how to manage those obligations and still go on about my research. But as you point out, there is a darker side to becoming your duchess that completely escaped me. I had not given thought to how much my life would change once we exchanged vows."

He moved over to sit beside her. "The change will mostly be for the better. We'll have each other from this day forward. You'll also be free to pursue your animal bones. The only difference is that you will do it with guards discreetly watching over you."

To his relief, she seemed to accept this very significant intrusion in her life.

"We have not discussed a wedding trip," she said after several minutes of their riding in silence. "If we must keep guards about us, then is travel overseas not made more difficult? Would you be averse to spending our holiday exploring my Devonshire caves?"

"And dig up those ancient animal bones you are determined to find? Sounds quite romantic."

She laughed. "Your sarcasm is duly noted. I suppose it is rather ghoulish to spend our first month of marital bliss in a dank pit, digging up dead things."

"Would you not prefer traveling to Italy? Or France? Greece? We could spend the entire year going wherever you like."

"With an entourage at our beck and call? What would you like to do, Ambrose?"

He leaned closer and took her hands in his. "I have already seen much of the world. The choice is yours, Adela."

She arched an eyebrow. "A year seems a very long time to be away, especially with all your business responsibilities."

"My brothers will take up most of the slack, Julius mostly because Octavian is still in the Royal Navy and I doubt they will allow him an entire year off to attend to the Huntsford interests."

"If the choice is mine, and you are not going to be angry about it, then I choose the Devonshire caves."

"Truly? Of all the beautiful places in the world, this is where you would most like to go? Ah, because your true heart's desire is to get that footnote in a book. *The Duchess of Huntsford, the former Miss Adela Swift, was the first to discover the massive bones of an extinct, as yet unidentified creature, in a cave not far from the Huntsford estate.*" He sank back against the squabs and regarded her affectionately. "It means the world to you, doesn't it?"

She nodded. "It is my dream. I don't wish to give it up."

He gave her cheek a light caress. "Nor shall you. Devonshire it is."

CHAPTER 8

ADELA WAS NOT used to all the attention now being foisted on her and quickly came to understand what Ambrose must have endured for most of his life. No wonder he held himself aloof and trusted no one.

It made the confidence he had shown in her all the more significant.

He seemed so content with his decision to marry her, she sometimes wondered whether she was trapped in a dream. But he was quite real, and she needed to do her best never to disappoint him.

Once his trust was lost, it would likely be lost forever.

Tonight was the night of Lord and Lady Knightly's ball. Ambrose had arrived to escort her and Eloise to this grand affair. As they rode in his elegant carriage to the Knightly townhouse, he reached over and took her hand in his. "Adela, are you all right?"

She smiled at him and nodded. "Yes, just preparing myself for the crush of guests we are about to face. Life was much simpler when I was merely a wallflower and soundly ignored. But I will have my three knights in shining armor to protect me...you, Eloise, and Phoebe, so I will smile and bear up gracefully no matter what is said about me."

"You shall have an entire army of protectors there tonight," Eloise remarked. "John and Sophie Farthingale will be in attendance along with at least thirty of their family members. Some of those Farthingale girls are married to Brayden men. No one tangles with a Brayden unless they have a death wish. My grandsons are equally fierce, so do not be fooled by how gentle and loving they are toward their wives."

Ambrose chuckled. "Satisfied, Adela?"

She nodded. "Yes, but I do hate the notion of others fighting my battles. Not that I am looking for trouble, however there are those who will attempt to cause mischief because this is in their nature. Is it awful of me to suspect Lady Felicity Rose will do her best to undermine me tonight? I suppose I will survive her insults. But I would be so much more at ease if she caught some inconvenient disease to keep her at home. Not life-threatening, of course. A splotchy, red rash of indeterminate cause along her arms and face would serve quite nicely."

Eloise chuckled.

But Ambrose's expression turned fierce. "I'll stay close. No one will dare insult you."

Adela liked that he could be apishly protective of her, for he did not usually show his feelings. He was always politeness itself and surprisingly indulgent of her, for who else would have agreed to digging up skulls in Devonshire on their honeymoon? But he could never be described as demonstrative in his affections.

For now, it was enough that he seemed to enjoy her company and did not tire of having her around.

Perhaps passion would come in time, for she knew he was capable of it. Had he not kissed her with fiery abandon? Those kisses could not count as true passion because he had used them as a means to an end, doing whatever was needed to gain her agreement to marry him.

Job well done.

Mission accomplished.

But she could not be angry with him for wanting to protect her.

She liked what she had seen of this private side of him. Had he not kissed her, she might never have known he had so much compassion within him. What he allowed others to see was the icier side of him, the one that required steady determination and cool calculation in order to effectively get his way.

Yet, it could not be overlooked that the kisses he had given her when convincing her to marry him had been exquisitely steamy and quite effective in rousing her desire.

One item she thought might be a problem was the matter of her father's consent. But his letter expressing delight and giving his hearty approval had arrived this morning, which was not possible unless someone had written to her father days earlier to request it. She did not think it was Eloise, but would not put it past her partner in crime, Phoebe, to have done such a thing.

The woman's instincts were uncanny.

Said consent was never in doubt since her parents had shoved her onto the marriage mart with precisely this objective in mind, although they never expected her to find such a prize as the Duke of Huntsford.

That he did not love her to distraction made Adela a little sad, but she was no enchantress and never the sort to steal a man's breath away.

It was enough that he easily tolerated her and appeared to enjoy her company.

She and Eloise were seated across from him in his carriage as it drew up behind a long queue of carriages outside Lord and Lady Knightly's splendid home.

"The house is ablaze in candlelight. How pretty it looks." Adela peered out the window as their carriage slowly moved forward toward the elegant townhouse.

"Is all arranged with Lady Knightly?" Eloise asked Ambrose as their turn came and a footman opened the door to assist them in descending.

"Yes, she and her husband will make the announcement of our betrothal as they are about to open the ball. Of course, everyone knows of it already."

"But this will make it official and irrefutable." Eloise nodded her approval.

Adela's stomach was in knots.

She took a deep breath and emerged from the carriage with a smile. She refused to be known as the cowardly duchess...or rather, cowardly duchess-to-be. She took Ambrose's offered arm so he could escort her and Eloise to the receiving line.

To her dismay, Lady Felicity Rose and her father were just ahead of them. Oh, how dearly she wished to avoid that girl. Lord Brynmore stood beside her, as ever the pandering toady.

Were The Fates contriving against her to put her in the path of the two people she hoped most to avoid?

She glanced at Ambrose, but his expression was stoic and completely unreadable.

If only she could appear so restrained.

Her blood was already boiling.

Ambrose sensed her mounting ire and shot her a warning glance. "Adela," he whispered in her ear, "you are my betrothed. You've won. Just smile and enjoy the evening."

Yes, he was right in theory.

In reality, it was hard to shed her hurt.

She was no diamond and would never be.

She still felt like a wallflower.

However, the pair surprised her. Neither Felicity Rose nor Brynmore turned around to acknowledge them. Well, that was satisfying. They behaved like scared mice, obviously afraid Ambrose and Eloise would give them the cut direct after having misplayed their hand. Indeed, what a delicious mistake on their part. Instead of humiliating her, they had put her straight in the arms of England's most coveted bachelor.

To see them crushed was most satisfying, not only for herself but for every shy debutante who had ever been teased and ridiculed by that loathsome pair. Oh, how she hated these mean-spirited *ton* games.

She was glad she had a duke and a dowager countess on her side.

As the last of the guests arrived, Lord and Lady Knightly moved off the receiving line to open their ball with a dance.

But before they did so, they motioned for their footmen to bring out glasses of champagne. Once everyone was served, Lord Knightly held up his glass. "It is with great honor, and humble appreciation of my long friendship with the Duke of Huntsford, that I announce his betrothal to the lovely Miss Adela Swift."

Cheers rang out among the crowd, and Adela was certain it

was her Farthingale supporters at their rowdy best, for it certainly was not Felicity Rose and her toady friends. She and Lord Brynmore looked mad enough to kill. This ought to have made Adela smile, for revenge was sweet, but it only made her worry about what they would plot next.

She shook out of the thought and stood beside Ambrose, a beaming smile on her face as they both accepted everyone's good wishes. The second dance was to be a waltz, and this time she did not hesitate when Ambrose swept her into his arms. They twirled in time to the music, following the other dancers as they moved in an easy flow around the dance floor.

She felt the heat of his gaze on her as he asked, "How are you doing, Adela?"

"Perfect." She smiled up at him. "I feel as though I am dancing upon a soft cloud."

"Have you been practicing? You seem relaxed, unlike last time when you were ready to cast up your accounts."

"I haven't practiced at all."

He eyed her curiously. "But you really have improved."

She shook her head. "The only thing that has changed is my trust in your lead. You are a very good dancer and I am no longer terrified of falling on my face. I trust you and am not afraid of anything when I am with you. Is this not a wonderful revelation? This is how I hope we'll move through our lives together."

Was it too soon for her to admit she was in love with him?

She dared not say anything yet.

Her declaration might scare him off.

It still scared her.

In any event, how could she be certain of her feelings in this short a time?

"Thank you, Adela. I hope for the same." His gaze drifted up and down her body. "You look very pretty tonight."

"It is another of Madame de Bressard's marvelous creations." The blue satin exactly matched the color of her eyes, that delicate blue with a tinge of gray. The fabric somehow fell across her body in such a way that it enhanced her best features and hid the worst.

As for Ambrose, he simply managed to look magnificent all the time, a big, handsome specimen of a man.

"Hold tight, Adela. I'm going to spin you outdoors."

"Why? Is something wrong?" She glanced around, worried Felicity Rose was about to swoop down on her and trip her, or step on her gown, or plot something fiendish to embarrass her.

"No." He cast her a rakish smile. "I just think it would be nice to dance with you under the moonlight."

She let out the breath she had been holding and laughed. "Spin away. I have no intention of stopping you."

Within moments, he had led her onto the terrace and down the steps into the small garden. To her dismay, there were other couples there already.

By the sounds emanating from the bushes, it appeared they were doing more than merely kissing.

She sighed, wishing Ambrose would kiss her.

As romantic as a dance in the moonlight was, could he not see his way to adding a kiss to it? However, she dared not say a word and risk irritating him by pushing him into doing something he was not eager to do.

The man knew his own mind and would not hesitate to seduce her if this is what he truly desired. That he did not seem inclined to do so proved she held no particularly seductive power over him.

A kiss would have sufficed.

It was not such a bad thing since he kissed divinely.

The moon was full and silver.

Distant torchlights cast a golden glow across the plant beds and walkways.

Ambrose drew her behind a rose arbor, her back suddenly against one of the empty trellises that was fragile enough to snap under pressure. He planted his hands on either side of her shoulders and leaned in deliciously close. "Adela, you make me ache."

"I do?"

Obviously, she knew nothing about men.

They weren't dancing, and he was looking at her as though he wished to devour her.

Which probably explained why he then bent his head to hers and kissed her with a raw hunger that caught her by surprise. Had she roused his passion? The notion was delightful. Or was this moment simply a matter of his *manly urges* coming to the fore as they might with any woman?

Eloise and Phoebe had lectured her earlier today on men and their urges. They were determined to explain what would happen to her on her wedding night.

Dear heaven.

It was the most embarrassing lecture she'd ever had to sit through. "Ambrose…"

"What, love?" He moved off her lips and was now kissing gently along her throat.

How easily he turned her body to fire.

"This manly urge you are having…"

He paused and chuckled softly while staring at her, his eyes as silver as the moon. "Do go on."

"Um, I understand that men are sometimes overcome by certain needs. My question is, is your need specific to me? Or would anyone do?"

"Blessed saints, what have those two old ladies been telling you?" he asked with a soft chuckle.

"Do you really want to know?"

He shook his head. "No, just forget everything they've taught you. I had better take you back inside."

"Oh, must you?" She could not mask her disappointment. "I did not mean to make you stop."

"I know, but it is best we do." He took her hand in his to lead her back inside. "To answer your question, it is you who brings out the wicked in me. No one else. This is why we had better go back inside. You look too delicious. I would not have stopped at mere kisses."

She smiled at him. "Truly?"

He nodded. "Truly, Adela. You are bewitching."

She shook her head and laughed. "Well, isn't that something? I have never been called that before."

"I shall have to correct this oversight."

She stared up at him, very much liking how they fit together as a couple. He was much taller and handsomely broad in the shoulders. She was not nearly as tall. In fact, she felt quite small beside him, but in a very nice way. Despite these differences, she could not get over feeling they were perfect for each other. "You are quite bewitching yourself."

He raised her hand to his lips and kissed it as they returned to the ballroom, a gesture noticed by everyone within close proximity of the doorway. "Men are not bewitching. That compliment is reserved for women."

"Then what are you?"

He grinned. "Magnificent will suffice."

She could not hold back her lilt of laughter. "Modest fellow, aren't you?"

"Never said I was. In fact, I am probably insufferably arrogant. But I am also happy, Adela," he said with a serious turn to his voice, now taking her for a stroll about the large ballroom under the watchful eye of curious onlookers. "I want others to know it."

"Is this why you have been so demonstrative tonight? You certainly have been behaving like the gushing bridegroom. But I know it is all calculated to play to our audience."

"The feelings are real. The only difference is that I choose to reveal them to others at this time. I suppose it could be construed as manipulative."

"Which got us into this trouble in the first place," she interjected.

"It is for a good cause in this instance. I am staking my claim on you, something made necessary because of that malicious bit of gossip about you fed to the scandal rags. Everyone needs to know the insinuations were ridiculous, that we dote on each other and have eyes for no one else."

"That is easy for me to do. I cannot stop looking at you because you are so handsome."

"I appreciate the compliment." When they reached the long table where the punch bowls were set out, he paused a moment to scan the room. "As for you...Felicity Rose and Brynmore have not taken their beady eyes off you the entire evening."

She glanced up in surprise. "You've been watching them?"

"Yes, of course. It bothers me they have not moved on at this point in the evening. This tells me they are plotting mischief, so I am not leaving your side at all tonight. One would think they would know better than to cross me, but those two are so full of bile, who knows what they will do? Come, let's keep walking. Brynmore is heading toward us and I think he will have the effrontery to ask you to dance."

"Ugh, I would refuse him."

"Let's not give him the opportunity to cause a scene." The supper dance was about to start. "Dance with me, Adela?"

"All right." She knew it was important for them to be mingling and looking happy, not to mention this was an easy way to avoid Brynmore's unwanted attention. Besides, she knew this reel and would not completely mess up the steps.

To her dismay, Felicity Rose and Brynmore also joined in the dance.

Ambrose had steered her far enough away from the troublesome pair that they might never encounter them as couples twirled and shifted forward in their positions as part of the reel.

However, it was not long before she noticed the pair skipping forward and cutting off other dancers to reach them.

Ambrose noticed it, too. "Botheration. What is wrong with them?"

"Brynmore would not be so stupid as to try something, would he?"

"The man is an idiot. Any man who grovels the way he does over Felicity Rose has to be a witless buffoon."

The pair were now upon them, Brynmore about to partner Adela as they met in the middle to spin around once before returning to their positions. He had just taken one of her hands in his and placed the other at the small of her back when Ambrose suddenly grabbed his arm and twisted it with enough force to bring Brynmore to his knees.

The oaf released her with a yelp.

"Drop it," Ambrose said, his voice a menacing growl.

In the next moment, a small pocket knife fell to the ground.

Adela gasped.

Another man picked it up.

She recognized him as the Duke of Edgeware, Dillie's husband. Dillie was right behind him, peering over his shoulder as he knelt to retrieve it. "Ian, what is it?"

Adela was curious to know, as well.

Edgeware glanced over at Ambrose who was still holding Brynmore in a tight grip that had the oaf still on his knees and squealing. "I don't think he meant you physical harm, Miss Swift. He likely intended to cut a few laces on your gown to make it appear shoddy work. The intent was likely to embarrass you."

"And I am certain I know just who put him up to it." She clenched her hands into fists, about to stride off to confront Felicity Rose, but Ambrose released Brynmore and put an arm about her waist to hold her close to him.

She frowned at him. "Why are you letting go of that toad?"

"Finn Brayden has hold of him now," he said, glancing at the big, dark-haired man who now had Brynmore by the scruff of his neck. Finn's wife was Belle Farthingale. In this moment, Adela realized what it meant to have the support of such a close-knit family, to have loved ones who looked after their own. It warmed her heart to realize she was now considered by the Farthingales as one of their own.

How was she ever to repay their kindness?

She loved her parents, even though she would never consider them competent in raising a child. Most of the time they forgot she existed because they were so caught up in their own thoughts. They did not mean to forget her...well, perhaps they did. To this day, they had not come to terms with her unexpected arrival. "Why will you not let me confront that horrid diamond? You know she is the one who conceived this spiteful plot."

"Which failed."

"But who is to know it unless we do something about it?"

"You are not to say or do anything to her, Adela."

"Are you serious? You would restrain me?"

He nodded. "Keep your righteous indignation to yourself."

She drew in a breath, not liking this at all. Was the odious girl

96 | MEARA PLATT

to get away with her mean-spirited schemes? "But I need to give her a piece of my mind."

"No, you do not. It is the last thing you need to do. Have you learned nothing after that gossip rag debacle? I will take care of it."

"You?" She frowned at him again. "Are you going to release me?"

"No. We've drawn enough of a crowd as it is."

Lord Knightly elbowed his way through the onlookers. "Huntsford, what is going on? Miss Swift, are you all right?"

Ambrose reported what had happened.

"Dear heaven," said Lord Knightly.

Lord Brynmore was promptly tossed out.

"He shall never step foot in my home again," their host muttered before ordering the musicians to resume the disrupted supper dance.

The crowd began to thin as the excitement was over and they all preferred to dance the lively reel.

Lady Felicity Rose was now off in a corner hiding behind her circle of friends. A few of those friends appeared to be edging away from the diamond, as though they wanted nothing more to do with her.

This delighted Adela.

Perhaps she would not need to confront her, for who was this diamond without others to do her cruel bidding? Ambrose now had a manly, quite apish look on his face as turned to Felicity Rose and her crowd. "Stay close to Dillie and her husband. Do not follow me."

"Where are you going?" But she knew by the determined glint in his eyes that he was about to issue a warning to the toadies still hovering around the malicious girl.

This is exactly what he did, striding toward Felicity Rose's circle with the intent of asserting his dominance.

He had forbidden her from so much as curling her fists, but he now had his own fists curled and was silently daring them all to fight.

Was it wrong of her to adore that surprisingly barbarian

quality about him?

Adela had to admit, she liked this protect-my-woman attitude. He had a warrior's agility and the prowess to pull it off.

They would have laughed at her and called her deranged if she had attempted the same, she supposed.

She had not seen the knife in Brynmore's hand, but had felt the slightest prick to her back just before Ambrose wrenched the bounder from her side and forced him to his knees.

Dillie and Finn Brayden's wife, Belle, joined her as she watched Ambrose in all his manly splendor. Their husbands had gone off with Brynmore to make certain he did not attempt to sneak back inside.

Dillie giggled. "They really enjoy behaving like apes. All this etiquette and civility grates on their nerves sometimes. Huntsford will come back to you with his chest puffed out and probably do something wonderfully stupid like sweep you into his arms. My twin, Lily, wrote a wonderful monograph comparing dominant male baboons to men. You should have heard the uproar she caused in the Royal Society. But those Fellows are all cowards, scared to death of any intelligent woman."

Belle, a pretty blonde with a sweet manner about her, chuckled. "You probably know this already, but Lily's husband, Ewan Cameron, is the Duke of Lotheil's grandson. He's a big, brawny Scot and fiercely protective of Lily."

Adela laughed. "Yes, I have been fully versed on your amazing family. I am so impressed by all of you, and readily see why your husbands adore you."

"Our big, apish husbands," Belle said with a giggle. "They are all this way, the wonderful proof of Lily's hypothesis."

"I doubt the Duke of Huntsford will ever be so brazen as to carry me off in his arms," Adela said, hoping not to sound wistful. "He is too controlled."

Belle shook her head. "No one is more controlled than Finn. His mind is all facts and figures, but even he has his wonderfully male baboon moments. Are you all right, Adela? Forgive me, may I call you that? We haven't been formally introduced, but you have met most of my family, and I already feel as though you are one of us."

"Please do. I adore your family. I wish I had grown up with siblings. But alas, there is only me."

Dillie inspected the back of Adela's gown. "Come upstairs to the ladies retiring room with us. There is a spot of blood at the small of your back. Huntsford is going to go wild if he sees it. We cannot have him kill Brynmore."

"Dear heaven. Please, let's go right now. I don't feel anything. Are you sure it is blood?"

Dillie nodded. "A very small spot. He must have nicked you while attempting to get at that first lacing. It might have happened while Huntsford grabbed his hand to draw him away. But don't even suggest it to Huntsford or he will never forgive himself."

"Take her upstairs, Dillie," Belle said. "I'll follow you as soon as I get some brandy to cleanse the cut. It cannot be deep, but if it broke skin, then it must be cleaned out."

Adela was not about to protest.

She and Dillie hurried upstairs.

The ladies retiring room was empty, which was a great relief considering the hour of the night and the crowd. But supper had now been called so everyone was on their way to the dining hall for the meal that was certain to be a feast.

Dillie quickly unlaced her.

Belle hurried in a moment later. "I have the brandy."

The mark on her back was little more than a pin prick, but it had drawn a drop of blood and Adela did not trust the condition of Brynmore's knife. It could not have been kept clean, for that toady was not a fastidious fellow.

Quite the opposite, he was lax and lazy.

She flinched only slightly as they used a handkerchief to apply the brandy to her skin.

Dillie then held the handkerchief to the spot and kept it there as they laced her gown so that the delicate cloth served as a makeshift bandage. They also managed to scrub out the tiny bloodstain on the silk.

Ambrose was looking for her, concern etched on his face, when she returned. "Dillie and Belle took me upstairs to calm me down," she explained. "Are you hungry? Shall we join everyone else in the dining room?"

He arched an eyebrow. "Are you sure you are all right?"

"Yes, I'm perfect." She wrapped her arm in his. "Did you scare off Felicity Rose's toadies? I think you must have enjoyed growling at them all."

His expression lightened and he smiled. "I did find it satisfying."

Later that evening back at Eloise's house, Adela told him the truth about why she had gone to the ladies retiring room.

He exploded. "Why did you not tell me sooner? I would have killed the stupid bastard."

"Which is precisely why I waited until now to tell you. Is this not the very same reason you would not let me approach Felicity Rose?" She matched his stubborn look with one of her own. "I do not need you killing a man over me."

"You need to see a doctor."

"Don't be ridiculous. I am fine."

He summoned Dr. George Farthingale, who happened to be having a nightcap next door with John and Sophie. Adela was now quite well versed in all the Farthingale family connections, and knew George and John were brothers.

To her relief, George Farthingale did not appear in the least incensed to be disturbed at this hour of the night over so small a matter. The ball had gone on into the wee hours of the morning, and he had also been in attendance. "Let me have a look at you, Adela. I understand my niece treated your cut. Dillie knows what she is doing. I'm sure she did it properly."

Adela nodded. "That's what I tried to explain to His Grace. But he is too thickheaded to listen."

"I am not thickheaded, but I do protect what is mine." Ambrose insisted on remaining in the room while the doctor examined her. He stood quietly with his arms crossed over his chest, looking every bit the fierce warrior as he observed all that went on. "Well, doctor?"

Since George Farthingale kept a spare medical bag at his brother's home – no doubt necessary when dealing with his family's own cuts, scrapes, and other more serious wounds – he had exactly what he needed at hand. "This tincture works wonders at preventing infection. Not that I expect one to develop, for Dillie and Belle did a good job in treating Adela. I am also applying a bandage to it, but its only purpose is to prevent the tincture from bleeding onto your gowns, Adela. Wouldn't want to ruin them. That ought to do it."

She cast him a heartfelt smile. "Thank you, Dr. Farthingale. I am so sorry we disturbed you at this hour of the night."

"Not at all," he replied kindly. "His Grace was worried about you, and rightly so. Having seen battle wounds and how quickly they can become infected, he had to be cautious and summon me. Well, good night to you both."

Ambrose nodded. "Doctor, I've taken you out of your way. May I give you a ride home?"

He shook his head. "Yes, I would appreciate that. Will you give me a few minutes to wash up and return my medical bag to my brother's house?"

"Yes, of course. I'll need a minute with Adela anyway."

She sighed. "You had better not lecture me."

Ambrose rubbed his hand along the nape of his neck. "I am not going to lecture you."

"Because I will stick my fingers in my ears and refuse to hear a word if you attempt it."

"Adela, I am not going to lecture you."

The doctor chuckled as he walked out. "You sound like a married couple already."

Adela gathered the bodice of her gown about her bosom as best she could, for she now felt the heat of Ambrose's gaze on her while she was very much unlaced.

Goodness, she liked that smolder in his eyes.

She cleared her throat. "Eloise and my maid will come up here any moment now."

"I know." He took a step toward her. "You should have told me, Adela."

"About Brynmore? I did, but I just waited until I felt it was safe to do so. Not that I feel very safe with you at the moment. I mean, you look as though you are about to eat me up."

"The thought did cross my mind."

She smiled. "Really?"

He nodded and took another step toward her, his own smile delightfully rakish. "It has been on my mind all evening," he said with a deliciously soft growl.

"Well, I suppose it is all right since we are betrothed and everyone will assume I have already succumbed to your will. Um...what are you going to do?"

"This." He drew her up in his arms and crushed his lips to hers with passionate urgency, while his hands now roamed along her body.

Dear heaven.

"Adela, stop me if you are not ready for something beyond kisses."

"Not ready? Dear heaven, you have no idea how long I've hoped for such a moment. It shall be a starred page in my diary."

"You keep a diary?" He laughed. "Of course, you do. You are one for keeping notes, aren't you? Do not write any of this down or Phoebe and Eloise will flay me alive."

One big hand delved beneath her loosened bodice and closed around her breast.

He stroked his thumb lightly across the bud of her breast.

Stars flashed before her eyes.

The world spun in circles around her.

"Adela, blessed saints. You are so soft and sweet, you leave me in agony. I ache to touch you." He kissed the swell of her breast and then put his lips where his thumb had stroked not a moment earlier.

"*Ambrose...*" She needed to marry this man tomorrow!

But tonight, the magical way he touched her and kissed her was all going down in her diary with double stars to note the page.

CHAPTER 9

AMBROSE ARRIVED AT the Huntsford Academy early on Monday morning, more frustrated than ever over his Bow Street runner's inability to find that lost book. He would not care so much if it were simply an ordinary book, but it was the only written account ever discovered to be attributed to the renowned archeologist of ancient Roman times, Jovian of Tarantino.

Adela had discovered something noteworthy in Jovian's manuscript, and every day that passed without its return was oversetting her even more than it overset him. "He studied cave drawings and inscriptions throughout the Roman empire and had his theories on what those dots and other markings represented," Adela had told him just last night, her voice delightfully impassioned as she lectured him.

"Adela, that book will be found," he had assured her.

"And if it is not? I agree with his theories and know how to prove they are not merely decorative designs, but mark specific information on the animals they hunt. Perhaps their migratory patterns and mating cycles. Who will listen to me if I cannot cite his research to support my own? As important as Jovian's work is considered, the archeologists working today seem to have forgotten everything he wrote about those cave markings."

This book and all it represented to Adela was very much on Ambrose's mind as he sent his driver around with the ducal carriage to pick her up this morning for Dr. Nordberg's lecture. A chaperone was not necessary now that they were betrothed.

He smiled when she burst into his office shortly before the noon hour. She seemed more excited about the professor's talk than their own wedding plans which Eloise and Phoebe appeared to have well in hand. "Good morning, Ambrose! Is he here yet?"

Ambrose chuckled as he rose and came around his desk to greet her. "I think you are more eager to see him than to see your own betrothed."

"Never." She cast him an impish grin as she reached up on tiptoes and planted a kiss on his cheek. "You have the finest bone structure of any man I have ever seen and I look forward to exploring it in intimate detail once we are married. Can you believe it? The wedding is less than a week away. When do your brothers arrive? I cannot wait to meet them. My parents are due to arrive on Thursday. Oh, and I've brought Marigold with me. She'll come up right after she finishes touring the Hall of Planets. I think she is a bluestocking at heart, isn't it wonderful?"

He laughed. "I'm not certain. As for Octavian and Julius, they arrived late last night. I've left word they should come straight here to meet you. In fact, they ought to show up at any moment, no doubt eager to plague me because they were sure I would never marry."

She laughed and shook her head. "Oh, dear. I hope they'll like me. Or do you think they'll find me crushingly dull?"

"You are not dull, Adela. You sparkle."

She dismissed the comment with a gentle blush. "I have also invited two of my friends to the lecture. We formed our own society of bluestocking wallflowers last Season when we realized we shared the same interests. Those endless rounds of balls and musical soirees were made tolerable whenever they were with me."

"Let me guess, you all went off to a quiet corner and spent the night talking about dead things. What a romantic thought, skulls and bones," he teased. "This must be why I never noticed you last Season. You were hiding from me."

"All you had to do was look in that corner," she said, her voice holding no reprimand. "But I cannot fault you. It must have been hard to see us with all those diamonds flinging their brilliance at you."

He kissed her softly on the lips. "I see you now."

"And I am still certain this is all a dream. Phoebe and Eloise are also walking on a cloud. Their first protégé lands herself a duke. Although I should not count my chickens before they are hatched. We are not yet married and anything can happen between now and then."

"Nothing is going to happen," he said, securing his hold on her as though she might slip away. "You will not get out of marrying me, nor do I have any intention of backing out. As for your dowager matchmakers, they had better quit while they are ahead."

"Why ever would they do so after this stunning victory? I have already enlisted them to help my friends, Syd and Gory. That is, Lady Sydney Harcourt and Lady Gregoria Easton. You'll meet them today, for I have invited them to join us for Dr. Nordberg's lecture. They are excited."

"To meet me?" he teased, knowing Adela and her friends found dead things far more fascinating than a living, breathing male.

"Yes, you," she said with a giggle. "And Dr. Nordberg, too. It turns out, they could not attend his lecture last week at the British Museum either and were devastated to miss the opportunity. Come to think of it, they missed this entire week of *ton* parties, too. I wonder why?"

"They might not have been invited."

"Perhaps not to all, but surely to Lord and Lady Knightly's ball. I'll have to ask them when I see them." She sighed and shook her head. "They really are eager to meet you. I've told them how wonderful you are. But do not be put off if they pay you little attention. They will have many opportunities to speak to you in the coming weeks and only this one chance with Dr. Nordberg."

She put a hand to his cheek and cast him a soft smile. "I will never forget your kindness in bringing him here for me."

"It is my pleasure. I knew it would make you happy."

"It has, Ambrose. No one has ever done anything so thoughtful for me. You did this even though I had just accused you of being inconsiderate and manipulative. I am so ashamed of my words. I wish I could take them back."

"No, you were right. Don't be ashamed. I deserved the set down. Your words struck home and I was angry with myself for being so callous toward you. Suddenly, it was important for me to make it up to you and this is the best way I knew how. I hope you will forgive me."

"Of course, I do." However, she pursed her lips. "But can you ever forgive me? Runyon has not yet returned your stolen book. I led that loathsome man here and now it is up to me to find the book and get it back to you. I will do it, I promise."

"Absolutely not," he said, his heart shooting into his throat at the very idea. "Put the notion out of your head immediately. I do not want you anywhere near that bounder. My Bow Street men will take care of him."

"But it has been days and nothing has happened."

He could see Adela's mind was already awhirl and she was going to fret about it through Dr. Nordberg's lecture. "Adela, stop thinking about Runyon."

"I cannot. He might sneak in here today because this lecture will draw quite a crowd. In fact, I would not be surprised if this is what he does, slip in and discreetly drop the book somewhere it will be found."

"What is wrong with that? Is this not the best solution?" Ambrose doubted that slimy lizard would do any such thing. On the other hand, Adela seemed to know the workings of the man's deceitful mind better than anyone else.

Perhaps she was right and the book would miraculously reappear today.

All the more reason to keep her close, for he did not want her confronting the sinister dolt.

That concern was set aside when he suddenly heard thundering footsteps outside his office.

Adela glanced toward the door. "What on earth…?"

Ambrose chuckled. "My brothers have arrived."

"Oh, my." She hastily drew out of his arms, her cheeks quite rosy with embarrassment when he refused to let go of her hand

and insisted on keeping her close. "What will they think?"

"That I like you." Which he did, but was not yet ready to reveal quite how much because it did not seem possible that Adela could so effortlessly make her way into his heart.

But he did release her as his brothers bore down on him with youthful zeal. "Oh, hell," he muttered with a deep, rumbling chuckle.

They were grown men, Octavian all of twenty-six years old and looking quite dapper in his Royal Navy uniform, although his present assignment was not at sea but in Oxford working with noted professors on secret government projects.

Julius was only a year younger and in charge of the Huntsford businesses in the north of England. However, he used Oxford as his base of operations.

They were excited to see him and had reverted to their silly childhood ways, pouncing on him as they used to do whenever they wished to irritate him because he was their older brother. In their eyes, just because they were all now older did not mean they had to behave like grown men.

He withstood their ebullience with patience as they finished playfully harassing him.

"Since you were holding this lovely young lady's hand, and smiling like a hyena as we walked in, I assume this is your Adela," Octavian said, now taking Adela's hand with gentle care and bowing politely over it. "A pleasure to meet you, Miss Swift."

"The pleasure is all mine, Captain Thorne."

Julius did the same. "You are even lovelier than our brother described. He said you were the prettiest lady in all of London and he was in raptures over you."

Adela shook her head and laughed. "Thank you, Lord Thorne. But I hardly think your brother was so effusive. He is the sort to take great care in what he writes down."

Octavian nodded. "We read between the lines. He is marrying you, so you have to be someone very special to him."

Julius motioned to the exhibition hall. "He said he met you here. This place is his labor of love. It must have swelled his heart with pride to know how much you appreciated all his hard work."

Adela nodded. "What he has done here is undeniably brilliant."

"He did this for our father," Octavian said, his voice laced with emotion. "He was a great man and we all loved him dearly."

Adela nodded. "It shows. And I look forward to helping him out here."

Ambrose took her hand again. "Adela has some excellent ideas we'll put in place after the honeymoon. Julius, we'll be gone for at least a month. Do you think you can stay on and manage this place while we are away?"

His brother nodded. "Yes, for certain."

"I intend to stay on, as well," Octavian said. "I'm due to give my report to the House of Lords, so I will help out whenever I am not stuck there or at the Admiralty offices."

One of Ambrose's clerks knocked at his open door. "Your Grace, Dr. Nordberg has arrived."

Ambrose winked at Adela. "Excellent, show him up here."

The young clerk cleared his throat. "And two acquaintances of Miss Swift's are in the library asking after her. They said to tell her...um, Syd and Gory are here."

"Show them up here as well," he said with a grin. "They can join us for our private luncheon before the lecture starts."

Julius shook his head. "Gory? Dare I ask? What does she look like? I shudder to think."

"She's lovely," Adela insisted. "Gregoria is her real name. While Sydney and I enjoy studying ancient dead things to piece together historical records, Gregoria's interests tend more toward the medical aspects of human life. Her greatest wish is to become a doctor, but her family will never allow it. So she tries to learn as much as she can on her own."

"Would her 'learning' happen to involve stealing cadavers?" Julius asked with a shudder. "Is this how she earned her pet name?"

Adela shook her head. "No, nothing so gruesome. She is quite brilliant when it comes to ancient medicines and forensic analysis. We call her Gory merely because her name is Gregoria. And I am almost certain she hasn't stolen any cadavers."

"*Almost* certain?" Octavian laughed. "Lunch should be interesting."

Ambrose asked his young clerk to also fetch Marigold from the Hall of Planets and bring her to the private dining room.

"At once, Your Grace," he said with a nod and hurried off.

Dr. Nordberg was a distinguished looking older gentleman of Danish descent who clearly had an eye for the ladies, Ambrose realized as he watched the man's eyes widen and wickedly gleam when introduced to Adela and her friends.

Even his brothers eyed the young ladies with more than a little curiosity, for they were quite pretty if one looked beyond the mops of hair haphazardly pinned up and the unfashionable clothes they wore. Sydney's hair was blonde bordering on ginger and Gory's hair was a blend of chestnut and red. They were of medium height, although Sydney was the tallest among them while Gory was about the same size as Adela.

Compared to the Thorne men, they all were small.

Adela made the introductions.

Ambrose exchanged amused glances with his brothers, for Adela's friends were studying them as though they were fossilized exhibits. He and his brothers were big men and resembled each other quite a bit with all of them having dark hair and gray eyes. However, this is where the resemblance ended. Julius had the more boyish face while Octavian had a brutish face, still handsome, but in a rougher way.

He wasn't sure where he fell, probably somewhere between his two brothers.

It struck him as hilarious that Adela and her friends were discreetly attempting to analyze their bone structures. Never mind that they were Thornes, sons of the former duke, and all of them wealthy in their own right. These ladies were not thinking of marriage, but of dissection...he had better feed them before they got ideas.

They all sat down as soon as Marigold arrived. "Your Grace," she said, her blue eyes bright and a big, dimpled smile on her pretty face as she hurried in, "what you have done here is astounding. I must return with my cousins and spend the entire day viewing the exhibits. Thank you for inviting me along."

He gave the girl a cordial nod. "It is my pleasure."

Marigold was also excited to meet Adela's friends and quickly struck up a conversation with Gory. "Women in medicine? I think it is an excellent idea. Are we not naturally more compassionate and attentive to details?"

Ambrose's brothers grinned at him.

Yes, another bluestocking in the making.

Since Ambrose was never one to chatter, he mostly sat back and sipped his wine while their luncheon was served. The fare was exquisitely prepared but not too elaborate or they would all be falling asleep during Dr. Nordberg's lecture. They enjoyed a choice of honey-glazed quail, salt baked trout, and savory pie along with a variety of vegetables set out for their repast.

Dr. Nordberg offered to show Sydney some of his bone samples after the lecture. "They are in a private room across the street at the British Museum," he said, eyeing Adela's friend a little too avidly.

Sydney's eyes lit up. "Oh, I would love that."

Octavian set down his glass of wine. "Sounds fascinating. I'll join you."

Ambrose breathed a sigh of relief. The Danish professor was renowned in his field and considered a serious scholar, but he was also a wolf, and Ambrose did not wish to see Adela's friend accosted.

It was obvious none of these young ladies, as clever as they were, had a clue about men and their baser urges. He'd noticed Nordberg eyeing Adela as well, but the old man knew better than to attempt anything with her, even though she looked delectable.

No doubt Eloise had not allowed her leave the house today without a thorough inspection. She was now betrothed to a duke and had to look the part. No pencils sprouting out of her haphazardly fashioned hairdo or gowns that hid ink stains.

Eloise must have given Adela's maid instructions on what gown to set out for today's lecture. Ambrose had to admit he liked her choice, for its soft lilac hue brought out the delicacy of Adela's features.

Her hair was also becomingly styled. Nothing too severe or intricate, just loose waves drawn back to follow the nature curl of those tresses.

He found it oddly arousing that beneath her veneer of polish beat the heart of a passionate bluestocking. Was she not the perfect blend of social grace, intelligence, and spirit? Was it any wonder he was in lo–

He took another sip of his wine.

Who fell in love in under a month? Or a year, for that matter.

How could one's heart just *know*?

Yet, he was undeniably attracted to Adela and looked forward to marrying her.

"Dr. Nordberg, have you collected skulls from around the world?" Adela asked. "And are you able to determine how old they are? And have you found bones or drawings and other depictions of beasts that are unknown to us?"

"I understand the Egyptians and various other ancient civilizations had mastered the art of brain surgery," Gory said. "Have you seen doctors perform this in our modern day? What medicines were used to numb the patient? Or does one's brain somehow adapt to the pain?"

"What significant cranial variations have you noticed between our modern day man and those ancient skulls found on your archeological digs?" Sydney asked.

Dr. Nordberg held his hands up in a gesture of helplessness. "Ladies, I shall discuss many of these topics in my lecture."

Adela and her friends were peppering the man with questions faster than he could answer them.

His brothers were highly entertained by these bluestockings.

Marigold remained mostly silent but followed their conversations with avid interest.

Well, he was glad Octavian and Julius had met them all, not only because they were Adela's friends. He hoped his brothers, who also happened to be sought after bachelors, would expand their search for the right woman by including intelligence and independent thinking to the attributes they wished for in a wife.

Had this not been his mistake all these years?

Was it any wonder he had never found the right woman for himself until Adela had knocked him flat? He understood the reason for his constant failure now. He was always searching among the *ton* diamonds, most of whom relied on their looks and nothing more to entice a man.

He now realized they were done a disservice by looking so beautiful, for it held them back from developing character, compassion, or dreams to strive for beyond catching a wealthy, titled husband.

What did these diamonds expect their life to be after marriage? Was this the reason so many unions crashed upon the rocks? As trained as these young ladies were to catch a man, they had never been taught what to do afterward. Yes, they were given lessons on how to manage a household, but they had no idea how to manage a man. So, to these diamonds, they had reached the pinnacle of their lives when making a match, and it was all on a steep downhill slope once wedding vows were exchanged.

Ambrose and his brothers escorted Dr. Nordberg to the lecture hall and, as members of the Thorne family, sat with Ambrose on the far side of the stage in the family's place of honor. He had invited Adela to join him, but she preferred to sit in the audience with her friends and Marigold.

He was not annoyed when she declined, understanding that she was not used to being the object of attention. She would have been uncomfortable seated beside him on the stage and gawked at by everyone.

However, he had overheard Adela muttering something about Runyon to her friends and experienced a moment's qualm over the whispered remark. Would she be so single-mindedly possessed as to tackle the fellow in the lecture hall if he dared show his face?

He rubbed a hand across the nape of his neck, imagining what The Tattler would report. Why had he not insisted she sit on the stage with him? Well, she probably would have leaped out of her chair and flown through the air to grab the bounder.

Gad, he knew she would do just that.

He did not wish to appear an ogre, but neither did he wish to see her hurt. She would be angry, but he had to rein her in for her own good. "Adela…"

She pretended not to hear him and scurried off with the other ladies.

"Adela, blast it. Come back here."

But she ignored him, refusing to look back even once.

"Blasted woman," Ambrose grumbled, keeping his gaze on his betrothed as she took a seat beside Marigold.

Octavian arched an eyebrow. "What was that about?"

"She thinks she is as mighty as a knight on Crusade." He quickly told his brothers about the stolen book. "I'm afraid she intends to take Runyon down on her own."

Julius laughed. "I'd love to see her try. I'll wager ten pounds she succeeds."

"Twenty and you're on," Octavian said. "She's too little to take down any man."

Ambrose then mentioned she had knocked him over.

Octavian groaned. "Why didn't you reveal that significant fact before I took Julius up on the wager?"

"Neither of you should be placing wagers on my future wife." He frowned at both of them. "Oh, hell. She's scanning the audience. She is convinced Runyon is going to show his face."

"What are you going to do if he does show up? Leap off the stage the moment you notice her get out of her seat?" Octavian thought the possibility hilarious. "I'd love to see my staid brother lose all sense of decorum and do just that. Care to place a wager on this, Julius?"

Their youngest brother smiled. "Done. Twenty pounds says he keeps to his seat."

"I say he leaps."

"Blast it, Octavian. I am not going after her. I have a Bow Street runner on the task. He is the best in the business and I've had him following Runyon around for days. If that little rat dares show his face here, my man will be on him before Adela ever gets close…I hope."

They settled into their chairs as the lecture began.

Since Ambrose had already heard most of it last week at the

British Museum, he kept his attention on Adela instead. As they neared the close of the first hour and were about to take a short break before Dr. Nordberg took questions from the audience in this second hour, he saw Adela's eyes suddenly widen. She whispered something to her friends and then clambered over them to race to the seat vacated by a gentleman wearing a dark hat and dark cloak who had just gotten up to leave.

She began to crawl under his empty chair.

Oh, dear Lord.

His brothers were trying hard not to burst out laughing.

"I knew I would like her," Octavian said, putting a hand over his mouth as he pretended to cough to mask his chuckles. "She has a very pretty rump."

Ambrose emitted a soft growl. "Do not stare at my betrothed's backside."

Yes, it was delightful, and she was wiggling it deliciously.

What in blazes was she doing?

Julius stayed quiet but now grinned from ear to ear.

Adela finally popped her head up and held up a package in triumph. But she quickly handed it to her friends and then sprinted out of the packed hall after the gentleman.

"Oh, hell." Ambrose turned to his brothers as he prepared to spring out of his seat. "She's gone after him. Pretend you know what you are doing up here. Blast the girl, I told her to stay put."

He shot out of his chair and darted out the rear of the stage, ignoring the shocked looks on everyone in the packed room.

Where was his Bow Street man?

He shoved open the door and scanned the hallway.

The lecture hall was on the upper level where his office and the general administrative offices were located, so no one would be up here unless attending the lecture or working for him.

His heart sank when he found it empty.

However, the exhibition hall's main floor was filled with visitors, he noted as he peered over the railing to the massive entry hall below and the crowd meandering toward one exhibit or another.

Where in blazes was Adela?

How hard could it be to spot her in that lilac gown?

CHAPTER 10

ADELA RAN OUT of the lecture hall and hurried down the back stairs in search of the black-caped man who had left the mysterious package beneath his chair. She would have seen him on the main staircase had he gone in that direction, so it was an easy deduction to guess he was fleeing out the back. But why was he running away at all? "You there! Stop! I want to talk to you!"

The man turned a moment, obviously having heard her, and then kept running.

She spotted him as he was about to enter the Hall of Planets, the most popular exhibit in the Huntsford Academy. "Drat," she muttered, knowing she had to get to him before he could shake her off in that crowd.

Her ridiculously fashionable slippers were made for sitting around and sipping tea, not for chasing scoundrels. Her gown was equally useless, not designed for any activity other than looking pretty while men ogled their fill.

She tore after him as best she could, racing past Mercury, Mars, and Venus before she spotted the perpetrator trying to blend into a crowd studying the rings of Saturn. The fool was too tall not to be noticed. But as she gained on him, he took off again toward the main hall from which he could then exit onto the street. "Stop him!" she called out to the guards, but the hall was too noisy and her cries drifted upward to be swallowed up in the ceiling.

With a final, desperate effort, she lunged at him, managing to grab hold of his cloak. But he did not stop running and merely dragged her along with him as he raced to the doors leading onto the street.

As she held onto him for dear life, two thoughts raced through her mind. The first, how ridiculous she must look clinging to this oaf's cloak and wiping the floor with her gown as he attempted to tear out of the museum.

The second thought was even more humiliating, for this man was not Runyon, so who was he and why was he desperately trying to get away from her? He was bigger and heavier set than Runyon, something she ought to have noticed immediately and left him alone.

She could not do so now.

If he had nothing to hide, why would he not stop?

And what was in that package he had left under his seat?

She would be in quite a bit of trouble if it had nothing to do with Ambrose's stolen book. Oh, Ambrose would be livid with her meddling, and perhaps angry enough to call off their betrothal.

But this still begged the question...if this had nothing to do with the lost book, then why was this man running?

"You meddlesome slut!" he said in a harsh rasp and was about to kick her in the ribs when a shadow fell over both of them and then a massive fist flew into the man's face.

He crumpled to the ground and lay moaning beside her.

She tried to catch her breath and rise, but that large shadow now put his hands gently around her waist and lifted her in his arms. "Blast it, Adela. You might have been hurt."

"Ambrose, I'm so sorry." She wrapped her arms around his neck and held on tightly to this wonderful man. "I thought he was Runyon. But he isn't and now I don't know what I've done. He left a package under his chair. I gave it to Syd and–"

"Hush, love. It's all right." He kissed her lightly on the brow. "We'll sort it all out. My guards will bring him into my office and we'll question him."

All eyes were on them as Ambrose carried her up the main stairs to his private office.

She expected him to be livid, but he said nothing as he set her down in the large chair behind his massive desk and showed nothing but exquisite concern for her. "You are going to have to stop tackling people in my museum," he said with aching tenderness. "First me and now this stranger. I cannot imagine what The Tattler will report if they ever catch wind of this."

She closed her eyes a moment and groaned. "I know. I am so very sorry. Are you angry? I would not blame you if you never wished to speak to me again."

"No, Adela. He may not have been Runyon, but something shady was going on. I just hope you did not meddle in something far more dangerous than retrieving my book."

"Will you let me stay while you question him?"

"Yes, but only because you saw what he was doing and can point out if he is lying to me. However, I will have you leave if I do not like the way he is looking at you."

"All right. Thank you, Ambrose." She clamped her mouth shut and said no more, completely stunned he was not shouting at her, calling her reckless and foolish, or threatening to end their betrothal.

In truth, he was being quite wonderful to her.

He shook his head and sighed. "Is life with you always going to be this–"

"Exciting?"

His gorgeous silver eyes lit up with mirth. "I was going to say *disruptive*. You must admit, for a quiet bluestocking, you have quite the knack for stirring up trouble."

He remained by her side as his brothers, Marigold, and Adela's friends hurried in. Syd had the package in hand. "Shall I open it?"

"No," Ambrose said, frowning at them all. "Who is attending to Dr. Nordberg? Did you leave him on stage to flounder on his own?"

Octavian frowned back at his brother. "We have better sense than that. Your head curator, Mr. Smythe-Owens, is handling matters. He'll do a far better job than either of us since he actually gives a fig about what those skulls and ancient relics signify."

"And you don't?" Sydney asked, inhaling a breath in outrage. "How can you not find them fascinating? The knowledge of the ancients is more precious than any Crown jewels."

Octavian glanced helplessly at Ambrose.

Ambrose shook his head and groaned. "All right, that will take care of Nordberg. My guards are about to bring the man in here. I'll ask him about this package before we tear it open."

"But it could be the book," Adela blurted.

Syd shook her head. "It does not feel like one."

"Oh." There went all of Adela's theories. Perhaps Ambrose was right and she was becoming so obsessed with retrieving his stolen book that she ignored all other dangers.

"Who are you?" Ambrose asked once the man was brought in and put into a chair in front of Ambrose's desk.

The man cast him a defiant glare.

Ambrose appeared not at all affected, but he had to be quietly seething in frustration. "Octavian, search his pockets."

It was a good thing Ambrose had ordered him searched because the man carried weapons. Two knives and a pistol.

Julius stepped forward to assist. "I'll check his hat and cloak."

Another pistol was found in the folds of his cloak.

Unfortunately, the man carried no identification and refused to give Ambrose his name when asked.

Ambrose tried again. "Who are you and what were you doing at the lecture?"

The man was obviously not talking.

Ambrose turned to Syd. "Give me the package."

Adela noticed a flicker of panic in the man's eyes.

She leaned forward, eager to see what it contained. "Bank notes? Who are they made out to?"

Ambrose groaned as he let out a breath. "Thomas Runyon."

She gasped. "Then this is about your stolen book, after all. I knew it! How much was he willing to pay?"

Ambrose quickly counted the notes. "One thousand pounds."

She gasped again. "And the exchange was supposed to be made here? Of all the brazen gall! How dare that little lizard set up the exchange under our very noses, intentionally rubbing the loss in our faces. Ambrose...er, Your Grace, I am so very sorry." She turned to this stranger who still appeared defiant. "And you were stupid enough to go along with it? You could have insisted on making the exchange anywhere else. Why here?"

"It wasn't up to me," the man said, finally breaking his defiant silence. "Runyon set the terms."

Adela glanced at Ambrose in dismay. "This means Runyon must have intended to show up here today. Oh, he might have been in the lecture hall waiting for the moment to retrieve the funds and hand off the book. I ruined it by jumping in too quickly."

The man laughed. "You'll never catch him now."

She glowered at him. "Yes, we will. Count on it. He will be tossed in the prison cell beside yours. You may as well give us your name, for we will find it out soon enough. These bank notes can be traced back to you."

But her heart was in her throat, for she might have interfered with Ambrose's Bow Street runners who would have been following Runyon here. If so, where were they now? And why had they not stopped Runyon here?

Perhaps they did not realize he was carrying the book to hand off to this stranger. But that did not make sense. How could they not realize it?

Obviously, this man seated before them was a middleman of some sort, for he spoke with an unrefined accent, and his clothes and shoes were not of good quality. He could not possibly have the funds himself to acquire Jovian of Tarantino's magnificent tome.

The man was no scholar but a ruffian off the streets.

Certainly not a nobleman. Ambrose and his brothers would have recognized him if he were one of them. But this man was definitely hired by a scoundrel with wealth and possibly a title attached to his name to secretly acquire that priceless book.

When continued questioning yielded no answers, Ambrose called in one of his clerks. "Summon the magistrate. This man is to be turned over to the authorities."

The stranger leaped up from his seat. "On what possible charges? Those funds are mine! I want them back."

"He is to be held on attempted assault on the Duke of

Huntsford's betrothed."

"She's the one who grabbed me!"

"Mr. Lewis," Ambrose said, his voice remaining steady as he addressed his clerk. "Send for the magistrate now."

"At once, Your Grace."

"I'll have yer little doxy brought up on charges herself," he threatened with a growl.

"Mr. Lewis, he is to be charged with attempted assault and violent threats to the safety of my betrothed."

Within the hour, the man was led away by the magistrate's constables. "I want my money back! He stole my money!"

The constables ignored his ranting. "Those notes are clearly designated for a Mr. Thomas Runyon. His Grace will see they are properly turned over to him. Now, unless you are willing to provide more information, shut up or we'll gag you."

Adela had at least a dozen questions for Ambrose which she began to rattle off as soon as the perpetrator was hauled away. "Should we not spread out and search for your Bow Street men?"

"No," Ambrose said.

"What do they look like? Do you know? Did you recognize any of them in the lecture hall? Surely, they must have heard the commotion? Do you think Runyon heard it and ran out? Why did they not stop him?"

"Adela—"

"Then they must have chased after him. How shall we find your runners? Runyon must have the book in hand as we speak. Do you think he'll go back to the place he retrieved it and hide it again? No, he couldn't. He'd be too afraid we are onto him. I wonder where he'll hide it next? But it might help to know where he stashed it the first time. We'll have to ask your Bow Street men for a detailed account of Runyon's movements."

Ambrose folded his arms across his chest. "Adela, do you ever intend to come up for air?"

"In a moment," she said before continuing. "Wasn't the Duke of Lotheil going to warn us if the Royal Society intended to deny Runyon's proposal? Do you think it was denied? Why didn't they tell us? Or do you think Runyon just got greedy and decided not to wait for a decision? I think we must find your Bow Street men and also talk to the Duke of Lotheil."

"We? Don't you think you have meddled enough?" His voice was a soft rumble, and she could not tell whether he was merely speaking to her gently because he cared for her and would never shout at her, or whether he was seething with anger and about to erupt.

"Um…" She knew better than to answer that loaded question.

"I am going to put you, Marigold, and your friends in my carriage and return you to Lady Dayne's home. Your friends may remain with you or be dropped off at their homes. It is their choice. But if I see any of your faces here again today, I shall have you bodily ejected."

Adela was dismayed.

She wanted to help bring Runyon to heel, but Ambrose would never allow her to do so now. She pinched her lips in order to keep her mouth shut, knowing she had likely pushed Ambrose to the extremities of his patience.

She understood he was worried for her safety.

But hadn't she proved she could take care of herself?

Well, perhaps not.

That awful man would have kicked her unconscious had Ambrose not arrived in time to stop that fiend.

Ambrose and his brothers escorted them to the ducal carriage and assisted them inside.

She peered back to watch the three of them standing like giant gargoyles, their arms crossed over their massive chests. "Oh, dear. I think he is going to send Octavian to follow us," she grumbled. "How dare he not trust me?"

"Should he?" Gory asked. "Where did you think to order the driver to take us instead of back to Lady Dayne's house?"

She sank back against the squabs and sighed. "What does it matter? The driver isn't going to obey me."

"His Grace did say to let Gory and me off at our homes," Syd mused. "But how is he to know where we live? Why don't you let us do a little snooping? Tell us where you think we ought to search and we can pretend to live close by. The coachman won't know the difference. We'll join you at Lady Dayne's once we are through."

Adela's eyes lit up. "You would do this for me?"

"Of course," Gory said, holding out her hand and waiting for her and Syd to place theirs on top of hers in a sign of their bond of friendship. "We know how much the loss of that book has upset you."

Adela set her hand atop Gory's, and then Syd did the same.

"May I join, too?" Marigold asked.

"Yes, of course. Friends forever," Syd muttered once Marigold had added hers.

"Forever," Marigold added with glee.

Adela nodded. "But you must promise me you'll do nothing foolish. Runyon is desperate and dangerous. All you are to do is find out if he showed up at The Red Drake earlier today and whether he later returned. Can you do this without attracting unwanted attention?"

Gory laughed. "I'm sure we can outsmart a few drunk men."

"No," Adela said. "Do not get overly confident or you will run into trouble. You must be clever about it. Although this tavern is close to the Royal Society, it does not mean it attracts a better class of people. We all know how nefarious these Fellows can be. Many of them are desperate to seek acclaim for themselves and will not hesitate to tread on anyone who dares get in their way on their climb to fame and fortune."

"We will be careful," Syd assured. "We'll meet you at Lady Dayne's within the hour."

Gory also appeared eager to investigate. "This is so much more fun than those tedious Society balls. I wish my uncle would just leave me in peace and stop being so eager to push me out of the house. Fortunately, his wife is a pinch-penny and will not allow him to spend on my clothes. So I've had to wear these hideous hand-me-downs and who knows where she got them from? They are five years out of style and the colors could not possibly be more unflattering to my complexion."

"But if Lady Dayne and Lady Withnall take you on as their protégé, then you will have a beautiful new wardrobe," Adela assured her.

Gory groaned. "Oh, that will never do. Let them take on Syd first. By the time they get around to me, I will be in my fourth Season and an utter joke."

"It should be my turn by then," Marigold said. "We can enjoy the Season together."

"That is very sweet of you," Gory said, "but I have no intention of wasting my life on a fruitless endeavor."

Adela took her hand. "Don't you wish to be married?"

"To one of those clowns on the marriage mart? No. I plan to save up enough funds to get me to Scotland. They do not frown on women holding positions of knowledge there. My father was an earl, so that should lend me some standing."

"You could find yourself a Scot to marry right here. Some of them come down to London for the Season. Any one of them would take you back to Scotland," Syd suggested.

"That won't work. Then I would have to be his wife, and if he is titled, then he will expect me to carry out the duties of a lady."

"But were you not trained for this?" Adela asked.

Gory arched an eyebrow and cast her a wry glance. "Like all the other *ton* diamonds? Yes. But I just want to be left alone to learn all I can about medicine. Why should my uncle care? He inherited a prosperous estate and does not need to marry me off to secure the family's fortunes. I've begged him to let me be, but he ignores all of my pleas."

Adela frowned. "Why do you think he is pushing you out in Society, Gory?"

"I don't know." She shook her head and sighed. "It has nothing to do with his caring for my welfare. I think he wants me out of the house and away from him and his wife. He wants me away and married to some clunch who will keep me out of his hair permanently."

"Then should he not be putting some effort into marrying you off?" Adela asked. "Surely, a few new gowns cannot be too much of an expense for him to manage."

"I thought the same, but those two – my uncle and his wife – are acting very strangely lately. Something about this inheritance business does not feel right, but none of the solicitors will tell me anything, nor will my father's bankers give me the time of day."

Syd took her hand. "Perhaps this shall be our next investigation. Imagine the doors that will be open to us once Adela is a duchess. No clerk is going to condescend to the Duchess of Huntsford."

"Oh, look! We are passing near The Red Drake now." Adela knocked on the roof of the carriage to gain the driver's attention. "My friends wish to be dropped off here."

The driver drew the team to a halt and one of the footmen positioned at the rear of the carriage climbed down to assist Syd and Gory.

"Thank you," they said, tittering as they scurried off.

The footman and driver both turned to Adela and eyed her warily, no doubt ready to report this suspicious action to Ambrose.

Oh, dear.

Perhaps *this* would tip him over the edge and cause him to end their betrothal.

Well, the damage was done.

No going back now.

She sank against the plush squabs as the carriage rolled on. "Marigold, I'm so sorry. We are setting a terrible example for you."

"Not at all. This is the most fun I've had since arriving in London." She leaned forward and gave Adela's hand a light squeeze. "Please do not worry about me. I think I am clever enough to understand what you are doing is dangerous. I would not have followed your friends to that tavern. Nor would I have chased that bounder through the museum."

Adela breathed a sigh of relief. "Good."

"But I do see the importance of making something of myself beyond the role of wife. Oh, I would still love to marry. But the man must be someone like these Thorne men, encouraging to all who seek knowledge and not threatened by ladies who have a little brain matter between their ears. Julius seemed awfully nice. Do you think he is in love with anyone? He was paying a lot of attention to Gory. I like her, too. Do you think he will ever notice me?"

Adela cast her a sympathetic smile. "I wish I could be more helpful, but I only met His Grace's brothers today. I know as much about them as you do. But Marigold, I know you will charm dozens of men when you have your come-out. Maybe Julius will be among them, assuming you are still interested in him a couple of years from now."

Marigold nodded. "I suppose."

To Adela's surprise, the Duke of Lotheil's impressive conveyance was standing in front of Eloise's home when they arrived.

Marigold gave her a quick hug. "I shall tell Aunt Sophie I had a marvelous time with you today, but will not reveal any of the sordid details. I'm sure they'll find out soon enough since this seems to be what we Farthingales do best, nose about and snoop."

Adela watched her run to the Farthingale house next door, making certain the girl made it inside when the faithful Farthingale butler, Pruitt, opened the door to allow her in. Only then did Adela hurry through Eloise's gate, now curious about what the duke had to report.

Watling opened the door to her.

She tore past the dear butler and scurried into the parlor where she knew Eloise and the Duke of Lotheil would be found.

Indeed, Eloise was seated on her silk settee and the duke was in the chair beside hers, the two of them having tea. "Is this other than a social call, Your Grace?"

He inspected her up and down. "Good grief, Adela. What happened to you?"

She glanced down at herself, only now realizing how badly her gown was soiled. Well, she had held onto the scoundrel and been dragged like a big, purple mop across the massive entry hall. Her hair probably looked a mess as well, the pins dislodged as she tore down the stairs and lunged at Runyon's cohort.

She brought over the fireplace stool and sat on it rather than damage Eloise's exquisite silk chairs. Once settled, she told Eloise and the duke all that had transpired. "This caught us by surprise.

We did not think Runyon would attempt to sell the book until he had heard one way or another from the Royal Society on his proposal. Has a decision been reached?"

The duke nodded. "Yes, the board met last night to vote on all the proposals submitted. But we were not to reveal our decision for another few days. Runyon must have bribed one of our clerks to give him an advance warning."

"Or bribed one of the directors," Adela mused.

Lotheil shook his head. "I cannot imagine any of them breaking their oath or agreeing to something so low."

"You have too much faith in the honor of those men. I can attest to the presence of several scoundrels on that board." Adela knew exactly who they were since those wretches did not bother to hide their disdain for women in their midst. Of course, they would always be on their best behavior around the Duke of Lotheil. "Runyon may not have the funds with which to bribe them, but he may have knowledge of secrets with which to blackmail them. This explains why he was so quick to sell that rare book. He must have put all in place and just been waiting for word on his proposal before taking action. I just don't understand why he would go out of his way to make the exchange under our very noses. It seems so reckless."

"We know the man is arrogant," Lotheil said.

"Oh, the fiend." Eloise set a hand on her heart, for she was obviously distressed. "It seems you have thwarted his plans. Adela, you must be careful. Who knows what he might do to you? He surely sees you as the cause of his continuing misfortunes."

"Well, I am not going to sit around and wait for him to cause trouble, am I?" She was debating whether to tell them what her friends were doing when they were suddenly distracted by a commotion at the door.

Watling hurried in, his face a little pale. "My lady, Miss Adela's friends are here...um, escorted by the Duke of Huntsford's brother, Captain Octavian Thorne. He does not look happy. Indeed, not happy at all."

Adela shot to her feet. "I knew it! He was following us!"

Octavian marched in with her two friends in tow. He wasn't

escorting them so much as hauling them in by the scruff of their necks like little, wayward pups. His expression was thunderous. "Ambrose warned me you three would try something foolish."

He took a moment to bow to Eloise and Lotheil before continuing. "I caught these two attempting to question some gentlemen, and I use the term loosely, for they were scurvy knaves if I ever saw any. They were at a tavern not far from the Royal Society."

"The Red Drake?" Lotheil said.

He nodded. "The very one."

Sydney tipped her chin into the air. "We were merely trying to question the tavern maids."

Gory cleared her throat. "But some of those dastardly patrons overheard us and decided to meddle. They did not appreciate our attempts to pry information about one of their own. You see, they also happened to be Fellows in the Royal Society. We tried to explain that Runyon was not to be trusted, but they refused to listen and attempted to toss us out."

"We couldn't let them get away with that, could we?" Sydney said, looking wonderfully indignant.

Adela listened in dismay as they related what happened next. "Syd, you threw a punch? Is this why you are nursing your hand?"

Her friend nodded. "I think I might have bruised a bone when my fist connected with the pompous blackguard's jaw."

"I'll take her to see Dr. Farthingale before I personally escort her home," Octavian said, his expression still thunderously dark. He spoke quietly, but Adela could see he was a raging storm.

She now turned to Gory. "Are you all right?"

She nodded. "Not a scratch on me. I am fine...but Captain Thorne..." She winced as she pointed to the black eye he now sported, which must have contributed to his ire since it could only have been acquired when he ran in to rescue her friends.

Oh, Ambrose was definitely going to call off their betrothal now.

Well, that should not stop her from doing everything possible to find his book. "Were you able to get any useful information out of the tavern maids before the fight broke out?"

"Yes," Sydney said. "Apparently, Runyon had come in the day your notes and that book were stolen. They could not recall if he ran in with a bundle, but they do remember he left soon after without anything in his hands."

Adela frowned. "Drat, can they not say for certain?"

Gory shook her head. "No, but does it not make sense? Where else was he going to hide the book between the time he stole it from the Huntsford library and arrived at the tavern? The book was likely hidden in the tavern all along. Perhaps buried up in the rafters or under a floorboard. I tried to tell Captain Thorne that we ought to go back in there and search for your notes since those might also be hidden there."

"I was not about to risk your lives to retrieve them," he said with a growl.

"The Fellows in the Royal Society are scoundrels, not killers. They would not have done us serious harm," Gory insisted. "At least, I hope not."

The Duke of Lotheil's expression was now thunderous, as well. "Give me the names of those who accosted you. I shall see them tossed out. It is one thing to forbid women into our membership, but quite another to attack a woman!"

Eloise rose. "No, you shall not take this any further. Adela and her friends were as much at fault. Did Huntsford not tell you to come straight back here? And yet, you ignored his warning. A warning issued out of concern for your safety. How do you think he will respond when he hears what you have done?"

"Call off the wedding," Adela said in a tight whisper. "I've certainly given him ample reason. But how can I not do all in my power to get that book back to him? It is all my fault it was stolen. No matter what happens, he deserves to have Jovian's masterpiece returned."

"My brother is not going to call off the wedding," Octavian said with a note of amusement mingled with his anger. "Nor does he care about the return of that book if it places your life and that of your friends at risk. I'm sure he will be along once he has attended to Dr. Nordberg, and then all will be resolved."

Adela fought back her tears because she knew exactly how this incident would resolve...Ambrose free again to find himself a proper wife and glad to be rid of her.

Octavian ignored all three of them as he addressed Eloise and Lotheil. "I cannot wait around here for Ambrose to arrive. I'll escort both of these young ladies to Dr. Farthingale's infirmary and then I will deliver them home. Lady Dayne, where do they live? I do not trust them to tell me the truth."

Sydney gasped. "We would not lie to you!"

He arched an eyebrow. "Beyond the lies you have already told?"

"Oh...that..." Adela's friend clamped her lips shut and nursed her hand, making not the least fuss when Octavian took her gently by the elbow and did the same with Gory.

But they had not taken a step out of Eloise's parlor before Watling hurried back in and announced, "The Duke of Huntsford and his brother, Lord Julius Thorne."

Ambrose took one look at Octavian's black eye and Sydney's swollen hand, and his expression darkened. To make matters worse, Gory now had a bruise forming on her jaw.

Adela stepped forward. "Um...I can explain."

He cast her a murderous look. "Do not bother. Where is Marigold? Is she all right?"

"Yes, we would never let her come to harm," Adela assured, realizing how lame she sounded while her friends stood beside her nursing their injuries. "She's safely back with John and Sophie."

"Blessed saints," Ambrose muttered, staring at her.

These Thorne men had the most expressive silver eyes...that is, when they chose to reveal their feelings and not hide them behind a wall of steel. Ambrose's were not so much silver now as stormy gray.

Quite dark and ominous.

She had never seen a man so furious, other than Octavian.

The two of them were frightening, even though she knew these men would never raise a hand to her or her friends.

Still, she shook inside.

These Thorne men had lost all respect for her, Syd, and Gory.

All Adela could do was brace herself for the tempest about to unleash.

But Ambrose merely stood there, seething.

Adela did not mind that he looked as though he wanted to throttle her. She could endure his anger. It was the hurt...the look of utter betrayal in his eyes that shattered her.

Yes, betrayal and disappointment.

She had lost his trust.

Oh, that precious trust destroyed and she had only herself to blame.

She reached out tentatively, hoping to set her hand upon his arm in order to mollify him.

"Don't," he warned.

She dropped her hand to her side. "Will you at least let me—"

"No." His gaze bore straight into her soul.

Indeed, his precious trust was lost.

Could she ever reclaim it?

CHAPTER 11

AMBROSE WAS FURIOUS.

He had sent those three home for their own protection, done all he could to make certain they would be delivered to safety, and how had they repaid him? By kicking him in the teeth. Purposely ignoring his warnings and traipsing off on their own to a *bloody* tavern, no less. "Is this how little you think of me, Adela? What if Octavian had been more seriously hurt because of your actions? Or Marigold harmed? What kind of example are you setting for that girl? Do you think the blasted book is worth risking any of your lives?"

Perhaps he had come on a little too strong, for Adela looked ready to burst into tears. "You are right," she said in a ragged whisper. "I put everyone in danger with my foolish actions and do not expect you ever to forgive me. How can you when I've betrayed you and forever lost your trust?"

The tears now began to flow. "I wanted so much to find that book for you, it blinded me to all reason. My behavior was inexcusable. Do what you must. I know I have bitterly disappointed you."

He sighed and took out his handkerchief to dab at the tears streaming down her cheeks. "Adela, I am not calling off our wedding."

"I would not blame you if you did. I have behaved deplorably in front of Dr. Nordberg and your brothers. You went out of your way to engage him for the lecture, all as a great kindness to me, and I raced off halfway through it like a crazed madwoman. I must appear so ungrateful to you."

She now turned to Eloise. "And to you, as well. I cannot seem to get out of my own way. I've ruined all your efforts to turn me into a proper lady. But that theft eats at my soul. It is such a precious book and my heart will never recover until it is properly returned undamaged."

Ambrose dabbed at her cheeks again. "Adela, forget about the book."

"How can I? But I will go about finding it with far more care from this moment forward. No more running off like a thoughtless peahen."

"We are getting married at the end of the week. Just think about the wedding plans, will you? Leave the search to my Bow Street men. Despite appearances to the contrary, they do have the matter well in hand. They will question the man now in the magistrate's custody and trace the payment. We'll soon know to whom Runyon meant to sell the book. They will also tear apart The Red Drake tonight."

"But they must keep their eyes on Runyon at all times. Did I not tell you he is as sneaky as they come? Do you know yet whether he showed up at the lecture hall? Or whether he had the book? And what happened to your Bow Street men? If he was at the Huntsford Academy to make the exchange, then where were they? Did he give them the slip?"

Ambrose put his hands on Adela's shoulders. "Stop. Are you going to pepper me with questions as we stand at the altar and take our vows?"

She sighed. "Are you certain you still want to marry me?"

He nodded. "Never a doubt."

She cast him a fragile smile. "Even after today?"

"Yes, Adela. Even after today."

"I don't deserve your kindness or forgiveness. And I am devastated to have lost your trust. This hurts me more than anything, yet I have no one to blame but myself."

"You haven't lost my trust." He couldn't believe he was now consoling her when he ought to be ranting and raging at her.

Chasing after that stranger had been foolish in the extreme. The man carried a veritable arsenal on him and could have used a gun or knife to stop her. As if this was not bad enough, she then compounded an already dangerous situation by sending her friends into that tavern on their own.

Well, they had gone in willingly but this did not absolve any of them.

Bluestockings were supposed to be clever.

One would never guess it by their reckless actions.

Yes, he was frustrated.

Enraged.

But all he wanted to do was take Adela in his arms and kiss her.

She glanced up in surprise. "You still trust me? How is that possible?"

Because he loved her.

Fool that he was, he had fallen more deeply in love with her when he saw her clinging for dear life to that knave's cloak, this little warrior in her elegant lilac gown never giving up because she was determined to get that book back for him.

Nothing on heaven and earth was going to stop her.

This is how deeply she would love and defend their children.

This is how fiercely she would love and defend him.

She was going to completely disrupt his orderly life. Shatter his peace. His solitude would be flung out the window.

And he did not care.

He wanted Adela in his life, desperately wanted her with all her foibles and passions and stubborn determination.

She repeated her question. "How can you still trust me?"

"Because your motives were selfless. You behaved like a peahen while trying to help me."

Her gaze turned hopeful. "Well, yes. That is true."

He tucked a finger under her chin. "But that does not mean I have calmed down about it. I am still furious, Adela."

"As you ought to be," she assured him, clasping her hands to stop their trembling.

He wanted to take them in his, but thought better about

encouraging her or her friends to pursue the matter of Runyon on their own. Adela would take advantage of any softness he showed her. Not that he meant to remain frowning at her, but all would be lost if she knew how much he truly cared for her.

"Octavian, Julius, and I will take you and the ladies to Dr. Farthingale. Once done there, we'll drop them off at their *real* homes, and then finish up the day by tying up any loose ends."

"Yes," Adela said. "You must find Runyon and that book. He probably has it on him now and must be searching for another place to hide it. Do you think he knows your Bow Street men are following him? That could be a problem. Although he must have eluded them today. What if he loses them again tomorrow? You really must bring him in today. Are the bank notes not enough to connect him to the scoundrel we caught today? I–"

He kissed her to stop her from talking.

A short, but urgent kiss.

"I should go with you," she said, the moment he took his lips off hers. "After all, they are my friends and I feel responsible. I would also have so much useful information to convey to your Bow Street runners."

"No."

"Ambrose…um, Your Grace, am I not safer in your company? This way, you will know where I am at all times."

"If you promised to stay home with Lady Eloise, then I would not have to worry about you. Will you promise me, Adela?"

She stared at him with pinched lips. "But I can help you."

"Adela, will you promise me?" He took her hands in his, trying not to laugh at her deliciously stubborn look. Why was this so difficult for her? He did not want her anywhere near him or his Bow Street men when they caught up to Runyon.

He wasn't certain what had been meant to happen this afternoon at the lecture hall, only that Runyon was somehow involved.

Adela's concerns were not unfounded, for he also wondered whether Runyon had been at the lecture. How else were those two knaves going to successfully make that exchange? Yet, he also knew Mr. Barrow and his men had not lost sight of Runyon, so he should have seen them and Runyon there as well.

But he had not recognized anyone, not at the lecture nor while tearing through the Hall of Planets after Adela and that stranger.

Something about the entire incident did not feel right.

Octavian was now frowning at him. "Anything more I should know?"

Ambrose shook his head. "I'll be meeting my Bow Street man later this evening. We'll learn more from him. Will you come to the meeting with me?"

His brother nodded. "Absolutely."

Julius nodded as well. "Wouldn't miss it."

"Me, too," Adela blurted.

Which reminded Ambrose that she had not actually promised him she would stay put. "Are you going to promise me you'll stay home tonight?"

She cast him that pinch-lipped look again. "No, I do not wish to lie to you." But she sighed and shook her head. "I'll agree to stay home but only *after* we've met with Mr. Barrow. How does that sound? I think it is a fair compromise. I will not get into harm while I am with you and your brothers. Mr. Barrow certainly is no threat to me. So let's hear what he has to say, then take me home...and I promise to remain here the entire evening."

He arched an eyebrow. "And your friends?"

Adela glanced at her partners in mischief, the young ladies she called Syd and Gory. "I will not involve them any further. I do not wish to see them hurt any worse than they already are."

He now turned to her two friends. "I'll have your promises, too."

They glanced at Adela.

She nodded.

"All right," Syd grumbled. "No more interference from us. Promise given."

Gory muttered a reluctant agreement. "Promise."

"I'll take you both home after Dr. Farthingale tends to you," Octavian said, looking upon them with genuine concern. But this was his brother's nature, to be protective of those he considered weaker. In truth, all the Thorne men were fashioned this way.

Ambrose was frustrated as blazes over Adela and her stubborn independence. Not that he wished to stifle her, but she was no match for a man's strength and had no training in battle tactics. She was fortunate that stranger had not done her serious harm.

"Give me a moment and I'll change out of this gown into something more practical," Adela said and hurried upstairs.

Her friends followed.

Julius chuckled. "Do you think they're hatching new plots?"

Ambrose rubbed a hand across the nape of his neck. "I hope not."

Octavian rolled his eyes. "How can you be so naive? Of course, they are."

Eloise offered him and his brothers a cup of tea. "I hope you are mistaken, Octavian. Adela has given her word and I believe she will keep to it. I expect her friends will do the same. But you must not treat them as fragile flowers. They are clever and observant, and it sounds to me as though Adela's quick action thwarted Runyon's scheme."

Ambrose settled his large frame in one of the chairs. "Possibly, but none of it makes sense yet. Where was Runyon in all this? I am worried he never meant for the exchange to occur with this particular man. Or rather, this man's employer. Runyon was merely using them as a diversion, I suspect. Which raises the question, what was he doing in the meanwhile?"

Julius pursed his lips in thought. "Perhaps your Bow Street man will clear things up shortly. I must admit, I thought your Adela was brilliant. But you are right, she could have been badly hurt."

The Duke of Lotheil cleared his throat. "I'll see what I can do at my end, at the very least discover the identity of the sneak who warned Runyon of our decision."

Eloise took a sip of her tea and then set the delicate cup down. "And Phoebe and I shall continue with the wedding plans since none of you seem to have put it as a priority. Honestly, Ambrose. Are we to have no input whatsoever from you or Adela? This is the most important day of your life and it seems to have slipped your mind completely."

Octavian arched an eyebrow in surprise. "Men never think about such details. Those are a woman's domain. Ambrose, are you sure she wants to marry you? I've never heard of a young lady not putting her heart and soul into wedding plans, especially when the man she is about to marry is a duke."

Ambrose ground his teeth. "This is Adela we are speaking about. If it does not concern skulls, bones, or hideous mythical creatures exhumed from deepest recesses within the earth, then it rates low on her list of priorities. But she does wish to marry me, as I wish to marry her. Eloise, just get her to the church at the appointed hour."

The dowager laughed. "She loves you, Ambrose. She will be there."

Eloise had stated it so casually, Ambrose wondered whether this was true. Did she love him? He certainly hoped so, for he did not want these feelings to be one-sided.

He would not say it…and could not say it, but there was no one else for him.

He had to be in love with Adela if he still wanted to marry her after the spectacle she put on today. She had also wheedled her way into his meeting with Mr. Barrow. Why had he agreed to it?

The answer was as simple as it was appalling.

He loved Adela and could not seem to deny her anything.

It did not take her long to change out of the pretty lilac gown he hoped could be salvaged by Eloise's staff. She now wore one of her serviceable muslin gowns, a plain dark blue with only a hint of lace at the collar, and had donned walking boots that were obviously more comfortable than her elegant slippers since she skipped down the stairs with an agile step.

Ambrose took Eloise's hand and bowed over it. "I shall have her back by early evening."

Octavian next bid farewell to Eloise with a rakish grin. "And I shall see that he sticks to his word."

Julius grinned. "And I shall try to keep them all out of trouble because I am sure our lovely bluestockings are not through running us ragged."

The Duke of Lotheil strode out with them, his purpose to

immediately open a Royal Society investigation into who had told Runyon of their decision.

Adela and her two friends scampered into Ambrose's carriage and took the bench opposite his while Julius rode up front with their driver and Octavian climbed into the carriage and settled his large frame beside Ambrose.

Perhaps they should have better arranged the seating, Ambrose thought. Despite the lavish size of the carriage, he and his brother were cramped because of their broad shoulders. Also, they were both big men and did not have the luxury of stretching their legs while the ladies sat across from them. Those three seemed to fit just fine, snuggled together like contented kittens and none of them complaining as they rode off.

"You may have to put Dr. Farthingale on retainer," Octavian teased.

"He does not need to bother with me," Gory said, lightly rubbing a finger across her bruised jaw. "This bruise is nothing. I'm sure it will be gone by tomorrow."

"But Syd appears to be hurt," Adela remarked, her brow furrowing as she regarded her friend. "Do you think perhaps your hand is broken?"

Her friend nodded. "It could be, but it was so worth punching that pompous toad."

"Bluestockings," Octavian muttered.

Syd glared at him. "What of it? I'd punch you for that remark. But it would hurt me more than it would hurt you, so what is the point?"

"The point is," Ambrose said, leaning forward to lecture the three of them, "that you had better be careful who you choose to attack. Not all men are gentlemen, and you could have gotten hurt far worse than a broken bone in your hand."

Gad, he could see the defiance in their eyes.

Why could they not be more biddable?

He supposed he would find them quite dull if they were.

He, Adela, and Julius waited in Dr. Farthingale's antechamber while Syd, Gory, and Octavian – who complained there was nothing wrong with him even as the skin around his eye socket had turned purple – were tended to by the ever-patient doctor.

Adela cast Ambrose a wry smile. "When your brother complains, he is merely being manly. But when we complain, we are accused of being difficult and irrational."

"Octavian is the size of an ox. You are…"

She arched an eyebrow. "What am I?"

He let out a breath. "An angel."

"Oh." She blushed and smiled at him. "You really must stop saying nice things to me. You make it very difficult to be angry with you. Although I suppose I was the one entirely at fault today."

"No, Adela." He took her hand in his, liking how small and soft it felt. "You were hoping to make things right. Just know that I care more for your safety than anything else."

Gory joined them in the antechamber. "The doctor is binding Syd's hand right now. He has your brother lying on his back on the settee with a cold cloth on his eye. It'll be a few more minutes yet before he is done with them."

Adela patted the chair beside hers. "Sit down and we shall all wait together. Shall we review today's events? Perhaps we will come up with some leads?"

Ambrose laughed. "Here's a novel idea. How about we discuss our wedding? Do you have any notion what Eloise and Phoebe are planning?"

Adela shook her head. "Oh, yes. I am quite aware."

He arched an eyebrow, dubious as to her response.

She sighed. "They've selected the gown I am to wear and I've already had two fittings for it. They've reserved the church. They've gone over the wedding breakfast menu with my friend, Viola. She is Lady Ardley, recently married to Alexander Dayne, Viscount Ardley."

Ambrose nodded. "Go on."

Adela cleared her throat. "We are very fortunate to have Viola's assistance. Her culinary skills are astounding, and she has volunteered to plan the entire menu with your cook. Phoebe and Eloise have also retained musicians to play. I hear they are excellent. Are you sure you wish to turn our wedding into something as grand as a state affair?"

"Adela, I am a duke. It is expected."

"It is an awful lot of fuss for just one day," Gory commented.

"Indeed," Adela said, "but I shall go along without objection since it is obviously important to you, Ambrose. Eloise completed the guest list early in the planning. It was easy for me to provide my part since I had only my two best friends and my parents to invite. Well, of course I included Eloise's grandson, Viscount Ardley, and his wife, Viola. I insisted Eloise invite her entire family as well as all the Farthingales. Do you mind, Ambrose?"

"No, it is the right thing to do. They have all been extraordinarily kind to you and very helpful."

"Then there are your friends and family. I saw the list you gave Eloise. It is quite extensive."

"As I said, it has to be. Most of the guests are already in London so they will not be put out by the hastiness of our wedding plans."

She cast him an affectionate smile. "I still cannot believe you are marrying me."

He grinned. "I should be angry as blazes, but I am relieved you are all right. I suppose eventually I shall have a good chuckle over the sight of you hanging onto that bounder's cloak. But not yet."

"Yes...well, about the wedding." She resumed ticking off the remaining chores to be done, and then took a soft breath. "So you see, there is nothing for us to do but find your book."

He groaned. "I do not care if we ever find it."

Adela's widened and she frowned at him. "Never say that. Yes, you do care. As does every scholar who has made it their life work to discover everything they can about cave drawings, extinct animals, and our ancient origins."

He leaned back in his chair and sighed. "Do you know if Eloise has ordered a wedding cake?"

"Who cares about–" She stopped as Gory kicked her foot. "Um, yes. Wedding cake is also to be taken care of by Viola. She assured me there is to be an entire table of sweets in the Viennese style in addition to the cake, puddings, ice carvings, and jellied molds. It will be a royal banquet and you will choke when you see how much this simple wedding is going to cost you."

Julius laughingly groaned. "Adela, he can afford it."

Ambrose nodded. "The royal family will likely attend. I am not going to stint on a single aspect of our wedding. Nor should you dismiss it as just another party. On this day of all days, I need you to look and act like a duchess and not as some straggling soldier who just wandered off a battlefield."

He glanced at Gory and the bruise to her jaw to make his point. His brother and Syd happened to walk out of the examinations room just then, further making his point. Octavian had a cold cloth pressed to his eye and Syd had her hand bound and resting in a sling on her arm.

Ambrose rose. "Are we done? Good, let's drop off Adela's friends then head to Mr. Barrow's office."

Gory cast him the most pitiful look. "My uncle is my guardian and he truly does not like me. Must I go home? Why can Syd and I not join you? We may have helpful information to contribute."

Syd nodded. "Truly, my family will not even begin to worry about my whereabouts until at least midnight. Besides, my parents are going to the theater tonight and I shall be left home alone. How is that safer than my being with all of you?"

Octavian stared at Ambrose.

He knew what his brother was thinking, that he ought to put his foot down and bring the matter to an end immediately. But Adela was casting him a pleading look and her friends looked so pathetic. Where was the harm in allowing them to join in the discussion?

"Oh, Lord help us all," Octavian said with a groan. "Ambrose, are you going to let them wheedle their way into your investigation?"

"We are involved already," Adela retorted.

"More deeply involved than you," Syd added, giving Ambrose's brother a marvelously indignant stare. "In fact, what good are you for anything other than providing the muscle?"

Ambrose could not suppress his laughter, for his brother looked utterly stunned. In truth, having grown up in a family of men, they had no idea how to deal with ladies. Their mother had passed away when they were young and their father had taken on the role of both parents.

Obviously, it was not quite the same.

Dr. Farthingale, who had come out of the examination room behind Octavian, was also laughing. "Captain Thorne, I learned early on not to fight that current. One must adapt when living in a household full of women. Do not believe the nonsense about men being king of their castle. It is completely untrue. Yes, they will love you and treat you like a king. But never forget that you are not the ruler of that kingdom. Nor should you ever wish to rule your home like a potentate. Women are the heart and soul of the family, and it is only by leaving them in charge that you will find happiness. This is because they are far more loving, competent, and observant than we are."

Ambrose did not feel quite so bad about caving to Adela's every whim now that he had heard the wise doctor give his speech. Apparently, capitulating was something most men did. In truth, he did not see the harm in having the ladies come along. They did not seem happy in their homes, the three of them misfits who had found each other and become more like sisters than friends.

The sun was still bright in the sky and the afternoon had warmed by the time they walked out of the doctor's infirmary. Gory, Syd, Julius, and Octavian marched ahead of them. Octavian helped Gory in first and then scooped Syd up in his arms.

"Eek! What are you doing?" she cried as he settled her onto the seat as though she weighed no more than a feather.

"I am the muscle, am I not?" he snapped back. "And you are the weak, helpless female."

Ambrose was not sure if Octavian liked Syd or not. But one thing for certain, he was not indifferent to her.

Good, he did not like being the only man in the family whose composure was in a roil over a woman. It was especially satisfying to see Octavian mystified because out of the three brothers, he was always the most cynical about women and ever so sure of himself. "Let's make a quick stop at the Huntsford Academy along the way," Ambrose said, settling onto the leather bench beside his brother.

"Why?" Octavian muttered.

"On the off chance something else turned up during our absence. It won't take us long and it is on the way."

"Is this your idea or are you once again indulging Adela and her wayward friends?"

Now Octavian was just getting thorny.

"The decision has been made and I am sticking to it." Ambrose wasn't having any of his brother's grumbling. "You can switch with Julius and ride up top with the driver, if all you are going to do is argue about it."

The Huntsford Academy staff were just closing up the main exhibit halls when they arrived.

Ambrose merely intended to ask them a few, quick questions and resume their ride to Mr. Barrow's office, but Adela and Gory immediately hopped out after him. "What are you doing?" he asked, trying to hold back his exasperation.

"Now that the museum is closed, we ought to conduct a search," Adela said.

Ambrose crossed his arms over his chest, hoping to convey how heartily he disapproved of the suggestion. There was not a chance Runyon had dropped the book somewhere in there today. In fact, he doubted Runyon had ever stepped foot back in his museum after accidentally stealing the book last week. "Why?"

"Is the reason not obvious? We caught that bounder with the bank notes in your lecture hall. Why would he be there, tucking the bag under his chair, if not to make the exchange? What I don't understand is why none of us caught sight of Runyon. He must have attended the lecture or been lurking somewhere close by."

"To see the mayhem he would stir?" Ambrose pursed his lips. "Doubtful. None of this smells right to me."

Adela studied his expression. "What do you mean?"

"We keep mentioning Runyon, but where was he in all this? Not in the lecture hall or even the exhibition halls because the Bow Street runners would have been on his trail. And that man you caught…everything feels wrong about him, too."

"Oh, Ambrose, do you think Runyon was merely toying with

us today? Purposely sending us off on a wild goose chase?"

He nodded. "It is a distinct possibility. Why would he have that man leave bank notes totaling one thousand pounds on the floor beneath his seat in a crowded lecture hall and then simply walk out empty-handed?"

Gory nodded. "Yes, he was not even looking around for that book. It was as though he had no intention of retrieving it."

"It is likely he was merely instructed to drop the package beneath his seat and walk out." Ambrose ran hand through his hair. "We need more information from that man in the magistrate's custody. I think he was hired to play a game designed to vex you, Adela."

"It seems to have worked," Julius remarked, also having hopped down from the carriage to join them. "You are concentrating all your attention here instead of where he must have actually hidden the book."

Ambrose nodded. "I would not be surprised if those bank notes proved to be forgeries and the man turned out to be working for Runyon and not some mysterious buyer."

Adela's mouth gaped open. "That would be dastardly, indeed. Why would that slimy lizard go to all the trouble? Merely to taunt us? All the more reason to search here. He may have had that man plant something nasty to harm visitors and cause you trouble."

Ambrose had kept his temper in check until now, but the thought of that bounder doing anything to his museum had him seething. "He wouldn't dare."

"I hope not," Adela said gently. "However, I am the bane of his existence and you are now betrothed to me and have put the Bow Street men on him night and day. It is quite conceivable that he has turned his outrage on you, too."

"Arrogant knave," Gory said with a huff. "He would rather blame anyone but himself for all his miseries."

Adela nodded. "I always knew he was fiendish and never to be trusted. We really must find that book, prove he stole it, and then have him expelled from the Royal Society. I will certainly urge the Duke of Lotheil to—"

"You will keep out of it, Adela. This is no longer a game."

"It never has been a game. Did I not warn you about these relic hunters? They are not scholarly academicians. They seek glory, not knowledge. I understand there might be some danger, and I will use proper caution. We all will, right Gory?"

Her friend nodded. "Absolutely."

"There, you see?" Adela turned back to him. "Caution is one thing, but you cannot ask us to sit home and cower in fear."

"I am not asking, Adela. I am commanding you to keep your nose out of it from here on out."

She huffed, obviously indignant. "Fine. If we are not going to search the building, then let's move on to the Bow Street office."

Julius had been listening to their exchange and now cleared his throat. "Ambrose, I could stay behind and search. Now that the visitors have all cleared out, it should not be too difficult to scout out the exhibits. I'll have the cleaning staff help me."

"That won't do," Gory insisted. "They may be good at finding lost mittens and scarves dropped on the floor or left on a bench. But a priceless book? Or what if that fiend has set an exotic poisonous spider loose in here? Or a snake? I'll know how to safely handle them. I'm staying with you."

Julius shook his head and laughed. "You are a very scary girl, Gory. Has anyone told you that?"

She smiled back at him, appearing to be not at all offended. "All the time."

By this time, Octavian and Syd, no doubt wondering what was taking them so long, had descended the carriage to join them.

"I'll search with you," Syd insisted, wincing as she began to remove her arm from the sling.

Octavian immediately stopped her. "Are you mad?"

"Perhaps, but I am staying to search."

He shook his head. "Then I am staying, too. You are as helpless as a bird with a broken wing. Someone had better look after you since you obviously have no intention of looking out for yourself. Are all bluestockings this foolhardy?"

"Are all duke's brothers this oafish?" Syd shot back.

"If there is a poisonous spider and it bites you on the rump," Octavian muttered, "rest assured I will not be sucking out the venom."

Syd gasped. "You are appalling!"

"Children, behave yourselves," Julius said with a chuckle, now turning to Ambrose. "You and Adela are the best ones to talk to Mr. Barrow anyway. Come back and pick us up once you are done. I expect Octavian and Lady Sydney will have killed each other by then, but Lady Gregoria and I will be ready and waiting for you."

Gory nodded. "We'll be hungry by then. Your Grace, I think you should take us all out to supper afterward."

"Gory! That is very forward of you." But Adela's eyes brightened. "However, it is an excellent idea. We can all compare notes while we dine. In fact, why not dine at The Red Drake and we–"

All three brothers howled in disapproval of the idea.

Adela sighed. "All right. Perhaps it is not the best plan. But what if Runyon went there today to make certain the book was still safely hidden? We cannot dismiss that it might still be there. Should we not search the tavern as diligently as my friends and your brothers are about to search here?"

"No." He took Adela by the elbow. "Mr. Barrow and his men will deal with it. Come along, he'll be waiting for us."

He nudged her along toward the carriage.

"Will my friends be safe with your brothers? Octavian really did look exasperated with Syd. He doesn't hate her, does he?"

Lord, these girls were clueless.

"No, he doesn't hate her." Good grief, Octavian was going to bust a spleen forcing himself to keep his hands off Adela's friend. Syd riled his brother as no other young lady had ever done before and was it not obvious Octavian was doing his best to behave and not go at her friend like a rutting stag?

Ambrose did not know if his brother's feelings ran deeper than lust, but he was not about to pry. He had his own female woes to deal with, namely keeping Adela away from Runyon so the bounder would not shoot her.

He wanted Adela alive and ready to marry him.

He had been burning to claim her ever since she fell atop him that first day. After all his years of bachelorhood, all those introductions to genteel young ladies and *ton* diamonds without so much as a skip to his heart, Adela suddenly appeared and his heart would not stop soaring. Indeed, she set his heart to rampantly beating every time he laid eyes on her.

What should any sensible man make of this situation?

Could he ever reveal his feelings to her? And yet, how could he not?

But to cede power was not in his nature.

Adela was staring at him as they sat opposite each other in the carriage while it rolled and jounced toward Bow Street.

"What?" he grunted, not reconciled to the impact she had on him. It was not only his heart at risk. All his bodily organs began to spasm whenever she was close.

"It is nothing." But her hands were clasped and she was nibbling her lip, a sure sign she was fretting.

"What, Adela?" he asked more gently.

"Hypothetically speaking, at what point will you decide I am not worth the headache and break off our betrothal?"

He arched an eyebrow, for the question took him by surprise. "Hypothetically speaking?"

She nodded.

He cast her a wry smile. "At no point whatsoever."

She blinked. "No, I am serious."

"So am I. The only way I do not marry you is if Runyon manages to kill one of us before our wedding day. It is this coming Saturday, if you will recall?"

"Is it?" she teased. "It entirely slipped my mind."

"Adela!"

She scooted to his side. "Of course, I remember. I am still in shock over it. I did not think anyone would ever have me. And now, to be about to marry you...would you be very angry if I told you something?"

He took her hand in his. "Of course not, Adela. I don't want any secrets between us."

"Well, it cannot be much of a secret...however, it is something important for you to know."

He gave her hand a light squeeze.

"Oh, Ambrose..."

"What is it you wish to say to me?"

CHAPTER 12

ADELA HEMMED AND hawed as she struggled to find the right words to express herself. She was well educated, much of the knowledge acquired on her own after her parents determined she needed to concentrate on finding a husband rather than pursue higher learning. But these words she wished to say to Ambrose were quite difficult to summon.

And yet, she knew it was the right time to tell him what was in her heart.

He gave her hand another light squeeze as his carriage rolled toward Bow Street. "What is it, Adela?"

She looked up at him, soaking him in and knowing she would never have enough of this wonderful man. "I love you, Ambrose."

She released a breath and awaited his response, but her words hung heavily between them like an enormously mammoth beast just sucking up all the air.

Indeed, she did not think Ambrose was able to draw a breath.

Had he paled? It was hard to tell in the dimness of the carriage.

The prolonged silence was humiliating.

She released another breath, this one ragged as she struggled to maintain her composure. Why had she opened her big mouth and upset their amiable coexistence? "I am so sorry, I mistook the situation entirely. Seems I am book smart, but utterly stupid about men."

She paused to sniffle and calm her breath, for how could she now take back those impulsive words? The answer was, she could not. "I thought you would be pleased to know my feelings since you seem determined to marry me despite the fact there is no need."

"There is a need."

"No, there never was. I could have ridden out the scandal caused by Lady Felicity Rose's mischief."

"And blended into the wallpaper again?"

She nodded.

"No, you could not." He hauled her onto his lap and kissed her with surprising fervor. "You are no drab thing, Adela. Do you have any idea how brightly you shine?" he said in a husky murmur, still holding her gathered in his arms after ending the kiss. "I hoped you would come to care for me in time."

She sniffled again and laughed. "Come to care for you? I am in a headlong tumble. I loved you within five minutes of meeting you," she admitted. "It is possible I loved you before ever meeting you because I *felt* you in my bones the moment I walked into the Huntsford Academy and browsed the spectacular exhibits and your library. I knew at once the man who created all this had to be someone special. Even though you were furious with me for knocking you over, I could not help thinking you were the handsomest and most extraordinary man alive."

He kissed again, this time softly on the lips.

She sensed he wanted to say something to her, but he was obviously struggling to find his own words. When none came, she rested her head against his shoulder. Her mind was more at ease now that he had not pushed her out of the carriage or railed at her for daring to embarrass him.

But anger and cruelty were not in his nature.

He was incredibly considerate and would never say anything hurtful to her.

He was also incredibly honest.

This was likely the reason he had remained silent and not responded with an *I love you* back to her because he was not going lie about his feelings and make her hope for possibilities that could never be at this early stage of their acquaintance. However, he could have said something. Anything. Perhaps gently reminded her it was too soon for them to know their feelings for each other.

It did not matter.

She had put him on the spot, completely caught him by surprise.

To his credit, he seemed to have reconciled himself to her revelation and was being very gentle with her.

Perhaps she ought to have stopped talking, but she could not seem to stop herself. The silence between them, even though his touch was kind and caressing, was unbearable to her. "I know I may appear to be single-minded in my pursuit of Runyon, but that is not so. I am constantly thinking of our wedding plans and forcing myself to believe they are real and not some cruel hoax. You are a king of the swans and I am a common goose who somehow got shoved in among the flock of female swans who adoringly trail you. How can we possibly be a good fit? Me a nobody and you a duke?"

She shook her head and glanced up. "This is why such matches are frowned upon in Society, is it not? Dukes do not marry so far beneath their station, do they? Not that your title has any significance beyond it being a part of who you are. There is so much more to you than merely your title. Oh, stop me from talking. I have said too much…more than enough."

"Adela, we have arrived." He pointed out the window toward Mr. Barrow's office. "We'll continue this conversation later."

She nodded.

What was he thinking now? That she had opened her mouth and revealed feelings he hoped never to hear again?

He could not climb out of the carriage fast enough, obviously relieved to have an end to this conversation.

But he tucked her hand in the crook of his arm and surprised her by keeping hold of her hand once they settled beside each other in Mr. Barrow's office.

Was this not a brazen show of affection on his part?

Well, she supposed a betrothed couple about to be married were allowed such liberties. How else was he to calm her when she had threatened to turn into a watering pot in his carriage? He must have been worried she would do the same in Mr. Barrow's office.

"It is a pleasure to meet you, Miss Swift," said the Bow Street man who looked like a street tough with his bulbous, red nose and big, portly body. However, there was no mistaking his spry, physical strength or his very intelligent eyes that she expected missed nothing when on assignment. Even here, she had no doubt the man was thoroughly assessing her. Not in a lascivious way, not at all. He seemed to be peering into her soul to determine whether she was worthy to marry this duke.

"Thank you, Mr. Barrow. His Grace speaks very highly of you. Can you give us any information on Mr. Runyon's whereabouts today?"

They each exchanged bits of information, taking care to recount every detail. Having met this Bow Street man, Adela now felt more reassured that the Jovian book would be found. "What about those bank notes? What do you make of those?"

He nodded. "They are forgeries, Miss Swift."

Ambrose had suggested as much earlier, but her eyes still widened in surprise. "How can that be? They looked quite real."

"Yes, but all a hoax. I believe the man in custody was also duped. He thought he was working for someone other than Runyon. But I have one of my runners well placed in the bank and he quickly confirmed this was all a ruse."

Adela glanced at Ambrose and suddenly gasped. "Of course, this is why he went to see Hollingsworth in Oxford. This is where he got those fraudulent notes, and I'm sure he took more than one thousand pounds worth of forgeries. He has probably been paying his landlord and the tavern keepers with them, as well as teasing us. I told you these relic hunters were an unsavory lot and not above treachery in any form. Oh, how it galls me those thieves are admitted into the Royal Society while honest, intelligent ladies are not. But why go to all the trouble? Just to have us running wildly in every direction?"

She shook her head, for her mind was now awhirl with questions. "Mr. Barrow, you have mentioned you searched The Red Drake and Mr. Runyon's residence several times and found nothing, not my notes or the book. And again today, you seem convinced those articles were never at The Red Drake. So it is obvious he must have made another stop within those few hours after running off with them. If not his home or the tavern, then the Royal Society seems the most likely place he would have gone."

"The Duke of Lotheil has permitted us to search there as well. Believe me, Miss Swift, we have left no stone unturned. It is possible he immediately sent everything off by post to some location where he could later retrieve it. I have a man investigating the possibility now."

Adela pursed her lips in thought. "I do not believe he would do this, hand off that precious book and worry someone might open the package before he got there to claim it. Or that it somehow might be lost. No, he is not one to let go of a thing. So, he must have stopped elsewhere. But where? I don't suppose we can abduct him and hold him prisoner until he divulges the hiding place?"

Ambrose gave her hand a light squeeze. "No, Adela. As tempting as it is, it will not work. The magistrate has already brought him in for questioning. Runyon knows I have Bow Street runners following him. He also knows the Duke of Lotheil is onto him. It cannot have escaped his notice that we have searched all his known haunts and are breathing down his neck."

"And he mocks us for it. You are playing by gentlemen's rules, something he would never do. He is not scared of any of us. Indeed, he thinks we are all fools for not using more sinister means to get at the truth."

"What do you suggest we do? Beat the information out of him? I would not rule it out if lives were at stake, but they are not."

Adela knew he was right, but the situation was still frustrating beyond belief. "I know, but it still galls me he has that priceless book. Are you sure there is nothing more the authorities can do?"

"Miss Swift, the magistrate held him for hours beyond his questioning at my request," Mr. Barrow said. "This was done as a favor to me. The only evidence we have is your word against his, and he is a Fellow in the Royal Society."

"So it is presumed he must be honorable? Which he is not," she said with a huff.

Ambrose sighed. "Lotheil will have him kicked out soon enough. But that still leaves us right where we started. Not a clue what he did with your notes and the book. Keep on it, Mr. Barrow. He may have been clever in hiding those items, but he has to retrieve them at some point. We'll have him then."

They were about to leave when one of Mr. Barrow's confederates hurried in. "Oh, I beg yer pardon. I did not realize ye had company."

Mr. Barrow rose to greet him and his eyes suddenly glittered in expectation. "Stay, Mick. This is His Grace, the Duke of Huntsford, and his betrothed, Miss Swift." He turned to her and Ambrose. "Mick is my best man and I've had him on this case from the start. What have you found for us?"

Adela held her breath.

Could this Bow Street runner be bringing news they were longing to hear?

"Runyon has a sister living in London. I left George and Wills to watch her residence, one of them will follow her if she leaves holding a bundle. Of course, they will report back at once if Runyon turns up there."

"And will follow him when he leaves?" Adela asked, her heart leaping into her throat. This had to be where the wretched sneak had gone after stealing her notes and the book.

"I already have two good men on him to follow his every movement," Mr. Barrow said.

Adela glanced at Ambrose, for it must be costing him a small fortune to keep all of those men to the task night and day.

Ambrose's face was stoic, nothing but steel in his expression and in his eyes. "You see, Adela. We have just put the noose around his neck. All it required was a little patience."

And a deep pocket, which he had. But she was not about to point this out to him, for it would only offend him.

He rose and held a hand out to her. "Do you wish to wait here or join us?"

She hopped to her feet. "Join you, of course. Where are we going?"

"Down the street to the magistrate's office," he said, wrapping her arm in his.

She inhaled sharply. "Are you going to order the magistrate to conduct a search of the sister's home?"

He nodded. "Mr. Barrow and his men will accompany him."

"What about us?"

Ambrose shook his head. "No, we are returning to the Huntsford Academy to pick up my brothers and your friends for our dinner engagement."

"But–" She stopped herself, now realizing she could no longer behave like an opinionated bluestocking who blurted her every thought. She had to start thinking like a duchess. "Yes, of course. Um, should you not let Mr. Barrow know where he can find us later? I'm sure he will have news to report as soon as his search has been conducted."

Ambrose's lips curved in the barest hint of a smile. "You will find us dining at the Wilton Hotel, Mr. Barrow. However, if the search takes longer than anticipated, report to me at my home. It does not matter the hour. I will instruct my staff to wake me."

"Yes, Your Grace."

"And what of me?" She turned pleading eyes on Ambrose. "I will instruct Watling to have me wakened no matter the hour. Will you send word to me if your book is found?"

Ambrose grinned. "Yes, for I doubt you will rest at all until the matter is put to rest one way or another."

They all marched off to the magistrate's office.

Adela marveled at how quickly Ambrose was shown into the magistrate's office and how quickly the search warrant was issued. They could not have been there more than ten minutes before the magistrate, his constables, and the Bow Street runners were armed with warrant and ready to march off to the sister's home. Yes, this is what it meant to be a duke, and why so many of them had elevated opinions of themselves.

It spoke well of Ambrose that he showed more of a level head than she had, for she was incensed and thirsting for Runyon's blood. She would have enjoyed smashing her fist into that wretched man's nose and hearing the crunch of cartilage.

However, she was not truly bloodthirsty and would have felt ill if he were truly beaten up.

That Ambrose restrained himself and did not consider giving the man a thorough beating spoke volumes about the goodness of his heart. He had conducted himself in a more civilized fashion than she had.

They climbed back in his carriage to return to the Huntsford Academy and pick up the others. Ambrose settled across from her, easing back against the squabs and stretching his large frame so that he took up most of the seat.

He looked more relaxed than she had ever seen him, and this made her smile. "You seem confident they will find your book."

He grinned at her, finally allowing his satisfaction to show. "Yes, it is the only place it can be. Your notes, too."

"I hope so. It will be nice to have them back. But I will not fret if they are not among the items found. The knowledge is still up here." She tapped a finger against her forehead. "I can reconstruct the research."

She cleared her throat. "You handled this sad affair beautifully. Better than I ever could. It would have been so easy to beat the truth out of him. You could have gotten away with it, for your privilege of rank would have protected you. But you chose to act honorably, even if it was the most frustrating thing imaginable...well, it was to me. You were solid in your resolve and knew it would end in our favor eventually."

"Nor was it easy for me. I wanted to pound that craven scoundrel to dust. But this is not what men go to war and fight for. We fight to live in a civil world where our loved ones know they will be safe. It may be imperfect and often frustrating, but no family should ever fear of a child or parent or sibling suddenly being hauled off to prison, being beaten or worse, perhaps never being heard from again. Some like Runyon think they are getting the better of us, but they are not. They always get caught in the end."

"Well, he is not caught yet."

"He will be. This is the breakthrough in the investigation we were all hoping for."

She nodded. "I am very proud of you, Ambrose. I knew you were a man of valor, but did not realize how profoundly honorable and blessed with good sense you are. I will do my best to be a good duchess. Seems I have a lot to learn from you."

"I am not perfect by any means, Adela." He leaned forward to take her hand. "I know you wish me to say something about your declaration in the carriage earlier."

"My blurting that I love you?" She shook her head. "You needn't. I just wanted you to know my feelings. It is not something I ever expected to say to any man, quite frankly. I don't know why I was compelled to tell you in that moment. The need bubbled up inside me and I did not want to keep it from you. But I know it is too soon for you to feel this way about me."

She sighed and continued. "Perhaps you will never love me. We cannot force someone to love us, can we? Being the man you are, I know you will always be kind to me. Oh, here we are, back at the Huntsford Academy. I hope Syd and Octavian have not killed each other."

Ambrose chuckled. "Julius is the youngest of us, but he has a good head on his shoulders. He will keep them from taking a hatchet to each other."

"Well, Gory will not mind having their cadavers to study if Julius cannot stop them before they do each other in," she said with a light laugh.

They entered and soon rounded up the four of them.

"Find anything of interest?" Ambrose asked.

Octavian shook his head. "No venomous snakes or spiders. Just lost gloves and handkerchiefs, a few pouches. But there was nothing nefarious in them. No explosives."

Adela gasped. "Did you really think Runyon would blow this place up?"

Octavian shrugged. "It cannot be overlooked."

Her friends were also gaping at him, for the three of them were stunned by the possibility. How could any scholar ever think to destroy a place of higher learning such as this magnificent structure?

"Dear heaven," Adela said, clutching her stomach. "He

couldn't be that mad."

"The mind is a tricky thing," Gory said. "Who knows what any of us is capable of when pushed to the edge?"

"Well, on that jolly note...let's eat. I'm starved." Julius took both Gory and Syd by the elbow and starting for the exit.

Adela followed them, surprised when Ambrose and Octavian hung back.

Octavian had looked serious the entire time. She assumed it was just his nature to be stern and brooding, but what if it was not?

What were he and Ambrose discussing with such seriousness?

Had he noticed something dangerous?

CHAPTER 13

AMBROSE INSISTED ON having Eloise and Phoebe join them for supper. While he and Adela could have dined together without setting tongues wagging because they were to marry within a few days, Ambrose knew her friends required a chaperone. For the six of them to be seen alone would have landed them right back on the front page of the gossip rags. Adela's friends might not particularly care, but he did.

Someone had to look after these girls since their families were obviously neglecting them. It made him sad to think they were being treated as hopeless and discarded when they had so much more to offer than most young ladies who entered the marriage mart.

Well, he was not their father.

Why should he get involved?

He sent word to Eloise and Phoebe to join them at the Wilton Hotel for supper, so it was a lively party of eight who sat at the finest table in the hotel dining room. Ambrose did not stint on the meal or the wine and champagne.

Adela was excited about the mystery of the missing book coming to a resolution tonight and kept glancing toward the entry for Mr. Barrow to appear. "Why is he not here yet?"

"My dear, these things take time," Eloise said, patting Adela's hand. She and Phoebe had been brought up to date on all that had transpired during their busy day.

Adela smiled at her. "I know, but I cannot help wishing the

wait was over already."

"It will be," Ambrose assured. "I think the first thing you must learn as my duchess is patience."

"Yes," she said with a groan, "But it eats at my soul, especially because it is you I have hurt. I will not rest easy until you have the book restored to your library."

"Adela, I have told you before—"

"That it does not matter? But it does and I cannot absolve myself of the blame. However, I shall put it aside and think of happier things."

Ambrose arched an eyebrow. "Such as our wedding day?"

She laughed and nodded eagerly. "How do young ladies wait a year in the planning? These next few days already feel interminable."

Indeed, quite interminable for him as well.

He looked forward to waking to her warm body pressed against his, sharing his days and nights with her.

"Everyone seems to know you," Adela remarked as he acknowledged several old friends and acquaintances, some of whom were exceptionally pretty ladies he'd gotten to know rather well over the years, some more intimately than he should have. "Oh, heavens. That lady is so beautiful. Who is she?"

Ambrose stifled a groan, for Adela was referring to Lady Victoria Chambers, now the Marchioness of Windhurst and formerly one of his intimate acquaintances. Everyone thought he would marry her. Even he had thought to offer for her hand, but something always held him back. As lovely as she was, and as good as they were together in bed, he had never felt that mad, wild passion or any desperation in losing her. Nor had he ever been ready to sacrifice his entire being in order to make her happy.

Passionate detachment is how he would best describe his and Victoria's relation, and he felt it very much on her side, too. He was a title, first and foremost. She had never been interested in the rest of who he was.

Nor had she been willing to wait for him to come around, either. She wished to marry well and make it all happen in her first Season out. For this reason, it was not long before she gave him an ultimatum. He had one hour to decide whether to marry her, or she was going to accept the Marquess of Windhurst's offer.

He had allowed the hour to pass.

Afterward, he had felt only relief when she announced her betrothal to the marquess. As well, he had felt a little pity for the poor sod who was not so bad a fellow.

"Huntsford, you are looking well," Victoria said in her sultry voice.

He and his brothers rose to politely greet her.

"As are you," Ambrose replied, hoping he was mistaking the offer in her eyes. Did she really think to resume their intimate acquaintance? She had to know he and Adela were getting married in a few days. "I hope your husband is well."

"Yes, Windhurst is closing up our Harrow estate and will join me in a few days. Until then, I am completely carefree and quite on my own."

Ambrose glanced at her party of friends. "I am sure your friends will occupy your time until he arrives."

He sincerely hoped her marriage had not already fallen apart, for he did not wish her or her husband any ill. When she did not immediately move on, he had no choice but to introduce her to Adela, Syd and Gory. "Miss Swift and I are to be married on Saturday, as I expect you have heard."

"I had, but did not credit the gossip."

Phoebe decided it was time to chase Victoria away, even though he had no need of her interference. But the two dowagers adored Adela and were quite protective of her. "I am sure there is a lot of false information being bandied about," Phoebe chimed in. "You are wise not to credit any of it. Here is the truth from me now...the match between Huntsford and Miss Swift is a love match. Anyone who thinks otherwise is a fool."

Victoria did not look pleased as she took the hint and moved on.

The conversation now shifted to their upcoming wedding.

The two dowagers had been working hard to put all in place by this coming Saturday. Ambrose hoped this change in topic would distract Adela from thoughts of the Jovian book or Lady Victoria who had been declared an unparalleled diamond three years ago.

Eloise and Phoebe assured him they had the wedding plans expertly in hand, not even any last minute details to fuss over. "All that is left is for Adela's parents to arrive," Phoebe said. "We have received responses from most of those invited. Only a few stragglers have yet to reply."

Adela glanced at Ambrose in surprise. "You were right about all those quick responses. Well, I suppose no one is going to miss out on the Duke of Huntsford's wedding."

Eloise nodded. "My dear, it is likely to be the wedding of the Season. Most responses came within hours of our sending out the invitations."

Syd laughed. "Do not dare put your hand to your stomach, Adela. You are not going to be ill. You are the perfect wife for His Grace and he obviously knows it. Indeed, I think he must like you very much to put up with Gory and me."

"I am enjoying your company," Ambrose assured them. "As are my brothers."

Julius raised his glass. "Here, here."

Octavian simply drained the last of his wine.

Ah, yes. His big brute of a brother was rattled by Syd.

They soon moved on to topics other than his book or their wedding. Ambrose and his brothers found themselves opening up about their father and the impact he had on their upbringing. It was a very personal conversation that none of them had ever shared except with closest friends.

It seemed Adela, Syd, and Gory were now considered to be in that small fold. His brothers felt it, too. Octavian and Julius would have quickly changed the direction of the conversation if they were not comfortable discussing their boyhood years with these ladies.

Of course, Adela was to be his wife so it made sense she should be his confidante. Phoebe and Eloise had always been close family friends. He and his brothers valued their continuing friendship with these dowagers.

However, his heart tightened as he watched Adela and her friends. The obvious neglect in their upbringing was in stark contrast to the solid relations he and his brothers had experienced with their kind and encouraging father.

Phoebe's nose was twitching, a sign her agile brain was once again at work. "We have decided to take Lady Sydney under our wing and sponsor her next Season. Then it shall be Lady Gregoria's turn the following Season."

Since Ambrose already knew of this decision, he understood the information was for the benefit of Octavian and Julius, particularly Octavian.

Good grief, the little harridan missed nothing.

Octavian grunted. "Going to turn them into *ton* diamonds, are you?"

"And what is wrong with that?" Syd snapped even though everyone knew it was the last thing she wanted. Adela, Gory, and Syd were three peas in a pod. They were never going to giggle inanely, flap their fans, or bat their eyes at some nodcock with little brains and a title.

"There is nothing wrong with it, if this is what you truly wish to be," Octavian said. "But I do not believe this is what you want."

The blaze in Syd's eyes extinguished. "It is hard to know what I ought to be or should desire to be when all my life I've been told what I *cannot* be. Sometimes I feel so frustrated because everything of interest is denied to me. So what else can I do but turn into one of those flitting butterflies and hope to find someone who will not completely squash my dreams?"

"Oh, my dear," Eloise said, her voice quite motherly and consoling. "We have no intention of changing who you are. What Phoebe and I shall do is polish off a little of the dust around you so that your unique sparkle shines through. That is all. We changed nothing about Adela other than the style of her clothes and perhaps improved a little on the fashion of her hair."

"Then you sat back and allowed the right man to find her?" Julius asked.

Eloise nodded. "And your brother did. Is this not right, Huntsford?"

Ambrose chuckled. "Adela certainly made a stunning impression on me."

"The point is," Phoebe said, "perhaps we had no hand in your first noticing her. But you would never have considered her suitable to be your duchess without the polishing touches we added. Is that not so?"

He reluctantly agreed, for Phoebe was right.

His attraction to Adela was instantaneous, but he would not have leaped to marrying her, not even when Lady Felicity Rose planted that scandal in the gossip rags, unless he had already decided she was worth holding onto. As Adela often remarked, with a little help from friends such as the estimable Farthingale clan, the scandal would have blown over in a few weeks and she could have resumed her wallflower existence.

Adela always had the intelligence to match wits with him, but seeing her in her elegant gowns and liking the way her beautiful curls framed her exquisite face had sealed the bargain for him.

He wanted her as his duchess.

Julius raised a glass in toast. "Lady Sydney, may you find yourself a duke, as well."

She shook her head. "Oh, no. I would much rather find happiness. But that will require a special man who understands my very heart and soul."

"No," Octavian said. "You are asking too much of the man. What man can ever completely understand a woman? I am not saying this to be condescending. We are not raised in the same way. Indeed, we are pushed in different directions from the time of our birth. Even among you three who are the closest of friends, do you know what is in the other's heart or in her thoughts and feelings with perfect accuracy?"

Ambrose joined in the discussion. "Lady Sydney, I don't think it is the *knowing* that is as important as the encouraging and supporting what the other person hopes to accomplish whether you understand it or not."

Adela nodded. "Yes, I agree."

Syd took a sip of her champagne. "I shall defer to your greater wisdom, Your Grace. I think it is obvious I am still struggling to understand all this myself."

"Most of us do," Octavian said, his manner surprisingly gentle instead of his usually brittle demeanor. "We men have learned to hide our doubts and fears better. Is this not one of the greatest differences between men and women? You are permitted to express your feelings while we are ridiculed and considered weak if we do."

Syd cast him a heartwarming smile. "Why, Captain Thorne, are you human after all?"

He chuckled lightly. "Only on the rarest of occasions. Do not get your hopes up, for I am still a big, insensitive dolt."

Julius suddenly turned his attention to a table in a far corner of the hotel's dining room. "Gad! Will you listen to that woman cackling? It pierces one's eardrums."

Everyone glanced at the corner table.

Adela groaned. "Oh, no. Lady Felicity Rose and her circle of toadies. I hope they haven't noticed us."

"They have," Ambrose said. "She has had her eyes on you from the moment she walked in and saw you."

"Drat, the girl. What have I ever done to her?"

"Other than steal the duke she wanted?" Gory quipped.

"She has only herself to blame," Syd added. "Of course, a creature like that never sees themselves at fault. It is always others in the wrong who have thwarted their plans."

Adela nodded. "I wish I could simply walk over and shake sense into her. Oh, dear. Do you think she will walk over here and cause a scene?"

"Do not get worked up over her," Ambrose said. "She will not dare approach you. This is what comes of being betrothed to me. You hold all the power now and she knows it."

Gory set down her fork. "I find this all quite fascinating, these silent communications that flow about a room. Something even more fascinating is that you understand all their nuances, Your Grace. I must say, it is exhilarating to be on the winning side for once instead of being mocked, ignored, or scorned."

Adela nodded. "Yes, but we must not let that exhilaration go to our heads. We may have power now, but we must always use it for good, never for pettiness or revenge."

Syd smiled at her. "Why, Adela, you do have the makings of a duchess."

"Never mind about that nasty girl," Eloise said. "Look, Huntsford. Is that your Bow Street man?"

Ambrose turned to the entryway and the man now speaking to the steward. "Yes, it is."

Adela gasped and started to rise, but Ambrose motioned for her to remain seated. "I'll bring Mr. Barrow to our table."

The portly Bow Street runner could have been Sir Galahad as far as Adela and her friends were concerned.

"Is that a pouch he is carrying?" Adela was craning her neck to see what he had brought. "He did not have it earlier. I think that is a very good sign."

Ambrose crossed the room in a few strides. "Come join us, Mr. Barrow. I shall have the steward bring over a chair and place setting for you."

"Very kind of you, Your Grace. But I would like to get home to my wife, if you don't mind."

"Then I will not detain you long. However, it is late and I'm sure your wife has put away supper for the evening. Have a quick bite with us while you give us an account of what has happened."

He led Mr. Barrow to their table, ignoring all eyes upon them as this man was clearly not dressed for this fine establishment. However, Ambrose thought he was worth more than the lot of them put together.

The steward brought over a chair and the requested place setting. "Soup and some of your excellent cornbread for my guest," Ambrose said.

"At once, Your Grace."

Ambrose waited for Mr. Barrow to settle in the chair beside him. "Now, tell us what you have to report."

"All of it is good news so far."

"It is?" Adela appeared ready to leap out of her seat with joy.

"Yes, Miss Swift." He nodded in gratitude as an onion broth and cornbread obviously hot and straight out of the oven was set before him. Ambrose filled the man's glass with wine as he listened to the report. "I have your book and Miss Swift's notes in this pouch. They were there with Runyon's sister all along. She and her husband were appalled to learn he had turned them into his unwitting accomplices."

"I can imagine," Eloise said.

"Indeed." Mr. Barrow paused a moment to take a sip of his soup. "The husband vowed to murder Runyon if he dared come around to their house again. Poor fellow was obviously in dread fear we would arrest him and his wife. But I have been in this business for over thirty years and I know an honest man when I see one."

"So you are certain the sister and her husband were innocent dupes?" Ambrose asked.

"Aye, Your Grace. He's a hardworking tradesman and they have small children to tend and feed."

Octavian leaned forward. "Is this not more reason he would feel compelled to make some easy money?"

Mr. Barrow shook his head. "No, my lord. It is all the more reason to keep out of trouble. He makes a decent wage in his trade. They reside in a modest but solidly built house. They are not extravagant and do not appear to live above their means. But more important, they did not behave as though they were guilty."

"How might one who is guilty behave?" Adela asked.

"Oh, fidgeting. Eyes darting left and right. Palms sweating. But it's the eyes mostly that give a criminal away. Runyon's sister and her husband were scared out of their wits and clearly knew nothing of what was really going on. They gave us all we needed for the magistrate to serve an arrest warrant on Thomas Runyon."

"It must have been hard on his poor sister," Adela said.

"It was, Miss Swift. It surely was. She was in tears and begged us to be lenient with him. But he's a bad cove, that one. Thinks he is smarter than everyone and enjoys the cruel games he plays. He is filled with conceit and amuses himself by manipulating those around him. What sort of man puts a loving sister at risk or travels to Oxford merely to obtain forged bank notes to then use as a ruse? He's a right, evil puppet master."

Ambrose choked on his wine.

Adela's eyes rounded in surprise and she cast Ambrose a knowing grin, for had she not accused him of being this very thing? Of course, not evil. He may have done a little manipulation of his own, but it was never intended to hurt anyone.

"I expect the magistrate will find Mr. Runyon at his home. My men have been on the bounder's tail for days now and will be more than happy to turn him over to the constables."

"Will you send word to His Grace once Mr. Runyon is taken into custody?" Adela asked. "He is such a slippery fellow."

"Yes, Miss Swift. I shall keep him abreast of affairs until every loose end is neatly tied in a bow." He asked for Ambrose's permission to leave.

"Good night, Mr. Barrow. Thank you for all your good work. Come by my home tomorrow afternoon at four o'clock and we shall talk further."

"I will, Your Grace." He rose, bowed to the ladies, and strode out.

Adela was eager to look through the contents of the pouch, but Ambrose merely withdrew the book and handed it to her for her inspection. "I'll take the book but give you the pouch to take home with you. Search through it to your heart's content tonight. Let me know if anything of yours is missing and I will convey the information to Mr. Barrow when I see him tomorrow."

She shook her head. "I'm sure it is all here. Your man is incredibly efficient, isn't he?"

"Yes, quite methodical. After all his years on the job, I'm sure he knows everyone in London. There is not a mouse that passes through here without his hearing of it."

Adela now turned to her friend, Syd. "I wonder, do you think we could retain Mr. Barrow to look into your situation?"

Ambrose was immediately drawn into the conversation. "What is wrong? Why do you wish to retain a Bow Street runner?"

Syd blushed. "It isn't important. I could not afford his services anyway."

Octavian frowned. "Are you in any danger?"

"No," she said.

But Adela and Gory each responded with a yes.

"I am not," she insisted.

Ambrose did not pursue the matter further since Syd appeared to be getting overset.

"Perhaps you ought to come live with me now rather than wait until next Season," Phoebe mentioned.

"It isn't necessary. Truly, I would tell you if anything was amiss." Syd raised her glass and offered another toast, but her hand was shaking. "To the return of Jovian of Tarantino's tome and Adela's notes."

They all joined in the toast and dropped further conversation about Syd's circumstances. However, Ambrose had no intention of letting the matter drop altogether. He would discuss her situation with his brothers and Adela tomorrow. If Adela thought her friend was in need of Mr. Barrow's services, he would arrange for it and bear the cost. After all, she and Gory were the closest thing Adela had to sisters, and would he not be expected to help out a sister of hers?

Supper was now over and it was time for him and his brothers to escort the ladies home. Octavian took responsibility for escorting Phoebe, Gory, and Syd to their homes while Ambrose and Julius accompanied Eloise and Adela.

As they were about to walk out of the hotel's restaurant, Lady Victoria sent one of the stewards after him. "Your Grace, my apologies, but one of the patrons wishes a word with you."

Ambrose spared a glance at Victoria who was now coming toward him.

"Very well." He excused himself a moment, allowing Julius to assist Eloise and Adela into the carriage.

As he strode back inside, it did not escape his notice that Felicity Rose and her toadies were watching him. He saw a malicious smile upon that girl's lips.

Ambrose sighed.

This girl exuded envy.

She was going to cause trouble, likely more lies to feed to the gossip rags. But he was going to have Mr. Barrow keep a man on Adela until they were married on the chance her vindictiveness went further.

What was it that compelled twisted people like Runyon and this diamond to take pleasure in harming others?

He shook out of the thought and greeted Victoria with marked impatience. "What is it you have to say to me?"

"You cannot seriously intend to marry that girl. I know what Lady Withnall said, but really Huntsford, it cannot be true that you love her."

Since he had yet to admit it to Adela, he certainly was not going to reveal his feelings to Victoria. "I am marrying her because I want her as my wife. No one has coerced me."

She brushed her fingers lightly along his arm. "Come visit me tonight."

He shook his head. "No, Victoria. Not tonight or any other night. We are over. You made your choice and it is now up to you to make the best of your marriage. Is your marquess such a terrible fellow?"

"What has come over you? You used to be quite a lot of fun." She turned away and stormed back to her table of friends.

"Fun. Right," he said to himself with a snort, shaking his head as he returned to the waiting carriage and climbed in beside Adela. He needed to feel her body against his and inhale the sweet warmth of her skin.

Julius sat across from him beside Eloise, holding tight to the precious book and pouch.

Octavian rode with the others in Phoebe's carriage.

Ambrose and Julius would pick him up at Phoebe's afterward.

He liked having his brothers with him again, for their lives often took them in different directions to the far corners of England or the Continent. Even though they frequently corresponded on Thorne business affairs, it wasn't the same as sitting together in his study and enjoying a port or brandy as they spoke of whatever came to mind.

Julius must have been thinking the same thing, for he had a wistful smile on his face which broadened into a grin when the two of them exchanged glances.

Adela sat quietly as his carriage clattered toward Chipping Way.

He took her hand in his. "What are your plans for tomorrow, Adela?"

"Gory, Syd, and I thought we might spend the day at the Huntsford Academy, but we will stay out of your way. Our time will be spent in the library. Perhaps we'll take a break at midday and have lunch in a nearby tea shop. You could add a tea shop to your building, you know. I'm sure there is space for it and the patrons will find it very convenient."

He nodded. "Add it to your list of suggestions. You know I will listen to anything you propose."

"Well, it can wait. I expect you have a lot to do over these next few days. I'll try not to be too much underfoot."

"You are never underfoot. I am always happy to see you." Then it struck him why she was suddenly sounding so withdrawn. "Adela, whatever was between Lady Victoria and myself has been over for several years now and will not be resumed. I give you my word of honor."

"It isn't necessary, Ambrose. I trust you, truly I do."

"Then why the glum look?"

She let out a soft breath. "These diamonds are so beautiful, even that odious Felicity Rose. I still have trouble understanding how I fit into your heart."

Julius jumped in before Ambrose could fashion his own answer. "Gad, Adela. Isn't it obvious my brother is wild about you? You are genuine. A man always knows where he stands with you because you do not lie. Do you understand how precious that is to someone like my brother? On top of this, you are exceptionally pretty."

"Thank you, Julius. But I hardly compare to those beauties."

"Hah! You far outshine them. Do you not realize it? And I don't mean just in looks. It is the entire package of you, including your eccentric, bluestocking ways. I could go on, but I think you get my point."

Ambrose gave her hand a light squeeze. "Adela, I think you understand me well enough by now to know I will keep to my wedding vows."

She nodded. "I know, because this is the honorable man you

are."

"But you still look troubled."

She nodded again. "Not with you. Felicity Rose was there and likely saw you talking to Lady Windhurst. It is a very cruel thing to put her marriage in jeopardy because that wretched girl is so single-mindedly determined to hurt me."

He laughed lightly in disbelief. "You are concerned about Victoria? After her abysmal treatment of you?"

"She did behave reprehensibly, but–"

"Victoria knew what she was doing and will simply have to bear the consequences of her purposeful actions. Windhurst is a decent fellow and she was openly disdainful of him and their marriage."

"I do not disagree," Adela admitted. "What do you think will be the top story in the gossip rags tomorrow?"

CHAPTER 14

ADELA WAS SURPRISED when she opened The Tattler and saw not a mention of her or Ambrose or Lady Victoria. "Perhaps Lady Felicity Rose has reformed her evil ways," she said when Ambrose stopped by the following morning to pick her up on his way to the Huntsford Academy. They would also pick up Syd and Gory along their route. "I cannot find anything in this gossip rag about us."

"She hasn't reformed in the least, but a threat from me put a stop to the article they were planning to run. It did not hurt that I had Octavian with me. He is strong enough to smash their printing press with his bare hands."

Adela's eyes widened. "Dear heaven, what did the article say?"

He rubbed a hand across the nape of his neck. "Stupid words."

She rolled her eyes. "I know they had to be stupid, but what exactly were they? I'm sure you can recite them *verbatim*."

"Yes, but what is the point when you already know it is meant to be hurtful?"

"Ambrose, you needn't shield me. I'll only imagine something worse than they were going to print."

"Oh, all right. Here's what they were going to run...*Is Duke H already straying? It is rumored the rakish duke arranged an assignation with the married Lady W while at supper with his betrothed.*"

"It said more than that, didn't it?" She knew how petty Felicity Rose was and how hurtful she wanted to be. Yes, alluding to an assignation between Ambrose and Lady Victoria was hurtful enough, but the girl must have added something more to specifically ridicule her. "She referred to me as a country cow again, didn't she? Tell me the rest of it."

He winced. "No, it is utter rot and nonsense."

"Your expression tells me everything I need to know. I can fill the rest of it in. *Is Duke H already regretting his mistake in marrying the country cow? Will there be a wedding on Saturday? How long before Duke H forsakes his marital bed to join Lady W in hers?*"

"I'm sorry, Adela. I wish I could gag her. But at least The Tattler is not ever going to print any of that tripe Felicity Rose is dishing out."

"Let's hope you are right. In the meantime, I will try to harden my heart to such wicked comments. I suppose I will have to learn how once I am your duchess."

He put his arms around her. "I don't know that you ever will. It requires one to erect stone walls around one's heart and not let anything or anyone in. I hope you never have to do this. We can talk more about it in the carriage. Shall we go?"

"Yes, let's get out of here before Eloise wakes. It is one of her 'at home' days, and I do not want to be around if any of those clots who showed up last time dare to show up again today. Are you still planning on meeting Mr. Barrow at your home at four o'clock this afternoon?"

"Yes, do you want to join me?"

"Of course! I would love to be there to congratulate him on a job well done."

Ambrose rubbed a hand across the nape of his neck again. "About that…"

A chill ran through Adela, for she instantly suspected something was amiss. "Oh, no. What's wrong?"

"Nothing, I'm sure. It's just that Runyon slipped out the grasp of the constables who arrested him. It happened at some point after the Bow Street men had turned him over to their custody. Mr. Barrow's men are assisting in the search and will have him shortly. They will not take their eyes off him until he is securely behind bars, which he will be soon. How many places can he have to hide?"

"Not too many, I expect," she said, trying to hide her dismay.

Ambrose gave her cheek a light caress. "Adela, do not fret. They will catch him today if they did not already find him last night."

"They must not have come upon him yet or they would have sent word to you if they had. Oh, I hope he does not get away. Do you think he knows about the magistrate's men and your Mr. Barrow visiting his sister last night? He must have. That sort of news has a way of spreading like wildfire. He will not dare try to hide out with her. Too bad, for now we'll have to figure out another place where he might hide."

"It does not matter. I'm sure he has run out of places and Mr. Barrow will get him. Have you had a chance to sort through the pouch? Are your notes all there?"

She nodded. "I tore it apart the moment I got home last night. Everything is there. Have you restored the Jovian book to your library?"

"Yes. Julius took it over there this morning. It is happily back in its place by now."

"I'm glad. It's recovery is also worthy of a starred page in my diary. You know how much its loss tore me apart."

He gave her cheek another light caress. "I know, Adela. But it was never your fault. Gather your things and let's go."

She rushed upstairs to grab her notepad, work papers, reticule, and pelisse, then hurried back downstairs to the entry hall where Ambrose was now waiting. Watling had the front door open in expectation of their departure.

The sun streamed in around Ambrose, illuminating him where he stood.

She laughed and shook her head. "Figures."

"What?" He escorted her down the front walk to his carriage.

"You are always the handsomest man in the room, looking every inch the Greek god. Is it any surprise the sun chose to shine down on you just now?" She shook her head again and smirked. "And do you know how irritating it is that you always look perfect no matter how hard the wind is blowing? Your hair just naturally falls back into place while mine looks like it was attacked by a murder of crows."

He placed his hands on her waist to help her inside, and then settled beside her. "You exaggerate, Adela."

"No, it is all quite true."

He shrugged, his shoulder rubbing against hers as the carriage jerked and began to roll away from Eloise's house. "Glad you think so, but I am far from anyone's ideal. I need to tell you something."

Her heart fluttered.

Oh, dear.

Was he going to end their betrothal now?

She had to stop thinking like this. Always leaping to the worst possible conclusion when she knew he was not a knave and would never do anything to hurt her.

But he did not love her.

He would have uttered those simple words if he truly felt them.

I love you.

Being the honest man he was, he simply could not say them to her. This was why she continued to have these nagging doubts about their upcoming wedding. Was this not a perfect moment for him to end their betrothal?

After all, everything was back as it should be, his book returned and her notes recovered. Perhaps he still had feelings for Lady Victoria even though he had denied it last night. One's thoughts often became clearer after a good night's sleep.

Had the two ever been in love with each other?

Adela had no doubt they were once bed partners.

But Ambrose, despite their betrothal and his obvious knowledge of a woman's body, had never made any such overtures to her. Indeed, to her frustration, he always remained the gentleman save for a few steamy kisses and that one time he had touched her breast.

Dear heaven.

His hands and lips had felt so nice on her.

But who was to say he did not kiss all his female companions in this melting way? She was to be his wife, yet he hardly behaved as though he were besotted.

"Adela, are you listening to me?"

She nodded. "Yes, Ambrose. What did you wish to say to me?"

"I–"

He suddenly drew her off the seat and shoved her to the carriage floor as something slammed against the window beside her. He covered her body with his own, protecting her while glass shattered all around them.

Had someone thrown a rock at their moving carriage? They had just turned off Chipping Way onto the main thoroughfare which was still in a residential area and not as busy as the shopping streets even though there were several carriages passing by.

Was it possible theirs had been struck by mistake?

"Adela, are you hurt?"

"No, I'm fine." Her heart was in her throat so that her words came out in a harsh rasp. "Are *you* all right?"

"Yes, fine." He withdrew a pistol from the lip of his boot. "Stay here. Do not move. Do you hear me? You are to stay in the carriage."

He was off her and hopping out before she could stop him. The horses were agitated and the poor driver was doing his best to calm them down. Two footmen usually rode at the back of the carriage, and they now went off with Ambrose in search of the perpetrator. She wasn't certain what was going on, but did this incident have something to do with Runyon still being on the loose?

Was something more going on that Ambrose had not told her?

The carriage jerked back and forth, and she sensed the horses were about to bolt. Glass from the shattered window littered the carriage floor and the door stood wide open, swinging back and forth as the team shied and nervously stamped their hooves. Since the carriage was still rocking wildly and she feared the horses were going to take off at any moment, she decided to climb out and find Ambrose.

Would she not be safer with him?

She spotted him a short distance away, standing at an

intersection and obviously searching for the perpetrator. The footmen were also standing a short distance away, having spread out to search down opposite streets.

Who other than her Royal Society nemesis could have hurled something through the carriage window?

She knew it for certain when that bounder suddenly emerged from behind a row of bushes and raised his arm. Yes, it was Runyon for certain, although he looked rather haggard. Was he going to throw another rock?

Adela raced toward him and leaped on the wretched man before he could get off his throw. She landed hard on the ground atop him, but he easily tossed her off and was about to strike her when Ambrose grabbed the fiend and sent him flying through the air. "You are a dead man, Runyon."

Adela worried that his words rang too true, for Runyon howled and then landed with a hard thud on the ground. He now lay motionless in a crumpled heap in the middle of the road.

Was he dead?

He wasn't moving.

To her relief, it was not long before the bounder began to moan and attempted to sit up.

She tried to get up as well, but everything hurt. The breath squeezed out of her when she rolled to her side and also tried to sit up. Pain shot through her temples and she could not focus her eyes.

She tried once again, but her head was still spinning. She yelped as another jolt of pain tore through her the moment she lifted to her knees. She must have scraped them and also twisted her wrist when hurling herself at Runyon.

"Oh, dear." She sank back on the ground, her entire body uncooperative.

"Stay still." Ambrose knelt beside her and took her in his arms with exquisite care. "I don't know whether to throttle you or kiss you."

"Kisses are preferred," she said with a groan. "He was going to hit you with a rock. I had to stop him."

"It wasn't a rock. Blast it, Adela." He sounded exasperated as he rose, lifting her securely in the cradle of his arms. "All you had to do was stay in the carriage as I told you. What is it you don't understand about keeping out of trouble? Look at you now, you're a bloody mess."

"I couldn't stay in there. The horses were frightened and I knew I would be crushed if the carriage toppled. How is that safer?"

"Runyon had a pistol in his hand and might have shot you."

"A pistol?"

"Yes, and that is far more dangerous than the possibility of my carriage tipping over." Ambrose hugged her to him and began to walk away with her in his arms.

"Wait! Are you going to tell me this and then just have us leave Runyon lying there? He must be turned over to the authorities."

Ambrose turned around so that she could see Mr. Barrow and his associate, the man he had introduced as Mick the other day, holding onto Runyon and binding his hands to prevent him from squirming away.

The two Bow Street men kept him pinned to the ground, ignoring the wretch's howls and threats. Ambrose's two footmen were also beside the Bow Street men, assisting them in securing the bounder who was struggling fiercely to break free.

"Ambrose, will you tell me what all this was about?"

He sighed. "The magistrate's men and the Bow Street runners had trouble finding Runyon last night, as I told you earlier. Mr. Barrow was concerned and thought he might attempt to approach you before escaping to the Continent. I did not think the man would be so stupid. Regretfully, Mr. Barrow was right."

She rested her head against his shoulder to ease the throbbing in her temples. "What a fool. Well, if any good comes of it–"

"There is no possible good," Ambrose said harshly.

"Well, no one will ever believe him now if he tries to claim my work as his. And what a comeuppance for the Royal Society for admitting that wretch as a Fellow."

"Bloody blazes, he almost killed you and this is what you think about?"

"You must admit they are insufferable, stuffed shirts, except for the Duke of Lotheil, of course. But it was you he almost killed. His vengeance and his aim were on you. Good thing Mr. Barrow and his Bow Street men thought to follow us."

"They were trying to be discreet and would have had a clean shot at him had you not gotten in the way. Did it escape your notice that I would have had a clean shot at him, too? Adela, any one of us might have shot you instead."

"But you didn't. It all worked out in the end. They have him now."

"So what? This does not excuse your rash behavior."

She gasped. "My rash—"

"Yes! I told you to stay put and what did you do instead? You bolted out of the carriage and singlehandedly charged at him like a crazed, Pictish warrior."

"Which I might not have done had I known others were guarding us."

"I always have guards. Why do you think those two footmen ride at the back of my carriage? Because I wish them to serve tea?"

"But they were too far away from you to protect you."

"So you thought you would take over the task?"

"Yes, actually. I did not wish to see you hurt. What is so terrible about my saving your life?"

"And risking your own?"

"Well, it all ended well, so it is all right now."

"No, it isn't, Adela. Can you not see I am angry as blazes? You might have gotten yourself killed."

"So you've taken great pains to tell me. But what about you? He was about to shoot *you*. Was I suppose to just stand there and let him? Are you sure he had a pistol and not a rock?"

"Yes, I'm sure." He marched toward the carriage that stood quietly just around the corner from Chipping Way now that the driver had managed to calm the horses. "I would have handled it," he grumbled, confusing her as he strode past the elegant conveyance and continued onto Chipping Way. "I had already noticed his approach out of the corner of my eye. More important, I knew the Bow Street men were right behind him."

"I did not see them."

"Because your gaze was trained on Runyon and you were going to take him down without a care for your own safety. I'm taking you back to Eloise's. Your gown is soaked in blood."

She glanced down. "That is a bit of an exaggeration. At worst, there is a small stain on it. My knees must be bleeding. I scraped them when I fell."

"You've also scraped your hand and looks like you've sprained your wrist."

She rested her head against his shoulder once more. It pained her to hold it up long enough to frown at him. "But I saved your life. Does this not count for something?"

"No, not when you almost lost yours in the process," he said with surprising harshness. "I don't know if he would have summoned the nerve to shoot me, but I know for certain he would have shot you. Blast it! You could have gotten killed in the crossfire. Any of us could have taken a shot at Runyon and hit you by accident. How do you think this makes me feel? Knowing I almost shot the woman I plan to take as my wife?"

She closed her eyes in an attempt to stop her tears. He sounded so angry. What was she supposed to do? Just watch him die? That is what would have happened if Runyon truly had a pistol, which he probably did have since Ambrose was not the sort to be wrong about such things. "What were you going to say to me before Runyon tossed that rock and broke the carriage window?"

"He *shot* it out, no rock involved. He aimed high, so he was likely only trying to scare us...or taunt us further. But who can be sure what he intended? The man has been hunted for days and must be as crazed as a mad dog."

"I cannot believe he seriously meant to kill either of us. That is beyond anything a rational man would do."

"Who says he was ever rational?"

"But he was...at least, I thought he was. Although he has always been full of conceit, and not above climbing over others in order to get noticed. He did not care who he hurt in order to reach archeological acclaim. But to be a killer?"

"He wanted to steal your work, have everyone believe he was the brilliant one. Is it that much of a stretch to think he needed you out of the way?"

She shifted in his arms to look up at him, her bones aching with every movement. "I knew he was a ruthless character, but to go to such lengths?"

"Must a madman have a reason? He's caught now, hopefully for good this time and won't be able to harm you again." He softly cursed. "What foolish lack of judgment."

"Yes, he is quite the fool."

Ambrose growled. "I meant you."

"What?" This is what he thought of her for trying to save him? "I resent that you are angry with me over this. Why are you too stubborn to admit I might have saved your life?"

"Need I repeat, it was at the risk of your own? Am I supposed to be dancing a jig because of it? For pity's sake, Adela. Do you have any idea how narrowly we averted disaster? Forget about your damned, bloody knees. It could have been you bleeding to death on the street." He was still glowering at her, and if she were not in so much pain, she would have glowered right back at him.

"Put me down. I am fine," she said, unwilling to admit she had a single ache even though her knees were burning and her wrist was throbbing, not to mention she had ruined another beautiful gown.

"Stubborn girl," he muttered. "As for Mr. Barrow, he will give us more information later. Right now, let's get your scrapes cleaned up and see to your wrist. Anything else hurt?" He kicked at Eloise's door and stormed in the moment Watling opened it.

"Miss Adela! What happened to you? Are you all right?"

"I need clean cloths and some brandy," Ambrose said, in full ducal authority tone. "Send one of the footmen to summon Dr. Farthingale. Is Lady Eloise awake yet?"

"Yes, her breakfast has just been brought up. I'll alert her maid and have one of my boys send for the doctor. Hopefully, he is next door visiting his brother. He often stops by there on his way to or from a house call." Watling scurried off to tend to those chores while Ambrose, still unreasonably angry with her, carried her into the elegant parlor and set her down on the stool beside the hearth since she was too bloodied to sit on any of the fine silk chairs.

He knelt beside her. "Let me have a look at your knees. You took a bad tumble. You're still trembling."

"Because I am angry."

"So am I. You have to stop tackling people, Adela." He placed a hand under her gown and raised the fabric above her knees.

Oh, that felt nice.

"Blessed saints, look at you." He stroked his fingers along her calf, his gentle touch sending tingles up and down her body. There was something wonderful about his touch, for it was firm and confident, yet also exquisitely tender.

"I don't go around looking for people to knock down. In fact, I had never run over anyone before I met you. So, in a way, you are completely to blame," she said, trying to make a jest in order to lighten the situation.

He merely arched an eyebrow.

Sighing, she gripped her hands on either side of the stool to steady herself. But she had fallen atop her left hand and any pressure on it was painful, so she winced and let go of the stool with that hand.

This earned her another frown from Ambrose. "Your parents will arrive the day after tomorrow and our wedding is two days after that."

"I know."

He withdrew a handkerchief from his jacket pocket and used it to blot the blood at her knees. "This is how they will see you."

"I am not going to walk around with my gowns hiked up to my knees."

Her remark earned her another scowl. "You will be hobbling."

"No, I won't. Is this what has you so overset? That I will be a hobbling duchess on our wedding day? If that is all you care about, then–"

"Blast it, Adela! If you dare suggest I call off the wedding, I shall haul you over my knee and spank you."

She clamped her mouth shut.

But after a moment, she dared to speak up. "You wouldn't ever raise a hand to me, would you?"

He sighed. "No, of course not."

"I could not let him hurt you, Ambrose." She was on the verge of tears and needed to explain her motives so he would understand them and not believe her to be a reckless dolt. "I am not sorry about what I did. Why can you not simply accept it? He was going to shoot you."

"Maybe."

"Maybe? Is that not reason enough? Dear heaven, I did not realize he had a pistol in hand and thought he was just going to toss a rock. I'm glad I did not know. But I don't think it would have changed my actions no matter the risk. You are too important to me and I don't ever want to see you hurt."

She paused now that Watling had returned with clean cloths and brandy.

"Thank you, Watling," Ambrose said and gave a curt nod of dismissal which the dear butler ignored because he had no intention of walking out until he was certain she was not seriously harmed.

"Your Grace, I shall be just outside in the entry hall should you require anything more. You have only to call out and I shall rush in."

Adela could see the kindly, old man was overset by her condition. Even though Ambrose had dismissed him, he still stood beside her regarding her with fatherly concern. "Forgive me, Your Grace...but perhaps Miss Adela would like a nice cup of tea."

Adela smiled up at him. "That would be lovely, Watling. Yes, please."

However, she was not smiling when she returned her attention to Ambrose and the permanent scowl affixed to his face. Why was he still angry with her? In the first place, he had no right to be even the littlest bit miffed. "I thought you were different from the others."

He paused in his ministrations to glance at her.

"I thought you would understand and be appreciative," she said, taking a deep breath in order to muster her resolve. "Not that I need accolades, but I do not need to be frowned at and told my actions were heedless. Would you feel the same if I were a man and had brought Runyon down?" She answered for him. "No, you would not. You would have been thanking me and inviting me to share a drink."

"But you are not a man." To prove his point, he stroked his hand lightly along her leg once more, the rough pads of his fingers surprisingly arousing and sending her heart into flutters.

The gesture was blatantly seductive.

He saw her responsive blush and was ridiculously pleased by the way he had so easily disconcerted her. Well, he was not really gloating about it. But she caught the glint of satisfaction in his eyes.

Such gorgeous eyes.

What did he see when he looked at her?

A hoyden?

A hellion?

A mistake?

Was he now trying to think up a way to bow out of marrying someone so unsuitable to be his duchess?

If he wanted out, she was not going to stop him. "Is this what our marriage is to be, Ambrose? Me walking on eggshells, always afraid of disappointing you?"

He was frowning again.

This is what happened when a couple did not love each other…well, she loved him but he did not love her.

Was he going to run into the arms of Lady Victoria now? Her heart twisted just thinking of the possibility.

"This is going to hurt, Adela," he said gently, holding up the cloth he was now dousing with brandy. "In fact, it will sting like blazes. Just hold your breath."

"I don't care. I am already going to cry."

He sighed. "Why are you going to cry? I haven't even applied the cloth to your knees."

"I am going to cry because…" She released a ragged breath. "I wanted you to fall in love with me and now it will never happen. I can just imagine what is going through your mind, the regret that you did not accept Lady Victoria's offer of an assignation."

"Are you serious?" His eyes turned an even stormier shade of gray than they already were. "This is what you think of me? That I would rather be in the bed of a married woman? One who cares so little of her husband's feelings that she approaches me in front of her friends and even strangers who happened to be dining at the Wilton Hotel? Am I supposed to admire her more than the young woman willing to risk her own life to save mine?"

"This is precisely my point. You ought to be admiring me, but you are not. You look upon me as a disappointment and just wish me to go away, just disappear. Believe me, I know that look. I have been on the receiving end of it for much of my life."

"You do not disappoint me at all and I do not want you to go away." He sighed. "Hold still, I am going to apply the cloth to your knees now."

Pain shot through her the moment the brandy soaked into her skin.

She yelped and almost fell off the stool. "Ouch! That burns!"

He put an arm around her waist to hold her steady. "Close your eyes and rest your head against my shoulder while I clean out the other knee. I'm sorry it hurts, but it cannot be helped."

"You had better not be smug about this. Do you think I deserve to suffer because I got myself into this mess? Is this what you really wanted to say?" However, she nestled against his body because he was gloriously built and impossible to resist. His skin was warm and held a trace of musk so that she wanted to inhale him for hours on end. "Oh, never mind. I don't want to fight with you. I just want to rest in your arms."

"Adela," he said in a husky murmur, "we are not fighting. This is me being insanely worried about you and kicking myself for not protecting you better. I might have lost you. It is my responsibility as your betrothed to protect you. Same goes for when I am your husband in a few days from now. I want to shield you from ever getting hurt. Seeing you like this just tears me up inside."

"It does?" She glanced up and blinked away her tears. "Ambrose, do you think you will ever fall in love with me?"

He emitted a deep, rumbling chuckle. "Amazingly, yes. I fear it is inevitable."

She gasped. "Truly?"

He nodded.

"And you are not saying this to make me feel better because you think I came close to dying a few minutes ago?"

"No, it has been on my mind since we met."

"That sounds promising." But she could not hide her disappointment, for he did not love her yet. Although, what did it matter if he was slow to come around? Not everyone fell in love at first sight as she had done when meeting him. Indeed, most people did not. "I am sorry I worried you. But I love you, Ambrose. I could not sit there, dumb as a log, when I knew you were walking into danger."

"You are too brave for your own good." He said no more as they heard a commotion at the door and both of them turned to the doorway.

Dr. Farthingale rushed in, his scuffed medical bag in hand. "You are in luck. I happened to be next door having coffee with my brothers."

Adela knew he referred to John, who owned the Chipping Way house next door to Eloise, and Rupert, another of his brothers who did most of the traveling in the family textile business. The Farthingale fabrics were renowned throughout England, for Rupert often went to exotic locations to bring back the most exquisite materials. These brothers were a true family.

Ambrose and his brothers were the same way.

But what did she have? Parents who often forgot they had a daughter.

Gory and Syd who were no better off.

Gory's parents had died recently and she now resided with an uncle who wanted her out of the house but was still too miserly to give her so much as a new gown to enhance her allure. Syd's parents…there was something very odd going on in that house, but Syd refused to speak about it.

"I really ought to put you on retainer," Ambrose jested, stepping back to allow the doctor some space while he tended her. "Make sure you bring your medical bag to our wedding. I'm certain we'll have need of it, the way our luck is running lately. Adela, now you will have a sprained wrist to match Syd's injury."

Dr. Farthingale studied her for a moment. "And bruises to

match those Octavian and Lady Gregoria suffered."

"Oh, heavens!" Eloise cried out as she bustled in and immediately sank into a chair beside her. "What is going on? Adela, my dear, you look a mess. What happened?"

Adela groaned. "It is not as bad as it looks."

Her words did nothing to calm Eloise who was still gaping at her. "I did not understand a word of what my maid was rattling on about, and now Dr. Farthingale is here again."

Syd and Gory arrived shortly thereafter. "We knew something had to be wrong when you did not arrive to pick us up. You are never late." Syd's arm was still in a sling and a bandage protruded at the wrist just under her sleeve.

"I suppose this means no Huntsford Academy library for us today." As Gory shook her head, Adela could see the prominent bruise on her chin had turned an awful shade of purplish-yellow.

This was a good sign, was it not? It meant her bruise was fading, although it now looked quite hideous. A little powder would cover it up if it was not gone within a day or two.

"Huntsford's library? I should say not!" Eloise intoned. "Adela is to stay home the rest of the week. You are welcome to join her here, but there will be no running off to parts unknown."

"You are confining her for the remainder of the week? But it is just a library," Gory said, sounding quite dismayed.

"Mischief and danger seem to find you girls everywhere you go. You should all stay put and heal. The wedding is only a few days away and the three of you look like alley cats on the losing end of a brawl. Phoebe and I did not go to all the trouble of putting this affair together only to have you three hobbling into the church on crutches."

Adela had no intention of remaining confined until her wedding day. "I don't see the harm in going to the library tomorrow. Ambrose and his brothers will be there, too. With Runyon out of the way, I expect our day shall be quite ordinary and dull."

Ambrose had been standing beside her while Dr. Farthingale attended to her, watching as the doctor properly cleansed and bandaged her knees, and then securely bound her wrist. When the doctor finished and left, Ambrose knelt beside her once more. "I shall take my leave now, as well. My brothers will be wondering what happened to us. I had better go and tell them."

She started to rise, but he motioned for her to stay seated. "Have tea with your friends. I'll see myself out. Stay put, as Eloise said. I'll be back to see you later."

She cast him a wry smile. "I'll be right here. Not going anywhere since I am apparently under a prison sentence."

He kissed her lightly on the cheek. "Promise me, Adela. My heart is still in my throat over you. What happened this morning is no joke. Do not treat it lightly."

"I'm not. I promise you, I am still in turmoil over it."

This time, he kissed her lightly on the lips.

Her friends giggled.

He had yet to let go of her hands or take his gaze off her when Octavian strode in. The skin around his eye matched the purplish-yellow bruising on Gory's chin.

They did look a mess.

All of them did except Ambrose who still resembled a Greek god.

Fortunately, he and Julius had escaped injury.

Octavian took one look at her, then turned to his brother and groaned. "Bloody blazes. What happened?"

Ambrose let out a breath and groaned. "Adela happened."

CHAPTER 15

AMBROSE AND HIS brothers joined Eloise, Adela, her friends, and Adela's parents for supper on Thursday evening at Eloise's home. The small party was meant to give Ambrose a chance to meet her parents, something Adela had been fretting about for the past two days. Now, he understood why, for they were two of the most absentminded people he had ever met.

He could see Adela inherited her intelligence from both of them, but she had an organized mind while her parents were completely caught up in the most impractical thoughts to the exclusion of anything else. It quickly became obvious Adela had been the one to keep their household in order.

What had they done before she took over the role of adult in the family?

And what would they do now that she was not returning home to them?

Was this the reason Adela had begged for their wedding destination to be the Devonshire caves? This would allow her to look in on her parents and perhaps spend a few days putting their bills and household affairs in good order.

However, it tugged at his heart to realize she gave more thought to her parents than they did to her. While there was no malicious intent on their part, the fact remained Adela had always been an afterthought to them, and neither of them appeared to appreciate the truly wonderful girl she was.

This explained why she was so determined to have her

footnote in history. She wanted someone to remember her, and knew it was never going to be her parents.

They did not hate her.

Quite the opposite, they were amiable toward her as one might be to a good friend. But there was something lacking, a sort of distance kept between them and her.

No tender hugs.

No ebullient joy.

They were scholars and never the sort to physically abuse her, but indifference could sometimes be just as cruel.

He wanted to reach out and hug her then and there, but it was not something he could do around a dinner table.

"Your Grace, you and Adela are welcome to stay with us while you are in Devonshire," her father said, shoveling a bite of mutton in his mouth. "We have a lovely house in Dartmouth."

Adela set down her glass of wine after taking a sip. "No, Papa. We have already made arrangements at the Blue Rose Inn, a lovely inn overlooking Lyme Bay. His Grace and I would prefer to have our privacy."

"Ah, well. You will look in on us, won't you?"

"Yes, Papa. Just set aside whatever it is that needs attention and I shall take care of it during our visit."

"You ought to do it before you get caught up with your caves," he said, taking another bite of mutton. "Everything has become such a muddle since you left. I think we shall have to hire a bookkeeper to replace you."

"That is a good idea," Adela said, but Ambrose sensed she was hurt by the possibility she could be so easily replaced in their heart by a bookkeeper.

He was not going to stew about it or pass a remark since Adela seemed to be handling her parents quite well and did not need him to make something more out of a situation that was never going to change.

As for him, he would do his best never to take her for granted.

He would tell her that he loved her, and silently chided himself for failing to do it sooner. Was he not holding her at a distance, just as her parents were? And for what? Because he thought he might lose the upper hand if she realized how much he truly cared for her?

The discussion returned to their honeymoon plans and the cave explorations.

"I have never liked caves," her mother said with a wistful air. "My life's work is birds. We have so many of them around the countryside near our home. Warblers, terns, snipes, crakes, chuffs, godwits, geese. Some nest with us year round while others migrate and then return. We happen to have some blue tits nesting in the woodlands near our home this year that merit avid study. I do enjoy watching them. They are so pert and bouncy."

Julius grinned wickedly. "I love pert and bouncy–ow!"

Eloise, who was seated beside him, poked him in the ribs. "Behave yourself. I thought you were the sensible one."

He rubbed his ribs. "What did you think I was going to say?"

Eloise harrumphed. "It does not bear mentioning."

Octavian laughed and choked on his wine.

Ambrose glanced at Julius who was grinning back at him.

Oh, lord.

Julius was in his cups.

Perhaps they all were, but who could blame them after the week they'd had? It was a little too exciting for their tastes, and they were getting reckless while in the company of ladies, even though Adela and her friends were bluestockings and had no delicate sensibilities to speak of.

"Have you documented their migrations? Or studied their nesting habits?" Gory asked, apparently fascinated by the topic of blue tits and completely unaware of the turmoil this completely innocent conversation had created in the Thorne men.

Despite all their accomplishments, they were still crass, little boys at heart.

Julius maintained that grin on his face while he listened to Gory ask her questions.

"I am afraid my notes are quite scattered," Adela's mother continued, "and must be put in some logical order before I can present them to our local ornithological society. I was hoping Adela would forget her caves and help me out." She shrugged.

"But she always was her father's daughter and never really cared for my birds."

"Mama, that is not so. We spent many summers exploring their nesting sites."

"Only when your father was not taking you off to the caves." She waved her hand as though to wave off Adela's supposed slight throughout the years. "One can never reclaim the past, but we must ever look forward. We knew it was time for Adela to find herself a husband, so we kicked our little bird out of the nest and watched as she flew away."

"I'd say she did all right for herself," her father said with a chuckle. "A duke for Adela. Whoever would have thought it? Certainly not I or her mother. But we would have made a pretty penny had we wagered on her landing one. What do you think the odds would have been on that? A hundred to one, I should think."

"Oh, dear heaven," Adela whispered, taking another sip of her wine.

"Ambrose is quite enamored of her," Julius assured them.

Her father appeared startled. "Is that so? I thought it was some nonsense about her being compromised."

"Papa! I was not compromised. Do not believe anything you read in The Tattler."

Her father set down his knife and fork. "My dear girl, the where and how of your betrothal matters little at this point. You are about to marry a duke and that is the bottom line. But I must say, you certainly chose the right one. I cannot wait to tour the Huntsford Academy. I hear it is a marvel and just across the street from the British Museum. That is quite a lot for us to take in tomorrow. I doubt there will be time to pay proper attention to both."

"I shall give you a private tour in the morning," Ambrose said, "then afterward you can walk over to the British Museum and squeeze in a few exhibits there. I'll have my driver bring you back here in my carriage when you are done."

Adela's mother tittered with glee. "Adela, this is really quite well done of you. And here we thought your second Season would be as ill-fated as your first."

"Thank you, Mama." She turned to Ambrose and cast him an apologetic look.

He took her hand under the table, something he was able to do since Eloise had seated them next to each other. "I did not know your daughter in her first Season, but I would hardly call it a failure. She is a beautiful girl and was probably viewed as competition by many of the other debutantes. Some of them can be quite petty and malicious."

Her mother nodded. "Poor Adela was quite unprepared for any of it. I suppose the fault rests with me since I did not see fit to take it as seriously as I ought to have done. Fortunately, Lady Eloise came to our rescue. I expect my poor Adela would have remained a spinster if not for the efforts of Lady Eloise and her friend. I am sorry Lady Withnall could not be with us tonight. But I shall thank her personally tomorrow evening. We shall all be dining with the Earl of Trent and his family, is that not right?"

Adela nodded. "Yes, Mama. All of us are invited because Eloise is the dowager countess and mother to the earl. She is also grandmother to the earl's son, Lord Ardley. I met Lord Ardley and his wife, Viola, Lady Ardley, last Season and we became quite good friends. Viola is the one who introduced me to Lady Eloise and all the Farthingales."

"There is nothing wrong with being a spinster," Syd remarked, obviously sensitive to the topic. "Why does everyone think a woman is nothing unless she is married? It isn't as though the men are always such prizes."

Adela's mother reached over and patted Syd's uninjured hand. "I hear you are their next project. I'm sure they will find a charming man for you. Believe me, they worked a miracle on Adela and I have every confidence they will do the same for you and next for Lady Gregoria."

Ambrose's heart tightened. "I would hardly call our betrothal a miracle. Adela would have charmed me had we met last year, I'm sure."

"Lucky for us, there you were this second time around," her father remarked. "She caught you right well, indeed."

"I did not *catch* him, Papa. His Grace is not a trout. We...we somehow found each other and decided...oh, what's the use? Would you care for some more mutton, Papa?"

The conversation flowed quite lively after that, the topics turning to the parties planned for the duration of her parents' stay in London. He and Adela would not be here for them since they intended to leave for Devonshire the day after the wedding.

Adela was surprised to learn Syd and Gory were not going to most of the festivities planned. "Why aren't you going?"

Syd shrugged. "Who is to take us? Certainly not anyone in my family or Gory's. Besides, it won't be the same without you in our wallflower corner."

"And Marigold is still too young to join us at these affairs," Gory added.

"Thank goodness for that," Eloise muttered. "You girls have been too adventurous for your own good lately."

Julius cleared his throat. "Octavian and I shall escort Syd and Gory. It isn't right that you must miss out on these invitations."

"Phoebe and I shall serve as chaperones for you," Eloise added with a nod. "There, it is decided."

Gory clapped her hands. "Thank you. Go ahead, Syd. Wipe that frown of your face and be grateful we have good friends to help us out."

Syd's lips were tightly pursed as she nodded. "I do not wish to seem ungrateful, for I appreciate the gesture. It is exceedingly kind of all of you, but not necessary. I think I am better off staying at home."

Octavian frowned. "Why?"

Syd glanced around the table. "It is not anyone's business, is it?"

"I am making it my business," Octavian said. "What is the next affair after the wedding? I cannot even keep up with all these blasted events. Farthingales, I think. Or is it Lord Frobisher's soiree? No matter, whatever is next, be ready. Julius and I will come by to pick you up. Same goes for whatever else comes up. No one is going to give you trouble while I am your escort."

"Oh, isn't that charming," Adela's mother said. "Seems Adela's friends are about to make matches of their own."

Gory and Julius laughed.

Syd and Octavian each muttered an emphatic "no".

Ambrose simply took hold of Adela's hand again, happy to be out of the maelstrom of the marriage mart.

When the meal was over, Adela took him aside for a moment. "I must thank you and your brothers for being so patient with my parents."

"They are a little awestruck and unpolished, but haven't we had our fill of polite society? They were pleasant enough to me and my brothers." He was not sure he ought to say more because she cared for them and he did not wish to overset her.

She nodded. "It is also very kind of your brothers to look after my friends. I do worry about them. I grew up in an eccentric home, but I was never ill-treated."

Blast it, yes she was.

He had to say something but would try to be gentle about it. "I don't know, Adela. Some of the remarks your parents made...they don't seem to understand how lovely you are. Perhaps they did not treat you ill, but I'm not sure they appreciated you as they should have."

"I know," she said with a light tremor to her voice. "This is what comes of being an unexpected addition to a family they never intended to have. They are never going to be doting parents. But we grew much closer as I got older and could join them in their studies. Gory lost her parents and now has an uncle who has no use for her. Syd...I cannot shake the feeling that something is amiss in her home. It worries me."

"Octavian will look out for her. He is good at that sort of thing. He may appear stern and forbidding when he puts on that fierce scowl."

"Which he always does, it seems."

"Underneath, he has a very soft heart. If he has decided Syd needs protecting, then this is what he will do."

"Whether she wants it or not?" She sighed and shook her head. "It does not matter what Syd wants. She needs someone to watch out for her. I can see she is troubled. Why won't she confide in us?"

Ambrose gave her a kiss on the forehead. "I don't know. It may be she is embarrassed, or if it is something more sinister, then she may be afraid whoever she brings in to help her will be harmed. I'll talk to my brothers, ask if they want me to engage Mr. Barrow and his Bow Street men."

"Thank you, Ambrose. That will ease my mind greatly."

"Mine, too. I like your friends." He glanced toward the front door as his carriage was now brought around. "I'll see you tomorrow. Sweet dreams, Adela."

She smiled. "They shall be filled with you."

He kissed her soundly on the lips, a short but ardent kiss, for he dared no more. They hadn't a moment alone these past few days and he needed to tell her that he loved her.

But the moment never seemed right.

Now, his carriage was here and everyone was waiting for him to climb in.

He had not even thought to ask Adela if she intended to join her parents on their museum excursions tomorrow. He doubted she would, for Eloise had put her foot down on any running around on the day before their wedding, other than Lord and Lady Trent's party since Lord Trent was Eloise's son and she was not going to refuse that invitation.

He planned on escorting them to Lord Trent's, so perhaps they would have time for a private moment then.

But the following day proved just as hectic and any hope of a moment alone with Adela was not to be. To make matters worse, Lady Victoria was lurking in wait for him and ready to pounce the moment he arrived at the Trent residence. She made her way toward him even though he had not only Adela with him but her parents, as well. "Botheration, what is her game?"

Adela sighed. "Isn't it obvious? She wants you."

He placed a hand over Adela's as it lay on his arm, for he wanted to assure her there was nothing between him and Victoria. He also wanted to prevent her from bolting, for she was ever the wallflower at heart and detested the games often played within these sophisticated *ton* circles.

"Still acting the saintly choirboy, Huntsford," Victoria said with a lilting laugh and the undercurrent of a sneer.

She ignored Adela and her parents, but it was only Adela who understood the snub. Her parents, bless them, were too busy admiring Lord Trent's home and the dazzling display of finery to pay any attention to what was going on under their very noses.

"Dance with me tonight, Huntsford. I understand your betrothed has injured herself and must sit out the evening. Is it any wonder she has a reputation for being clumsy?" She cast him a cat-like smile and emitted a throaty purr. "You and I were always good together. There is no reason why we cannot be so again."

"No longer, Victoria," he said with marked impatience. "Go find your amusement elsewhere."

She tipped her chin in the air. "You'll sing a different tune once you are married and realize just how deadly dull your life has become." She now turned her spite on Adela. "Do you think you can hold him? I assure you, he will stray before the month is out."

Having cast her prediction, she sauntered off with a smug look of triumph.

"Adela…" His hand still covered hers and he had no intention of releasing it anytime soon. "I cannot apologize enough. Surely, you know it is not going to happen."

She cast him a sweet, genuine smile. "I do know, Ambrose. She thinks she is unsettling me, but I am more assured every time she opens her mouth and her bile spills out. I know you only a short time, but understand you better then she ever did. You would walk through fire before ever betraying your vows."

He breathed a sigh of relief. "I'm glad you know this. I hope one day we shall be able to walk into a party and simply enjoy it instead of being accosted by supposed diamonds like Victoria or Felicity Rose. At least that irritating girl is not here tonight."

"Thank goodness." Adela glanced around and frowned. "Nor are my friends here. Your brothers and Lady Withnall were to escort them. I wonder why they are delayed?"

"They'll turn up soon. Octavian is a bull, no one's going to stop him. Julius may appear cheerful and easygoing, but he can also be fierce when the occasion calls for it." He hoped his words calmed her.

However, he was now worried on her behalf.

They should have arrived by now.

He set the thought aside as Lady Eloise's grandsons, Alexander and Gabriel, and their wives approached. The wives, Viola and Daisy, broke with polite formality and rushed to hug Adela, something noted by all in attendance since he, as a duke, was usually the one fussed over to the exclusion of others.

Alexander Dayne, known as Lord Ardley, was the Earl of Trent's eldest son and heir. His wife, Viola, considered Adela one of her best friends. "Adela, we heard you were hurt!" Viola said with obvious concern. "You must tell me and Daisy what happened."

After affectionately greeting Eloise, who was grandmother to their husbands, and also gushing about Adela to her parents, who were obviously awed by the attention lavished on their daughter and themselves, Trent's daughters-in-law then took Adela from Ambrose's side and paid rapt attention as she regaled them with the tale of her last encounter with Runyon.

Ambrose had no idea what Adela was saying to them, for they were too far away for him to overhear. But he could tell by the alarmed arch of their eyebrows and the occasional drop of their jaws that his bluestocking betrothed was recounting the incident in minutest detail and perhaps embellishing a little along the way.

Not that the story required much embellishment, for she had been remarkably brave and he ought to have been more appreciative. He would have been, had he not been crazed with worry that she might have been seriously injured or killed.

Even now, the mere thought of her encounter with Runyon had his heart in a painful twist. They had come too close to disaster and it still haunted him. Not only might that foul relic hunter have shot her, but he and his own Bow Street runners might have accidentally done the same while trying to shoot Runyon.

Gabriel Dayne patted him on the back. "Be proud of her, Huntsford. My Daisy rode through the night and got herself stabbed while trying to save me. I would not be here today if not for her determination. Any man should want their daughters to be as valiant as those ladies."

Eloise heartily agreed. "They may be soft and little compared to you big men, but their strength of heart is more than equal to your own."

Adela's parents listened in awe as Gabriel related his story about Daisy. When he finished, Alexander laughed. "But my wife has something better. Viola is a master chef and you will never have a meal finer than the one you shall eat tonight. She supervised my father's kitchen staff, probably did most of the work herself, although she will never admit it to me since she is a viscountess now and not supposed to be seen in the kitchen. But this is her passion and her love, so I shall never deny her the pleasure."

Adela's mother shook her head. "My goodness, they are such accomplished young ladies."

"Accomplished in the ways that count," Lady Eloise interjected.

As Alexander and Gabriel moved on, taking Adela's parents with them so they may be introduced to their other guests, Eloise took Ambrose aside. "All right, even I am worried now. Your brothers are late. Not that I fear for them since they know how to take care of themselves. But it must mean something is wrong with one of Adela's friends."

He nodded. "I'll wager it is Syd. How could any of us overlook her distress the other night? I should have put Mr. Barrow onto her immediately."

"And I ought to have insisted she stay with me," Eloise added. "Oh, thank goodness! Here comes Phoebe. They were to pick her up along the way to serve as chaperone. But I don't see the others."

Everyone in the grand room suddenly stopped talking when the little termagant marched in. As she scanned the crowded gathering, several people looked away, trying to hide their guilty expressions. Of course, this meant Phoebe would immediately single them out.

Ambrose liked Phoebe, but she was a predator on the prowl

when it came to learning secrets others were desperate to hide. She was a tiny thing, needing a cane to assist her in walking, but one would think she was Attila the Hun, the way those guilty souls feared her.

Of course, she also had many friends who knew and trusted her.

But the *ton* was rife with secrets and Phoebe seemed to know every last one of them, particularly where infidelity, theft, or betrayal was involved. He would not be surprised if she had been recruited as an agent of the Crown at one point in her life. Perhaps she was still an active agent, he thought with some amusement. "Where are the others?"

"Unfortunately, I do not know. Your brothers never came by to pick me up. Something foul is obviously afoot and I do not like it one bit. I understand Syd was behaving quite oddly last night."

Eloise nodded. "Yes, I was just remarking to Huntsford upon it."

Phoebe pursed her lips. "I have yet to discover what she is trying to hide from us all. Quite frustrating, I should have begun my investigation sooner. She is a good girl and has courage, but is obviously scared about something."

"Oh, dear." Eloise now fanned herself to calm her obvious distress.

Phoebe placed a hand on her friend's arm. "However, I could be wrong and it is nothing but a silly, logistical misunderstanding. Your fretting won't help poor Syd right now. Nor should Ambrose go rushing off to track them down." She turned toward him. "You are getting married tomorrow. You have to think of Adela."

He raked a hand through his hair. "I am thinking of her. Do you believe she will stay calm or even show up to our wedding if she fears something has happened to her friend? And what of my brothers?"

"What about us?" Octavian said, walking in just then.

Julius and Adela's two friends were beside him.

Ambrose breathed a sigh of relief. "Blast it, Octavian. You gave us a scare. What delayed you? And why did you not pick up Phoebe first?"

"The blame is mine," Gory said. "I sent word for them to come straight to me. You see, I saw carriages in front of Syd's townhouse and trunks being loaded onto them. I was afraid her family was going to pack her off to parts unknown."

"Were they?" Adela said, now rushing to her friend's side.

Syd was not responding, so Octavian answered for her. "Yes, they were. But I put a stop to it. We knew there was no way she was ever going to miss your wedding unless forced to leave under duress. Something had to be wrong. Julius and I decided to get her away from her family. Um, they may have the constables come after me on some fabricated abduction charge."

Syd frowned at him. "You did abduct me."

"And you ought to be grateful for it," Gory shot back. "You are frightened to death, which is not like you at all. Why won't you confide in us? We were late because we had to return to my house so Syd could borrow one of my hideous gowns, although it seems to suit her rather nicely, doesn't it? Figures, she looks like an angel in it and I look like a turnip whenever I put that thing on."

"By the time we came around to pick you up, Lady Withnall," Julius said, his gaze on Phoebe as he explained, "you had already taken your own carriage to come here. Our sincere apologies. We hope you understand the reason for our rudeness."

"I do, dear boy. You did the right thing." She thumped her cane to emphasize her agreement.

Adela nodded. "Syd, this is very serious. You cannot keep us out of it any longer. We're not going to let anyone hurt you, so you may as well help us get to the root of your problem before the magistrate and his constables come after the rest of us."

Syd appeared on the verge of tears. "You are getting married tomorrow. I refuse to tell you anything before then. Your Grace, I hope you will protect your brother should anyone try to arrest him."

Ambrose nodded. "Of course, I will."

"I don't need anyone protecting me," Octavian shot back.

Syd frowned at him. "Nor do I."

Octavian merely growled.

"If your family is involved in something shady," Eloise said, "the last thing they will do is summon the authorities. But you must tell us everything after the wedding. I insist on your promise, Sydney."

Syd darted off toward the glass doors leading onto the terrace.

Octavian sighed. "She is either running off to cry or to escape. Either way, I had better go after her."

Julius held out his arm to Gory. "We had better keep an eye on those two. Syd is even more stubborn than Octavian, and he is the stubbornest man I know. He may need our help."

Gory turned to Adela. "You keep out of this for now. Meddle as much as you wish after your wedding, but do not let anything interfere with your happiest day."

Ambrose groaned inwardly as he watched the pair dash off.

He knew Adela was not going to sit back and do nothing. Why should she think tomorrow was going to be the most important day of her life when he had never told her that he loved her? Becoming a duchess was not a reason she considered of any importance. Nor did she think he would go to pieces if he ever lost her.

But she had turned him inside out during their encounter with Runyon.

Seeing her hurt had almost destroyed him.

Fortunately, the bounder was securely behind bars now and would remain so for quite some time to come unless sentenced to be hanged.

He fixed his gaze on Adela who was fidgeting beside him. "Despite appearances, Octavian has the matter well in hand. I've already told you I would put Mr. Barrow onto the task of assisting him. I'll do it this very evening. In the meantime, Syd will stay with you at Eloise's. No one in her family is to get near her until we understand what is going on."

Eloise nodded. "Syd and Gory already planned to stay over tonight. Their gowns are at my place and their guest rooms are prepared. Between you Thornes and the Bow Street men to guard us, we ought to be quite safe."

Ambrose certainly hoped so.

Runyon's misdeeds were an ugly business, but he sensed Syd's situation could be something just as sinister.

However, there was little they could do while Syd refused to cooperate.

"Adela, dance with me," Ambrose said, determined to enjoy this evening with his betrothed and not allow anything more to mar it. The music had started up and the orchestra hired for this splendid affair was now playing a waltz.

To his surprise, she readily agreed.

"This is so hard for me, Ambrose. I don't want to ignore Syd's problems, but I also do not want to do anything to ruin our wedding tomorrow. Please tell me your brothers and Mr. Barrow are up to the task."

"They are." He took her into his arms, drawing her close as they began to twirl along with the other dancers. "What about our honeymoon plans?"

Her eyes widened. "Do you wish to cancel them?"

"No, Adela. I thought you might want to do this." He loved the soft feel of her in his arms.

"What I want to do is throttle Syd for turning us all upside down. But I am hardly one to complain when I've done quite a job of aggravating your orderly life ever since I burst into it. I want her to be safe. And I also want time alone with you on a proper honeymoon, although I don't suppose a month or two in Devonshire digging up old bones is something you are desperate to experience."

"I will be with you, so I am certain to enjoy it," he said with a grin.

She smiled up at him. "I float on air whenever I am in your arms. Despite all the chaos swirling around us, I am truly happy when I am with you."

"So am I, love."

Her eyes widened. "Do you realize what you just called me?"

"Yes, Adela."

"Do you mean it?"

"That you are my love?" He drew her close so that their bodies were touching, and then whispered in her ear, "Yes, to the depths of my soul."

CHAPTER 16

AMBROSE LOVED HER!

To the very depths of his soul, no less.

That sounded quite promising.

Adela did not know if she ought to believe him, not that he was the sort to spout glib endearments for the sake of flirtation or seduction. But he knew she was distressed and may have embellished the truth a little to keep her focused on their wedding plans instead of her troubled friend.

Still, she was happy and her heart was in an absolute flutter as she donned her wedding gown and magnificent lace veil the following morning. She hardly recognized the face staring back at her in the mirror. For the first time in her life, she thought she rivaled the *ton* diamonds in beauty.

Is this what Ambrose saw when he looked at her?

Fortunately, her wrist had only been mildly sprained and hardly hurt anymore. She had removed the bandage this morning and only the slightest swelling was noticeable, nor were the scrapes on her knees visible since her gown covered them.

They were not very pretty to look at, though.

"Adela, come along or we shall be late," her mother said, scurrying into her bedchamber and bustling her and her friends out. "The three of you are to ride in the first carriage. We shall follow in the next with Lady Eloise. Don't you all look lovely, like three little wrens."

Gory chuckled. "I don't think I have ever been called that

before. Perhaps a raven or a blood-sucking bat."

Adela's mother shuddered. "Gregoria! That is utterly ghoulish."

She shrugged. "Sorry. You needn't worry, I'll be as chirpy as a nightingale for Adela's special day."

"And you, Sydney," Adela's mother asked. "How are you feeling today?"

"Quite happy for your daughter." Syd glanced at her arm. "I no longer need the sling and my glove covers the bandage to my wrist."

St. Ursula's Church was a charming building made of gray stone situated on the edge of fashionable Belgravia. The church, with its exquisite, stained glass windows and tall spire was nestled between two small parks. It had an elegant courtyard large enough to accommodate a dozen carriages arriving at once and an exquisitely cultivated front garden that was a riot of early blossoms in shades of white and brightest yellow comprised mostly of forsythia and daffodils. Behind these flower beds were trellises with leafy green branches entwined in them. Red rosebuds were beginning to show amid the green leaves and would burst forth in all their crimson splendor within a few weeks.

Adela smiled when she saw Ambrose and his brothers standing in the courtyard in their top hats and formal coattails.

"We're here," Gory squealed, her face pasted to the newly replaced window of Ambrose's carriage which he had sent to Chipping Way to pick them up.

"Don't they look handsome," Adela remarked, nudging Syd to join them in staring out the window.

Syd chuckled. "Yes, Adela. They are obviously the most gorgeous men in the world. My heart is thumping and bumping. Fetch my smelling salts, for I am in danger of fainting from the rapture of their magnificence."

She gave her friend a playful poke. "No sarcasm allowed today. They are handsome, and you know it. Especially Ambrose. He does look stunning, as always. It is quite irritating, don't you think? He doesn't even try to look good. It just flows naturally out of him."

Her friends giggled and began to tease her, neither of them holding back their good-natured jests. "I overheard the upstairs maids in my home playing a game one day. Do you want to know what it is?" Syd said, her grin quite broad.

Gory nodded. "Is it something bawdy? Then yes, absolutely."

Adela's eyes widened. "You cannot tell us now. Ambrose and his brothers are walking toward our carriage."

Syd laughed. "All the better. The game is called *Above the Waist or Below the Waist.*"

Adela gasped. "Syd, what exactly does that mean?"

"Honestly, Adela. This is no time to be prim. Isn't it obvious? On your wedding night, does he kiss you above the waist or move lower to–"

"Not another word! Syd, you are wicked!" Adela felt her face turn to flames. "Ambrose would never do such a naughty thing. He is a gentleman and will be my husband!"

Her friend waggled her eyebrows. "You cannot pretend to be calm about your wedding night. But the other part of the game is to wager on how far *you* will go when kissing him. Above the waist or below?"

"Oh, good heavens! I would never! It simply isn't done. Have you always been so wayward?" Adela buried her face in her hands and laughed. "Stop! My face is on fire and Ambrose will think I am ill if he sees me like this."

The three of them dissolved into snorting laughter. Of course, none of them had any experience with men so they had no idea what it all meant beyond what they overheard in whispered conversations or read in gothic novels innocent girls were never supposed to read.

Adela supposed it was harmless fun.

But really, her friends were too forward. However, it did her heart good to know Syd was back to herself and the three of them were behaving like silly girls. Since they rode alone in Ambrose's ducal carriage, no one could hear what they were giggling about, and she was glad her last few moments before becoming Ambrose's wife were spent in good humor with these friends she considered sisters.

Eloise's carriage followed just behind them carrying Eloise, Phoebe, and Adela's parents who were certainly having a far more serious conversation.

But Adela was glad to have this time alone with her friends, and quite relieved there had been no trouble from Syd's family after Octavian had abducted her.

Syd assured her there would be no arrest or further problems, but Adela thought her friend might have said this so as not to upset her honeymoon plans.

It had calmed them all when Syd appeared cheerful and much at ease this morning, and Adela hoped it was not merely an act on her part. Then again, even though Syd was not pleased with Octavian's interference in her parents' plan to ship her out of London, she also seemed greatly relieved by it.

Adela sighed, for her friend was quite complicated.

She stopped straining her mind about it and went along with their silly chatter.

Gory giggled again. "Can you believe it, Adela? Just look at us, all dressed up and looking quite splendid ourselves, if I do say so myself. I don't think I have ever looked this good. I'll have to ask Eloise's maid how she did up my hair. I almost feel like a diamond."

"You are one, Gory." Adela gave her a quick hug.

"So are you and Syd," Gory said. "In fact, we all look dazzling. Let the Lady Victorias and the Felicity Roses of the world bow their heads and weep."

They said no more as Ambrose and his brothers stepped forward to assist them out of the carriage. Julius winked at Gory as he helped her down. "Don't you look fetching? You'll have all your cadavers ogling you."

Gory's eyes lit up. "Why, thank you."

Syd groaned. "Only Gory would take that as a compliment. All right, me next. Here comes the beast," she muttered as Octavian stepped forward to assist her. "I really ought to be nicer to him, but he's just so…arrogant."

Adela smiled. "There's a bit of arrogance in all the Thorne men, but can you blame them? Women have been fawning over them throughout their lives. Don't scowl at him. He was sincerely worried about you last night."

"I know. He probably saved me from a dire fate, but don't you dare tell him I told you so or he will be insufferable forever more."

She hopped out with Octavian's assistance before Adela could ask what she meant by the remark.

Saved her from a dire fate?

Was her friend in mortal danger?

"Ready, Adela?" The wind was brisk as Ambrose helped her down, but Eloise's maid had attended to her hair so it was done up quite securely and would not fall out of its pins no matter how hard her veil tossed about in the breeze.

"Ambrose, you'll never guess what Syd just told me. She said her life was in peril...well, dire fate is what she said. I think something bad would have happened to her if Octavian had not shown up when he did last night."

He frowned as he nodded. "I'll convey the information to Mr. Barrow. He's here along with a half dozen of his runners. Syd will be safe while she is with us."

"What about afterward?"

"Octavian and Julius will look out for both your friends, as will Mr. Barrow and his men. I will keep them on to guard her night and day, if it is called for." He still had his hands around her waist and now released her to lead her into the church which was already packed with guests. "Adela, we are about to be married. Do you think you can concentrate on us for the next few minutes?"

She reached up on tiptoes and kissed him on the cheek. "Yes, Ambrose. I shall think of nothing but you for the rest of the day. You look wonderful, by the way."

He caressed her cheek. "So do you."

The ceremony lasted almost an hour, but most of it passed in a blur for Adela. This moment felt so much like a dream, she standing beside the handsomest man in England and about to become his wife. The flower arrangements in the church were magnificent, all handled by Eloise, Phoebe, and Sophie

Farthingale who had become adept at planning hasty marriages for her own family.

She felt a pang of regret in not having had more to do with the planning, but what could she have added to any of it? She knew about skulls and bones, not flowers, table settings, or the proper menu for a sumptuous wedding banquet. Her friend, Lady Viola, had made certain to take charge of the wedding breakfast menu. Last night's supper at the home of Lord and Lady Trent had been the best she had ever tasted. It was all Viola's doing, so she knew the food for today's celebration would be just as splendid.

What she did regret was not spending enough time with her parents, but they were caught up in the social whirl as much as she was, and had little time for her. Nor was her mother disappointed to miss out on the planning. Her parents had eloped because neither of them cared to wait months before marrying. Her mother never regretted her lack of an elegant wedding, for she had been an avid bluestocking in her day and disdained the heady whirl of *ton* parties.

As for the wedding night, she would soon find out all there was to know about it from Ambrose himself.

Eloise had tried to explain what happened when a husband *claimed* his wife, but Ambrose had laughed heartily when she repeated the advice given. Her mother had tried to educate her about such things before the start of her first Season. However, their conversation immediately reverted to birds and whether the male or female snipe sat on the eggs before they hatched, so that was not very helpful.

Ambrose would explain it better than her mother or Eloise ever could.

"Do you, Adela Swift, take Ambrose, Duke of Huntsford as your husband, to love and cherish..."

"I do," Adela said, hardly able to get the words out while her heart was beating so rapidly and her lungs felt as though they were about to burst.

This is truly happening.

Ambrose grabbed hold of her hand when the minister turned to him and intoned the similar question. "Do you, Ambrose, Duke of Huntsford…" He then droned on, listing a string of Ambrose's other titles and knighthood honors.

Dear heaven.

Adela's father was a knight, but nothing to compare with all the knighthoods Ambrose held. She ought to have realized he was not merely a duke, but also an earl and viscount. Not to mention his knightly honors which included Order of the Garter, St. Michael's Cross, and three other Orders with saints in their names.

She really had to study her *Debrett's Peerage.*

Ambrose seemed to know exactly what she was thinking and found her dismay amusing. She knew this was one of the reasons he liked her, this utter disregard she had for titles and other grants of prominence.

Of course, she would have to teach herself quickly now that she was to be his duchess. Miss Adela Swift's ignorance could be overlooked. Duchess Adela would be expected to know these things and those in power would be insulted if she did not.

Memorizing facts and statistics was rather easy for her.

She would master all the rules of precedence, titles, and terms of address given a few days of solid reading.

After their exchange of "I do" the minister pronounced them husband and wife.

Ambrose wrapped her up in his arms and kissed her with heartfelt joy. "Welcome to the Thorne family, Duchess Adela."

She smiled up at him. "Thank you for inviting me in. I love you, Your Grace."

They had no chance to say more as friends and family swarmed around them. To her relief, no one in the immediate royal family was in attendance. A crisis of a sort had come up, not that Adela wished ill on anyone. She hoped the crisis would pass quickly, but was glad not to have the pressure of royalty at her wedding beyond a few minor representatives, the most exalted of whom was an earl who was cousin to the king.

Ambrose had a broad smile on his face and was obviously quite happy.

So was she.

Her face was going to crack if her smile was any broader.

"Come on, love," he said, taking her hand. "Our carriage awaits."

He led her through the crowd of well wishers and helped her into a barouche festooned in garlands and ribbons. It was everything garish and not at all Ambrose's style, for it was obviously outfitted for newlyweds and meant to draw everyone's attention.

Ambrose winced. "Not my doing, but it is only a short distance to my home."

He climbed in beside her, taking her hand in his as though it was the most natural thing to do. The carriage bench was hardly big enough to accommodate both of them, especially with Ambrose's big shoulders and long legs, but Adela liked having to huddle against him.

As the church bells clanged, they made their way through Belgravia toward his impressive residence where the wedding breakfast was to take place. The glorious aromas of what was to be their feast carried on the wind. "Oh, heavens. Is that cinnamon? And warm apples? That is divine."

Ambrose nodded. "It is enough to make anyone hungry."

"I couldn't eat this morning. I was too excited." She turned to him as the carriage stopped before his home. "How do you feel, Ambrose?"

"Happier than I have ever been. I mean it, Adela. I have wanted to do this properly for days now, but we keep getting interrupted. Adela, I–"

Octavian yanked open the door. "Come on, you lovebirds. No dawdling allowed. The guests will arrive at any moment and you need to be standing on the receiving line."

"Blessed saints, will I never get the words out?" He kissed her on the lips with surprising hunger, but quickly ended it and hopped down. "Come along, love."

Before she knew it, they were greeting what felt like hundreds of guests.

"Two hundred and fifty, to be precise," Ambrose whispered. "That is small compared to what it might have been had we had a year to plan. The list would have stretched to a thousand, I fear.

Foreign dignitaries, royal relatives. Fortunately, those invitations could not have been received in time."

"Do you think they will angry?"

He shrugged. "Not if they think we had to marry in haste. Compromising scandals are forgiven."

"Well, I suppose we have Felicity Rose to thank for that."

"Gad, do not mention that malicious peahen. She will never be permitted into our home. Do not go soft on this, Adela. I do not care if she comes to you in tears and begging for your forgiveness. She will not really be sorry, only seek to manipulate herself into your good graces because you are now a powerful personage. Talk about puppet masters. That girl can scheme with the best."

"Speaking of powerful personages, I shall have my work cut out for me."

"Ah, the rules of peerage." He nodded. "I married you because titles were so unimportant to you."

"But I will have to learn now. I don't mind, truly. I will never care about your rank or how many grants of title you possess, but I will always care about making you proud of me. I don't ever want to disappoint or embarrass you...well, no worse than I already have done."

He chuckled. "You won't, Adela."

She smiled up at him. "I am immensely enjoying being married to you."

"The best fifteen minutes of your life?" he teased, removing his watch fob and pretending to stare at the time. He leaned over and gave her a light but surprisingly steamy kiss on her neck. "Wait until tonight, love. You'll enjoy it more."

She blushed.

Yes, tonight.

This was another area in which she hoped not to disappoint him.

Above the waist or below the waist?

She was not experienced in matters of intimacy, but hoped Ambrose would claim all of her. If the scorching look he was now giving her was any indication of tonight's activities, she was undoubtedly going to like it very much.

But she quickly shook out of the thought because she was not good at hiding her feelings and her expression might reveal too much. Fortunately, there was plenty going on to distract her. She concentrated on greeting their guests and making each feel welcomed.

People were always going to talk about her now that she was Duchess of Huntsford, but she hoped there would be some nice things said along with the disparaging remarks. She knew what it felt like to be given the cut and ridiculed. She never wanted anyone to feel this way when in her company.

To her surprise, a gentleman who introduced himself as a reporter from The Tattler showed up. Her resolve to be nice to everyone flew out the window. Adela curled her hands into fists and was prepared to bodily remove him all by herself, when Ambrose place a hand to the small of her back. "He is not here to harm us, Adela."

"Then why is he here?"

"A bargain struck with the rag's editor. He promised to run no more scandal pieces on us so long as I allowed him an exclusive report on our wedding."

Her eyes widened. "But that is extortion."

"On whose part? Mine or theirs?"

"Theirs, of course. You are utterly perfect."

He cast her an affectionate smile. "Glad you think so, but I am hardly that. We cannot avoid being in the public's eye, but we can – and I say this hopefully – exert some control over what is printed about us. Try not to tackle this fellow, will you?"

She shook her head and sighed. "Seems I have a lot to learn about Upper Crust politics."

"You will master it in time. In the meanwhile," he said with a glint of amusement in his eyes, "just look at me adoringly and keep out of fist fights."

She laughed. "I shall do my best to oblige both of those requests."

It turned out the reporter, a young man by the name of Mr. Hawkins, was an amateur archeologist himself. While Adela did not have time to engage in a lengthy discussion with him, Gory and Syd managed to keep the gentleman regaled with stories of their research findings.

Although Julius and Octavian remained ever watchful over her friends, they did not hover too obviously around them or interfere as they spoke to the reporter. That poor man was not likely to have much of a career at The Tattler, for he seemed too gentle and honorable for the usually seedy assignments. His editor was not going to print a dissertation on skulls, bones, or cadavers.

The day was a long one and the wedding breakfast was more of an all day affair with Ambrose's kitchen staff churning out food as fast as they could, many in resplendent molds or elaborate pies. Adela expected they had tapped London dry of brandy, ale, champagne, and ratafia punch since the Upper Crust knew how to consume their spirits. But everyone stayed merry enough and the musicians remained to the very end since many guests enjoyed dancing and did not want the music to stop.

It was almost midnight by the time everyone left, including Syd and Gory who were to remain with Eloise for at least another night. Ambrose's brothers had chosen to sleep at their gentlemen's club even though the Thorne townhouse was enormous and would easily accommodate all of them.

"Out of the question," Julius said, chuckling when she suggested they need not move out on her account.

Octavian merely arched an eyebrow.

She sighed. "Very well, but Ambrose and I shall be leaving tomorrow morning for Devonshire. I hope you will come by to see us off."

Julius bowed gallantly over her hand. "Wouldn't miss it, Your Grace."

Once they left, Adela's heart began to race faster.

The house was suddenly quiet, only she and Ambrose standing in the hall now that his head butler had locked up the house and secured the windows for the night. The candles in the chandeliers and wall sconces had all been doused, leaving them standing together by the light of a lone candle Ambrose held in his hand and the filtering silver glow of moonbeams shining upon the marble floor.

The silence struck Adela.

She was alone with him…completely alone for the very first time.

He held up the candle to illuminate their way as they climbed the stairs to his bedchamber. Well, she assumed this is where he was leading her when he took her hand and said, "This way, love."

She had never been upstairs in his home, certainly never seen any of the bedchambers, much less his. Her belongings had been moved over in the morning during the church ceremony. She knew the duke's suite was at the end of the hall. But he paused just short of it and released her hand to open another door. "These are the duchess quarters."

She glanced up at him in surprise. "Oh. I thought…that is…"

He smiled, his face exquisite by candlelight. "There's a lot we did not have time to discuss. I want you in my bed, Adela. But this is all new to you and I do not want to push you into sharing it with me every night."

"I see. I suppose you like your privacy."

He shook his head. "No, it is you I am thinking about. You will likely not believe me, but I enjoy having you around. In truth, it wasn't very long after meeting you that I felt the need acutely, as though a part of me was missing whenever you were not by my side."

"Truly?" His admission was quite something to absorb and she felt tingles all over her body. Having imbibed too much champagne did not help maintain her composure, for in addition to those tingles and the giddy whirl of excitement, she was feeling quite a bit tipsy, too.

He smiled and said no more as he led her into her bedchamber.

She watched him set the candlestick atop the bureau and then turn to her with a wry arch of his eyebrow and another melting smile. "I thought I would take over the task of helping you out of your gown this evening, but I can summon a maid to assist you if you feel uncomfortable disrobing in front of me."

She shook her head. "Not at all. What you just mentioned about my being a part of you, it is the same way I feel about you. I never imagined two people could feel so strongly connected to each other, certainly not in so short a time."

He laughed softly. "I know. Believe me, no one was more surprised than I. You blasted quite a hole through my protective barriers that very first day. Until you came along, those thick walls had been impenetrable."

"I have no barriers whatsoever. Every unkind remark I endured in my first Season struck straight through my heart. I expected the second to be the same, then you came along and everything changed." She smiled up at him. "I could go on for hours telling you how I feel, but that will likely drive you insane. So I will stop talking now and let you get on about the business of undressing me. But I must warn you, there are lots of buttons and laces. Donning this gown was quite the affair, much like a knight being placed in his suit of armor. It may take you a while to get me undone."

"Less time than you imagine," he said with a chuckle and removed the veil from her hair. "I am up to the task. However, we are in no hurry. We have the entire night to ourselves."

As they would from now on, Adela marveled, still not quite believing this man was hers. After so many years of being irrelevant, first to her parents and then on the marriage mart, this felt like a miracle.

"You seem lost in your thoughts," he said, now working on her laces. "What are you thinking, Adela?"

Since she had her back to him as he undressed her, she turned her head slightly to smile at him. "Goodness, so many things. Do you really want me to keep talking?"

He kissed the curve of her neck. "It will put you at ease."

"All right. But you will believe me foolish."

"Not at all, love." He took little time managing the laces and began on the full row of her buttons which were tiny in addition to being delicate. "What's on your mind?"

She could hardly fashion a thought while his hands were on her body, a knuckle grazing here and fingers stroking there. Each light touch had her heart beating faster and her legs turning to butter. She was already feeling warm and tipsy, unable to cool herself while he stoked her flames.

"Well, on my mind?" She ran her tongue along her lips while attempting to compose a thought. "Um...in the stories I've read, the man is usually in a hot frenzy and the couple are soon tearing off their clothes and tossing them everywhere. But you are being quite methodical about your seduction of me."

"Ah, and that disappoints you?" He kissed her once again lightly along the curve of her neck, the soft sensuality of his lips wreaking havoc on her concentration.

"No," she said, releasing a breath as fire shot through her when he began to lightly suckle her neck. *Dear heaven.* Did he think she could string a complete sentence together? "Ambrose..."

"Yes, love."

"You are making me forget what I wanted to say." She sighed as he kissed her throat. "Whatever you are doing is quite effective. Is it all right if I ask you questions?"

"I would expect nothing less from you," he teased and kissed her again in another sensitive spot along her neck.

She was the expert on skulls and bones, but his knowledge of the female anatomy was clearly far superior. "How are you getting on with those buttons?"

"Almost done, love. Does it feel slow to you?"

"Yes...no. I am anticipating the rest of what's to come, but enjoying what you are doing. Mostly it feels wonderful." She clutched the gown to her bosom as it began to slip off her shoulders. "Oh, you've finished. Quite well done of you."

"Thank you," he said in a husky murmur.

"What happens next?"

"I slowly peel the rest of the garments off you."

"Slowly?"

"Yes, love. There are two reason why I am taking my time with you," he said, drawing her into his arms and seeming not at all put out by her questions or impatience. "First, this is your wedding gown and something you might treasure enough to pass down to our daughter, should we be so fortunate as to have children. Do you really want me to tear it off you?"

"No."

He trailed more kisses along her shoulder as he eased the gown off her. "Second, this is your first experience. I would scare you if I went too fast. What might be thrilling when read in a book would put you off if it actually happened to you, at least until you trusted me."

"That makes sense," she said, allowing him to remove the gown off her body completely and set it on the chair beside them.

"Do you trust me, Adela?"

"Yes. But it isn't you I am worried about."

He tucked a finger under her chin and tipped her face up to meet his gaze. His eyes had a soft glint to them, hopefully a sign of his approval as she stood beside him wearing only her thin chemise. "Are you worried I might find you wanting?"

She nodded. "Seems everybody else who matters to me has. I don't think I've ever made anyone proud of me."

Her admission truly tore at his heart.

"The lack was in them, love. Never in you. Nobody else matters here and now but you and me. You won't disappoint me. It will never happen. Do you not see how we are made for each other?" He removed his jacket, waistcoat and cravat in quick order, then turned back to her. "Help me off with my shirt."

Her fingers were nimble but shaking so that she did not think she was of much help. In spite of her fumbling, he soon had the cufflinks set aside and the shirt off him.

Her heart almost stopped when he turned to her and she saw the beautiful maleness of his torso, the sculpted tone of his muscles, and the magnificence of his bare chest.

No wonder women panted after him.

He was taut and lean, radiating power and strength.

Divine did not begin to properly express her thoughts.

Dear heaven.

In theory, she had known he was big and strong, and had broad shoulders. But this…she was unprepared for the way he sent her senses reeling.

She ran her hands lightly along the length of his arms, and then stroked her fingers ever so cautiously against his chest to feel the soft hairs sprinkled upon it. His body twinged a time or two. She hoped it was from the pleasure of her touch. If she was affected by their undressing, was it not right that he should be as well?

His breaths came a little faster as he unpinned her hair and ran his fingers through it to shake loose her curls.

She closed her eyes and sighed.

"I thought I could be patient and take things slow," he said with a gentle laugh, "but it appears I cannot."

She opened her eyes in surprise.

"Lord, you're beautiful." He groaned and scooped her up in his arms to carry her to bed. "Are you ready?"

Her body was in flames.

Her pulses were throbbing in places she had no idea existed until this moment.

He set her down on the bed and then stretched out atop her, resting his weight on one elbow so as not to crush her while he reached between her breasts and tugged on the tie string of her chemise.

It sprang open for him.

She wasn't certain what to expect next, but she suspected she would like it, if the heat in his gaze was any indication.

"I knew you would be this lovely," he said in a deep, raspy rumble as he nudged the lacy chemise off her shoulders and then drew it further down so there was little of her body left hidden to his perusal. "Creamy soft and lovely."

No man had ever seen her like this.

She was quite brazen in many ways, but not in this very personal regard. In truth, she was modest about her body and never traipsed around her bedchamber unclothed even when alone. She always scrambled to cover herself as quickly as possible.

But with Ambrose...she felt completely comfortable.

Of course, this had to be the reason he had taken his time with her and patiently answered her questions. He was building trust and letting her know he would never rush her into anything. He understood her so well, as though he could see into her heart. "You are a wonderful man, Ambrose."

"Glad you think so." He cast her an affectionately wicked grin, then dipped his head to her breast and kissed her there. More than kissed her because his lips were now suckling the straining bud and she was going to shoot off the bed if he did not stop doing whatever he was doing with the light swirl of his tongue.

Was she supposed to explode like a fireworks display?

No one had adequately explained this to her before.

Is this what one felt when roused to passion?

Ah, passion.

No wonder poets made such a fuss about it in their verses.

She gasped as Ambrose moved off one breast and began to work his magic on the other with effortless skill.

Dear heaven.

Wondrously fiery sensations built within her body.

She clutched his shoulders, needing to hold tightly to them for fear she would shoot to the stars and turn to glitter against the sky.

So this was passion?

She was going to enjoy her wedding night immensely.

CHAPTER 17

AMBROSE PROMISED HIMSELF to take things slow, but his body was not cooperating. He had felt the attraction between him and Adela from the moment they first met and their bodies collided. One would think the passage of time and his prior experiences in the bedchamber would allow him some control.

Alas, it did not.

He was ravenous for Adela, his prized control on a very thin tether that was about to snap. But he had to hold onto that last frayed thread of restraint and remain gentle. Reading books about a sweet young thing being ravished by a dark, brooding nobleman might be appealing on the pages but not in actuality for someone as untried and innocent as Adela.

In addition, she was still bruised from her run in with that wretch, Runyon.

She was a brave girl when it came to fighting for others or for causes she believed in passionately. But for herself? She had been brought low by neglectful parents and spiteful *ton* diamonds. Was it any wonder she had little confidence in her own loveliness?

If only she could see herself as he saw her, the soft beauty of her face and her inner glow.

He loved the way she responded to him, the trust she had in his touch.

"Shift your hips upward, love. Just the slightest bit. Does it hurt you? The hip is still a little bruised."

"I'm fine. It doesn't hurt."

"Good." He slipped the chemise completely off her so she now lay fully open to his view. Exquisitely so, for her legs were long and slender, her skin soft and silky if one overlooked her knees. But those marks would soon fade.

Her breasts were glorious and large enough to fill the cup of his hands.

She had not seen him fully unclothed yet, for he had not removed his trousers. Nor would he before he gave her a first taste of pleasure. She was eager for it, but not merely because he ravished her senses. She was the most curious girl he had ever met, always thirsting for knowledge, so he wanted to give her time to experience each new sensation and absorb all its nuances before she began asking questions.

It was not long after he put his lips to her magnificent breast that she closed her eyes and sighed. "Ambrose…"

"Yes, love." He tipped his head upward to kiss her throat.

"I'm feeling a fiery heat rush through me."

He propped on his elbows and met her gaze as she opened her eyes with a starlight sparkle. "And you wish to know what it is?"

She nodded.

"Hard to explain. It is something you just feel, Adela. But you ought to save the rest of your questions for afterward. Pausing to talk at each step dampens the heat of the moment. Allow your body respond in the way it desires. Do not hold back or worry about fire sweeping through you. This is supposed to happen."

She nodded. "May I ask just one more question before we start again in earnest?"

He groaned inwardly. "Yes, love. Go ahead."

"When you put your lips to my bosom, I responded in a place other than there. Is this supposed to happen?"

"Yes. Are you referring to the tender spot at the juncture of your thighs?"

She nodded and started to clamp her legs together.

"No, love. Just relax. This is where you will feel the heightened desire no matter where I touch you because it is the core of your pleasure sensations."

"I did feel it already," she said, her body easing as he slid his hand lower to rest on the inside of her thigh.

He smiled. "You felt the start of it. You haven't fully experienced the rest of it yet. You'll know when you do. Clear your head of questions now and allow your body to show you the way."

Her eyes widened. "Are you sure it will instinctively know?"

"Yes, love. Hold onto the bed sheets."

"Why?"

"Because you'll need to cling to something when I make you soar."

"Sweet mercy."

He kissed her deeply and then proceeded to leave no part of her body unexplored, for he was no less affected than she was.

Her curves were perfection, and she was heaven to the touch.

His urges were purely sinful, for she set him on fire and all of him was burning.

He shifted lower to settle his shoulders between her legs, knowing this was a shockingly intimate thing to do. But what he intended next would also thrill her and give her the adventure she craved but had only read in books until now.

As for him, he wanted to hear her soft, shattering cries, to call out his name and clasp his shoulders as she begged for mercy.

He wanted to give her the best night of her life...which he proceeded to do with the first soft lick of his tongue at her core.

She responded immediately, her innocence almost causing him to spill himself because he was already so aroused by her.

She tasted so sweet, like nectar on his tongue.

Her skin was soft and as fragrant as orange blossoms.

The soft purrs coming from low in her throat excited him beyond bearing, for she was soon hot and moist for him, calling his name softly and trying to keep her composure as her sensibilities abandoned her.

He ought to have warned her this would happen, but he did not want her dissecting the moment instead of simply feeling the passion build within her. A few more breathy moans from her and he knew she was close...so close.

Let yourself go, love.

He had barely finished the thought before she erupted like a little volcano, clinging to the bed sheets and then to him as he arched up to watch her beautifully responsive face and her eyes fill with wonder. "Adela...sweetheart, you are ready for me."

He drew off his trousers and took her back in his arms as he entered her slowly, her slickness easing his way despite how tight she was and how urgently he needed to embed himself inside her. "I love you," he whispered. "I love you so very much. You are heaven in my arms. You will always be my heaven."

He finally got out the words he needed to say because he wanted her to know their marriage was going to be real in every way.

"Ambrose...I...ah..."

"I'll try not to hurt you, but this time might be a little uncomfortable because it is your first." He felt the rapid beat of her heart and the warmth of her skin as she held onto his shoulders and at his instruction wrapped her legs around his hips to draw him inside her, to urge him in so that their bodies entwined and blended into one.

His heart filled with pride, for she had accepted him as her husband with her heart and now also with her body. In claiming her, he was also giving himself to her. Heart and body. Their marriage would never be a tug of wills over who would surrender and who would conquer.

They both surrendered and both conquered.

He moved inside her, slowly thrusting in and out, still careful with her but also enjoying her expressions as the fire built within her again, just as it was building inside of him. Well, he was on a short fuse, a roaring flame heading toward a powder keg.

Lord, she had him wild.

He could not get enough of her, the perfect way she fit against him and the way he fit inside her, the arousing scent of her and the silkiness of her skin, the softness of her lips as he kissed her, needed her. Wanted her.

They erupted together with spectacular effect, her kittenish moans and his grunts filling the air as their bodies wrapped around each other and they soared to the stars.

"Ambrose, that was…" She laughed when they finally began to regain possession of their senses. "That was something indescribably splendid. I had no idea. We were quite hot and frenzied, weren't we? Just like in those books."

"Yes, love." His entire body was drenched and drained, as he expected it would be because he cared so much for Adela and was moved beyond words to be the first ever to share this intimacy with her.

Of course, he would be the only man ever to claim the honor.

Adela was always going to be true to him as he would be to her throughout their marriage.

He rolled off her exquisite body and now drew her atop him so that her ample breasts pressed against his chest and that wild mane of dark hair spilled over both of them in a glorious tumble. "Ambrose…"

"Yes, sweetheart." He brushed back her hair and tucked a loose curl behind her ear. "Go ahead, ask your questions."

"You don't mind?"

"No." He grinned. "How could I mind anything after what we did?"

"Does this mean you liked it? How was it for you? Not that I wish you to compare me to any of your prior conquests, but did you enjoy it?"

"Yes, I did. Was I not quite vocal about it? But the greatest pleasure for me was in having you as my partner. It is a different thing altogether when love is involved, Adela."

"How?"

"A man's heart does not have to be involved to perform the physical act. The engagement is ephemeral. Once it is done, it is done. But with you, our coupling is an act of love, and that never leaves one's heart. Each time we join, it will bring us closer, bind us to each other in a marriage that will become stronger over time."

"I think it is already strong for me. I love you that completely."

"I love you, too. Never doubt it. But we are still new to each other, and there are those who do not wish to see us happy. We already know how manipulative and intentionally hurtful some people can be. However, there will come a point in time where nothing can ever shake the trust we have in each other. You are my wife, Adela. I shall love and honor you to the end of my days."

"You make it easy for me to do the same. I thought I would have to guard my heart or risk being hurt by you. But I realized soon after you proposed to me that it would never be so. And today, as we stood in St. Ursula's and exchanged vows, there was something in your eyes, a soft look and at the same time a glint of steel, powerful and determined. I knew your pledge to me was unbreakable from that moment on." She inched up to kiss him on the lips. "Hearts are quite fragile, quite easily shattered. I knew I could give you mine, set it in your hands, and never worry you might damage it."

She emitted a breath and cast him a shaky smile. "In truth, I sensed early on that you would be the one to heal mine."

He stroked her hair as she spoke, amazed by how easy she made it to love her. He knew his feelings ran deep for her, but had not quite understood the significance. "Always, love. I will always look out for you and protect you." He kissed her on the forehead. "Remember that whenever I irritate you and you want to kick me out of our bed."

"I never shall." She laughed. "Oh, I'm sure I will rile you far more than you will ever rile me. I am the impulsive one who rushes to act, while you always keep calm and never jump in until you've thought things through quite thoroughly. Although, we did marry in haste. From what I have learned of you, this is completely outside of your character."

"I did not need any further convincing or assurance about your being the right one for me. In truth, I knew it after our first conversation."

"How is it possible? I called you an idiot."

He kissed her on the forehead. "No one has ever dared call me that, although I hope not to give you cause to call me that again."

She turned surprisingly serious. "You will always have the truth from me, but never the insults. I've seen how damaging those can be. I'm so sorry I called you those horrible things. I was lashing out in frustration, just shooting my mouth off to an interfering stranger who was holding me back while Runyon, that horrid creature, stole my dreams. The insults weren't personal. I was not trying to belittle you, just trying to get you to let me go. But what I said was wrong. I will never treat you that way again."

"I would have done the same if the situation had been reversed."

"I don't know about that. I've never heard you say something cruel to anyone. You shouldn't be so quick to dismiss my actions. I should have been more polite to you."

"As you watched your life's work slipping away? Don't be too hard on yourself, Adela. Your feelings were honest and have always been so. I liked that you did not turn into a fawning toady when you realized who I was. I fell in love with you because you took me to task and did not indulge me when you learned I was a duke. Well, it did not hurt that your breasts were exquisite, too."

She gasped. "Ambrose!"

He arched an eyebrow. "What? Is it so awful that I liked the entire package?"

"I suppose not. I was gawking at you to the point of embarrassment. I'd never met a handsomer man. I loved your bone structure."

"Gad, no mention of bones tonight," he said with a groaning laugh. "We'll be digging them up soon enough in Devonshire. Speaking of which, we had better get some sleep if we mean to get an early start in the morning."

"Do you know why else I am in love with you?"

"Why, love?"

"Because my hopes and dreams mean something to you. I thought I would have to give them up or somehow negotiate a role for myself beyond being your wife. But you are supporting me, indulging me. This is so exciting, Ambrose. Within a few days we'll be digging in those caves. I'm so grateful to you whether or not we ever turn up a single bone. Oh, but I am talking too much and you wish to sleep. Will you stay with me the entire night?"

"Yes, unless you prefer that I go."

"Good heavens, no. I want you and your big, warm body beside me always."

"Then here is where I'll stay." With that assurance, Adela snuggled cozily against him and soon fell asleep in his arms.

Ambrose lay awake longer, realizing this was a first for him as well. He had never made it a habit to spend an entire night with any of his conquests. Waking up to a woman in his bed was something he had not experienced before...well, they were in Adela's bed in her duchess quarters, to be precise. He did not care where they slept once they returned from their honeymoon, whether in his ducal chamber or here. The point was, they would always sleep together and wake to each other each morning.

He expected he was going to like opening his eyes to find Adela smiling at him, her exquisite, slate blue eyes bright and filled with love.

They awoke shortly before dawn and made love again.

Her body was soft and delectable.

He could not keep his hands off her.

They were both grinning and breathing heavily as they soared together and eventually calmed. Ambrose held her in his arms and caressed her as she fell back to sleep since it was still early and the sky was yet dark. He had no intention of nudging her out of bed before they needed to start their day.

But it was not long after daybreak that his valet arrived at his bedchamber to assist him in preparing for their journey. He had assigned a maid for Adela, but knew he would shock the girl if she walked in to find him naked in Adela's bed.

They would have to work out a sensible schedule on their return because he wanted her to share his bedchamber and not keep separate quarters. For now, they simply needed to cover themselves, for there was certain to be confusion on this first day of their married lives.

He nuzzled her neck, careful not to scratch her with the rough stubble of his beard. "Do you wish to sleep longer, love?"

She yawned and stretched like a kitten, then turned toward him and placed her open palm against his cheek, apparently fascinated by those rough bristles. "I'll get up with you. I can always sleep in the carriage later if I'm tired."

"I left instructions last night for baths to be sent up for each of us. I'll return to my own bedchamber now since I hear my valet marching back and forth, impatient to attend me. Your maid should be knocking on your door in a few minutes. I had better go, but I didn't want to slip out of bed without telling you. Just come into my chamber whenever you are ready."

She nodded. "I won't take long."

"No rush, sweetheart. We'll leave for Devonshire after breakfast and that won't be for several hours yet. My brothers will join us this morning, but the meal won't be anything elaborate. Just a bite to hold us until we stop at midday for a more solid repast at one of the coaching inns. We'll need to rest the horses anyway."

Adela drew the sheet over her body and stared at him as he rose and began to gather his clothes. He winked at her as she ogled him. "Like what you see?"

"Yes, immensely. You are not bashful, are you?"

"No. But I know you are." He picked up her nightgown and robe and set them close to her on the bed. "I'll shut the door between our chambers to lend you privacy as you dress, but I'll never lock it unless you prefer I do."

She shook her head. "No, I hope we never lock the door to each other. Oh, but you'll have your valet and other servants to attend you. Would they ever open this door?"

"I would behead them if they ever did."

"Ah, that ought to get the message across," she said with a lilt of laughter.

He grinned. "A little too harsh?"

"Perhaps a little apishly possessive. Threatening to discharge the misdoer ought to be enough."

He came to her side of the bed and kissed her. "I'll put the key on your side of the door. Lock it when you are dressing. Unlock it when you are done. Then I won't have to kill any fool on my staff."

It was not long before he heard the household begin to stir.

He entered his bedchamber and greeted his valet. "Good morning, Saunders."

"Good morning, Your Grace."

Since the door between his room and Adela's had been left ajar for the moment, he was able to hear the knock at her door when her maid arrived. He also heard the clunk of metal and thud of heavy footsteps as servants brought up her bath and pails of water to fill it.

Adela's voice was gentle as she let them in and thanked each of them for their service. Once all but her maid had departed, she shut her door, and then shut the door between their rooms which she then locked.

A few minutes later, his tub was brought up and readied for him. He shaved and took a leisurely soak. His efficient valet was particularly chatty this morning, peppering him with questions about which cravats he would like to take on his honeymoon trip and should he also pack His Grace's formal attire?

"No formal wear, Saunders. We are going to be digging for ancient bones the entire time." A good suit or two would do for the evenings he and Adela dined out. But he expected they would have supper in their room most nights, and perhaps not get out of bed for days at a time if Adela was feeling particularly amorous toward him.

However, those cave fossils were stiff competition for her attention, so he doubted there would be much romping in the bedchamber when they only had a month or two to collect bone samples and document the drawings found on the cave walls.

"You will be digging for bones, Your Grace?"

"Yes, Saunders." He finished rinsing the soap out of his hair and off his body, then rose from the tub. "Her Grace is an accomplished archeologist and we shall be spending our days on an actual dig site. Who knows? We might unearth a pirate's treasure along with elephant bones and the remains of giant birds."

"Fascinating," Saunders said, his manner earnest as he handed over a large drying cloth. "This is something I long to do once I am pensioned off. As a boy, I used to explore our Cornwall caves. But I never found anything of historic significance. The bones of a dead pirate was my most spectacular find. He wasn't dead all that long, it turned out. They arrested one of the local men for the murder. Apparently, it was a squabble over smuggled goods."

Ambrose laughed as he dried himself off. "Those Cornwall pirates are notorious. Our Devonshire rogues are tame by comparison. We shall let you know what we find. Have you ever been to the Huntsford Academy?"

"Not yet, Your Grace. It only opened recently and I haven't had the chance." Saunders took the cloth and put it in a pile with other items to be laundered. He continued to chatter away while Ambrose reached for the clothes neatly set out on his bed. "But I plan to go while you are on your honeymoon trip. I shall have time to fully enjoy the exhibits then. Couldn't see spending that admission price if I only had an hour to wander about. But it's well worth the full day's cost."

"There will be no charge to you, Saunders," he said, silently kicking himself for being an unmitigated dunce. This project had consumed his attention for years, but not once had he thought of his own staff. He knew nothing of their interests or opinions. "Go whenever you like. I'll provide you with a special pass. Bring a guest. Or do you have family in Town? Nephews and nieces who might enjoy the outing? The pass shall cover all of you."

"That is most generous of you, Your Grace." He cast Ambrose a smile as bright as any Crown jewel.

In truth, it wasn't generous of him at all.

He was ashamed of himself for not giving more thought to this man who had served him faithfully for over a decade. Why had he not asked Saunders even once what his interests were? The talk had only been one way, him spouting about his plans and Saunders listening attentively. He thought his valet was merely listening out of duty as any good servant ought to do. But he was listening out of a thirst for knowledge and a love of history, science, and learning. All this time, Ambrose had no idea.

Not an inkling.

Not a clue.

And yet, it was something he could have discovered with just one question.

He continued to silently kick himself as he finished dressing.

Even that reporter from The Tattler had been spellbound by

Syd and Gory's knowledge of the ancient world and the mysteries it held.

"What a clot you are," he mumbled under his breath.

"I'm sorry, Your Grace. Did you say something?"

"No, Saunders. Just muttering to myself."

Adela had been going on about making his exhibits available to everyone. She understood the true value of his project, its appeal to young and old, rich and poor, scholar and stable hand, members of the royal family all the way down to menial laborers. Indeed, those who could least afford the cost of admission were likely to appreciate his exhibits the most.

"There, Your Grace." Saunders nodded in approval as he tied the perfect knot in his cravat.

Ambrose was just sticking a pin in his cravat when he heard the click of an opening lock, and then Adela knocked on the door between their two rooms. He crossed his large chamber in two, long strides and opened it wide to allow her in.

Big eyes and a bright smile met his gaze.

"Come in, love," he said.

Her hair was damp since she had just washed it. She now had it drawn back in a loose ribbon in order for her curls to dry while they were downstairs eating their breakfast. He must have been hungrier than he realized because Adela looked delicious and he wanted to devour her.

She wore a travel gown in a striking, dark blue hue, one of those exquisitely vivid Venetian colors. He approved of this elegant gown, no doubt a very practical addition to the finer silk ones Eloise and Phoebe had ordered for Adela from their talented modiste.

"You look beautiful." He leaned in to kiss her on the lips.

She blushed.

Saunders grinned.

Adela's maid giggled.

"You look quite dashing yourself," Adela said, "but you always do."

He took her hand in his, not caring what anyone thought of this show of affection. But neither Saunders nor Adela's maid seemed to mind. He supposed they found it romantic. It was certainly out of character for him.

But so was their brief courtship.

Their hasty marriage.

Certainly their odd honeymoon destination.

They walked downstairs and were about to enter the dining room when his brothers arrived with Syd, Gory, and Marigold in tow. Also with them were Viscount Ardley and his wife, Viola, who now rushed toward Adela to give her a hug. "I hope you don't mind. Alexander and I will be returning to Ardley later today and we wanted to see you off first."

"How could I mind? None of my good fortune would have happened if not for meeting the two of you. I am eternally grateful for all you've done for me." Adela then greeted the others effusively and peered toward the front door. "Is that everyone?"

Gory nodded. "Yes, just us. Your parents were too tired to join us."

"All the excitement was too much for them," Marigold said kindly, no doubt noting the disappointment on Adela's face. "I know how they must feel, for London quite overwhelms me. I'm glad I've made good friends among you. I feel I am such a burden to my family, otherwise."

"You a burden?" Julius remarked with a laugh. "You are the sweetest thing. I'm sure your family delights in having you around just as we do."

Marigold tossed him a beaming smile. "Thank you."

Adela appreciated the girl's attempts to excuse her parents. She ought to have expected their decision to sleep in rather than join their newly married daughter. After all, they had been ignoring her for years, treating her as a visitor rather than one of the family. A welcome visitor, to be sure. But never a beloved daughter. It still hurt after all these years. Was there nothing she could ever do to shine in their eyes?

She forced a smile and tried to shrug off their absence, for she had Ambrose now and things would be different. "I'll see my parents in Devonshire soon."

Ambrose took her hand. "We'll make it a point to visit them

several times before returning to London. We'll have plenty of time to discuss this on our journey. Come, the salvers have been set out on the buffet. Let's eat before everything gets cold."

"You don't have to ask me twice," Julius muttered and held out an arm for Gory and the other for Marigold.

Octavian sighed and held out his for Syd. "Do you think you can stop glowering at me long enough to allow me to escort you into the dining room?"

She tipped her chin in the air and marched on ahead of him.

Ambrose stared at his brother. "What is that about?"

"I don't know. I suppose she is still angry that I thwarted her family's plans to take her away the night before your wedding. And yet, she was so relieved. Did you see how happy she was yesterday? Smiling at everyone and glad to be in attendance? She even smiled at me. I ought to have been suspicious and realize she was merely trying to throw me off my guard."

Octavian raked a hand through his hair, obviously worried as he continued. "I caught her crying her heart out this morning. I think she is going to run off again soon."

Adela put a hand to her throat. "What are we to do? I should have asked earlier, did her family leave Town without her?"

Octavian shook his head. "Yes, but they've left some of their staff behind. An unsavory lot, if you ask me. They look more like prison guards than travel companions."

Ambrose frowned. "Where do you think they'll take her?"

"North to York, that's what their servants told Mr. Barrow when he questioned them. But I don't know if that is to be her final destination. She won't tell me anything, of course. She's furious I caught her sobbing and accused me of spying on her when all I meant to do was find her and let her know Julius and I had arrived to pick them up."

Adela appeared genuinely distraught.

Ambrose knew he had to do something for her friend. "Whatever you need, Octavian. Just tell me and I will order it put at your disposal."

"Nothing for now," his brother said. "The Bow Street men and I will try to piece together what is going on. We won't let her come

234 | MEARA PLATT

to harm."

Ambrose nodded.

Adela thanked him profusely. "Thank goodness for you Thorne men. But Octavian, don't you have a report to give to the members of the House of Lords?"

"The report is written up. Someone else will explain it to them if I am not around to do it. They won't understand any of the science anyway. In fact, Ambrose can present it for me since you and he will be back in London by the time I am due to stand before them. Do you think you will be away longer than a month?"

"Yes, it is quite possible," Ambrose said. "Likely we'll be gone two months, at least."

His brother sighed. "Well, Julius understands the science as well as I do and is certainly more adept at the politics of presenting it. I'll ask him to do it if the need arises."

Ambrose did not think it was wise, for Octavian would have to answer to the Admiralty if he pawned so important a task off on another, even if he or Julius were to be that other. However, his stubborn bull of a brother was a grown man and not about to listen to his older sibling lecture him.

Adela was still fretting. "You are risking a lot for Syd. Let me try to talk to her. We can delay our departure for an hour while I do."

Octavian shook his head. "It will only be a waste of time. She won't listen to reason. Gory has already tried to pound sense into her. You are welcome to do the same, but I don't think she will oblige. She is determined to undertake her mission, whatever it is, on her own."

"But she promised to tell us after the wedding," Adela said. "She would not break her word to us."

Ambrose put an end to the conversation by reminding her their other guests were waiting for them in the dining room. "My brother is on the task. And look at her, she's smiling and chattering away as though nothing happened this morning."

Adela sighed. "But we all know it did."

"Don't ask me to change our plans, love. Syd is set on her path, whatever that is. Octavian will do all he can to protect her while we are away. It is not your fault she remains stubborn. She has made her choice, as foolish as it may be. Are you now going to set aside your dreams over a friend who is spurning everyone's offer of help? What do you want us to do? Spend our honeymoon holding her prisoner in our home?"

"No, you are right," Adela said with a groan. "Let's enjoy the morning with our friends and family."

The remainder of their breakfast passed without rancor, everyone enjoying themselves and wishing them well on their travels. It was soon time to leave, and their friends saw them to their carriage which already had their trunks loaded on it. They brought no entourage with them, for one of the inn's maids would be available to help Adela don her gowns if she was not pleased with Ambrose's assistance.

As for him, he required little help other than securing his cuff links to his shirt sleeves, something Adela could easily do. "Ready, love?"

She nodded and rushed to hug her friends.

"Enjoy your time," Viola said, kissing her cheek.

Syd grabbed her and gave her a fierce hug. "Be happy, Adela. You've married a very special man."

"Syd, you must promise me not to do anything foolish while we are gone."

"I have no intention of doing anything foolish. I'm sure Octavian will see to that." She cast Adela a wistful smile. "I promise you, I'll be here when you return. The family crisis has passed, although I'm not certain yet the resolution is to my liking. However, I will seek out Octavian if something more must be done. I know what he said to you about risking his career…risking everything to see me safe. It is more than my family would ever do for me, and I will apologize to him for my behavior this very day."

Adela hoped she meant it.

When Gory's turn came to bid her a safe journey, Gory merely grinned and gave her a quick hug. "All I want to know is…above or below? Syd and I have wagered on it."

"Gory!" Adela's face turned a fiery shade of red.

"I knew it! Syd, pay up. I've won the bet."

Adela scampered into the carriage. "Dear heaven."

Ambrose climbed in beside her.

He waited for them to be on their way before he asked what that exchange was about. "Above or below? What did she mean?"

Adela's face turned flaming red again.

"Blessed saints! They were wagering on our wedding night?" Of course, he had devoured her. Above. Below. Several times. What man in his right mind would ever keep his hands or lips off her gorgeous body? "Your friends are too inquisitive for their own good."

"It is harmless fun. They don't really understand what the wager is about. I don't think Gory or Syd have even been kissed yet. None of us were until you came along and kissed me. We are told so little, left so unprepared to face the important changes in our lives. Can you blame them for being curious? I hope they find the same happiness I have found with you, and that they enjoy the intimacy shared between a loving, married couple. Well, I don't suppose one needs to be married for *that* to happen, but as you saw from my response, reading about it and actually experiencing it are very different things."

"You were quite wanton last night," Ambrose teased.

She laughed. "Indeed, I was. Dear heaven, you were quite naughty in leading me astray. I think I need to fan myself."

He took her hand in his as their carriage rolled off. "Feel free to shed your clothes if you are too hot."

She gasped and at the same time laughed. "In a carriage?"

He arched an eyebrow. "Think of what we can do as the carriage bounces. I'll show you once we are outside of London and the roadway is clear."

"Good grief, you are serious. It sounds awfully wicked."

"It is."

"You know, we have only been married a day and I already feel thoroughly corrupted by you."

He cupped her face in his big hands and kissed her ever so gently on the mouth. "I'll never force you to do anything you–"

"Oh, I wasn't complaining about it. I am quite eager to be your partner in that sort of adventure. If I fall asleep, just wake me once the road is clear."

He threw his head back and laughed. "You won't regret it, love."

He said no more as their carriage slowly made its way through London and finally onto the less congested Devonshire road. Adela turned silent, but he could sense she was happy as she spent her time watching the scenery until she fell asleep against his shoulder.

He had kept her up much of the night and she must now be exhausted.

She was sleeping so peacefully, he decided not to disturb her.

They would have their romp in the carriage another day.

They had a lifetime of days ahead of them.

Besides, he did not mind just holding her in his arms.

However, the silence brought his thoughts back to Octavian. His brother had always been a restless fellow and was not pleased when the Admiralty promoted him to duties on land. He had wanted to remain in command of his ship, and not merely because the captain of a ship commanded the biggest share of spoils from any enemy vessel captured.

Octavian had amassed a sizeable fortune already and had no need to risk his life adding more to it. He chafed at being on land because he loved the sea and was fiercely loyal to the men under his command.

But those in the higher echelons knew his value and were grooming him for greater things since Octavian had brains as well as brawn. Coupled with his experience at sea, this made him the best naval officer to oversee the design of a new fleet of ships and accompanying weaponry. He had the battle experience and the scientific vision to advise on these designs as well as detect flaws. These advancements were vital to maintaining England as the reigning monarch of the seas.

Despite Octavian's grumbling, Ambrose knew this was no soft assignment. Within a few years, his brother would be elevated to the rank of admiral. The only way Octavian could sink his career was if he ignored his duties and ran off after Syd. She had assured Adela she would remain in London, giving the impression that whatever crisis had caused her family to attempt to drag her away was now over.

Could they believe it?

Adela did, but he was not certain.

What if she did run off again?

Was Octavian going to toss aside his promising career to go after her?

CHAPTER 18

ADELA'S CAVES WERE near her childhood home in Dartmouth, not very far from the charming Blue Rose Inn where they were staying for the month, perhaps two if their dig proved successful. The inn was a perfect retreat, having a lovely view to the sea, an excellent dining room, and an accommodating staff.

Ambrose had made sure to purchase ropes, pegs, lanterns, shovels, and pickaxes while in London, and had them loaded onto the carriage along with their trunks for the journey. There was a well-stocked mercantile not far from the inn where they could purchase anything they were missing, including ladders and working man's gloves, something they would need if it turned out they had a lot of digging to do. Adela's hands were soft and would blister easily. His hands were rougher, but not even he would escape blistered palms if they had to spend hours digging deep down.

"Ambrose, this is marvelous! When did you have time to take care of all this?" Adela asked, her smile radiant as he showed her their supplies.

"I am thorough about everything."

"I see that you are."

"So, when were you going to tell me?"

She shook her head in confusion. "Tell you what?"

"That you own the land where your precious caves are located."

She laughed. "I told you my family was not poor, nor are we

fabulously wealthy either. My grandmother left me an inheritance and I used it to purchase this property."

"A wise move, indeed. I think the treasure in these caves could turn out to be something quite valuable. Not necessarily in financial terms, but for the sake of your discoveries." In truth, her excitement for this project was infectious and Ambrose found himself eager to start on their hunt for bones.

He also liked the informality, feeling at ease in the simple work clothes he had brought along. Those consisted of dark trousers, coarse linen shirts, a durable leather vest, and old boots that were quite worn in.

The day was beautiful, the wind soft and fragrant as it carried the honeyed scent of wild flowers along with the salt of the sea off Lyme Bay. Adela's hair was neatly pinned back and she was also dressed for a day in the caves. She had donned her walking boots and wore a dark-colored gown of sturdy material that made her look like a prim governess...one he would very much like to seduce.

He cupped her cheek and drew her close for a lingering kiss.

She enjoyed it, he could tell by the sparkle in her eyes. But she poked him with her elbow and cast him an impish grin a moment later. "Don't you dare delay us. We have important work to do. Besides, my friends will be meeting us at the caves to help out."

"Cruel woman, denying me my pleasure."

She laughed. "I'll make up for it tonight."

He chuckled. "Assuming you don't fall asleep the moment your head hits the pillow. A cool breeze and a full day of physical labor will do that to you."

She reached up on tiptoes and gave him a quick kiss on the lips. "Oh, I'm sure you'll put the spark back in me if I start to nod off."

He picked her up and twirled her playfully in his arms. "It is all your fault, you know. You shouldn't look so tempting."

"Nor should you." She wrapped her arms around his neck. "The ladies in my explorer's club are going to swoon over you and your gorgeous muscles."

"How many of them have agreed to join us?"

"All the members, but we're a very small club. Only two men and three women, not including me. I sent word as soon as we arrived yesterday. They are delighted you are sponsoring our expedition."

He arched an eyebrow and laughed. "I am a sponsor now, am I?"

She nodded as he set her down. "We have agreed to name one of the fossil finds after you in honor of your generosity."

He gave a mock shudder. "Oh, no. I will not have a strange animal named after me. You are the one who wants the footnote in the annals of history."

"Very well, but it is your loss. I would love to have a primitive creature named after me." She took his hand in hers and led him to the inn's stable. "Come on. We mustn't be late."

The sun was still shining brightly and the air was dry when they met Adela's friends by the Devonshire caves. They were near the sea, so Ambrose could hear the distant crash of waves against the rocky coast. "In which cave shall we dig first?"

Adela pointed to the central one that also happened to have the largest opening. "We must start here. It is the one with the most wall drawings and likely to be the one used by these ancient tribesmen as their communal dining hall."

He noticed the ladies did not take their eyes off him as he rolled up his sleeves. They skittered into the cave after him and watched with grins on their faces as he began to dig where Adela instructed.

Their gawking was harmless.

Besides, Ambrose was used to being fawned over from an early age.

These ladies were more curious than predatory, unlike those in London's elegant society who were out for blood and would not hesitate to ruin the reputation of anyone who got in their way. No, these amiable spinsters, Miss Appleby, Miss Lansing, and Miss Gootch, who appeared to range in age from mid-twenties to mid-thirties, were too awed by his rank and respectful of his marriage to Adela to make any untoward advances.

The men in their club, Mr. Hastings and Mr. Collins, were

closer to forty years of age in his estimation, and were also awed by him.

Well, this is what came of being a duke.

At first, he thought to keep to formality and have them address him as Your Grace and do the same for Adela. But he quickly saw that wasn't going to last. Adela and her friends giggled every time they referred to her by that title, so he relented somewhat and allowed them to call her Adela. As for him, he remained Your Grace, merely to remind them all who was in charge.

Once they returned to London, he would insist Adela be addressed by her title. She had to get used it and learn to wield her authority. Even though her Dartmouth friends appeared unaffected by her rank, the London elite certainly would take notice of it. She had to learn that most people would look upon her differently now that she was his duchess.

However, he resolved not to interfere with these old friendships, although he hoped an occasional word would put a little caution in Adela. Most of her companions would remain on good terms with her, but some might seek to take advantage because of her elevated status. Perhaps not in this group, for they were excited by old bones and not trappings of wealth.

In truth, he was surprised by how friendly and lacking in guile they all were.

It was altogether possible he was the one who had grown too cynical over time.

"Adela," he said several hours later, resuming his digging after their merry group had enjoyed a picnic lunch in the nearby meadow, "I think I've struck something."

She gasped and scurried over to him. "Is it a bone? Be careful. Stop digging. I'll use the small spade to remove the dirt around it."

The others also stopped their work and formed a circle around the hole he'd dug, which was the deepest. This was not surprising since he had more muscle to put into the task than the other men. Mr. Hastings and Mr. Collins were older gentlemen and scholars, neither of them used to performing physical work.

Ambrose now held the lantern over the hole while Adela

carefully cleared dirt off the exposed part of the bone. But it was larger than imagined, so he and the men began to dig another hole beside it in order to reveal more of the bone. The ladies hovered at the edge with lanterns raised, the firelight casting a golden glow throughout the dank cave and seeming to bring the wall drawings to life.

Excitement sizzled through him, just as he knew it did with the others.

Adela's eyes were wide and sparkling. When she was not grinning from ear to ear, her mouth was open in wonder, and he could hear her soft gasps as they dug deeper to expose more of this single bone.

Even his jaw gaped open as they began to understand just how enormous this discovery was. "Adela, this is no mere footnote," he muttered. "You and your friends have uncovered what has to be the leg of an enormous creature no one has ever seen before. Some kind of giant lizard."

"Or a dragon," Miss Appleby remarked. "Just like those depicted on these cave walls. I knew they had to be real. Legends in myth often are. Besides, discovering the Devonshire Dragon sounds much better than discovering the Devonshire Lizard."

Adela nodded enthusiastically. "Oh, yes! What a wonderful addition it will be to the Huntsford exhibits. Everyone will marvel as they enter the Hall of Dragons. What dreams the children will have after seeing such a display!"

"It is just one bone," Ambrose reminded her.

"Oh, no," she said, shaking her head. "We are about to find many more right here. This cave is our portal to an ancient world, an inspiration to all who have the ability to imagine impossible things and make them come true. This is the stuff of dreams, the discovery of life beyond our known existence. It is wonder and hope."

"It is a miracle," Mr. Collins said.

Ambrose conceded the point.

Adela and the members of her club were right. This discovery filled even him, a cynical duke, with an indescribable feeling of elation. It brought him back to his boyhood days and the excitement he and his brothers felt with every little find they made while exploring the grounds of their Huntsford estate with their father.

The Fellows in the Royal Society who had rudely dismissed Adela would now be green with envy. The Duke of Lotheil would not mince words when excoriating them for their failure to admit women into their membership. Of course, the Fellows would not be moved despite the enormity of this find. If anything, Adela's accomplishments were likely to put them in greater fear of being outdone by a woman.

As for the British Museum, their curators had been more polite about ignoring Adela. He expected they would now clamor to purchase as many giant lizard bones as could be found. He and Adela would decide later whether any should be sold or all retained for the Huntsford collection.

Whatever happened, he would make certain Adela and her companions in their explorer's club were properly acknowledged and rewarded for their find. This was perhaps the most important archeological discovery to date in England. Unearthing Roman ruins or shards of pottery left behind by the ancient Celtic tribes was one thing. Those were modern history compared to the truly ancient history this bone and the others to follow represented.

His mind was already awhirl, dreaming up the fascinating lectures Adela and her friends could put together surrounding this discovery. And why not a special series of lectures for children, too?

His brothers would have a hearty laugh over the change in him.

He had closed himself off very early in his life, needing to adopt a reclusive nature as a shield. No one but Adela had ever breached that barrier. However, his position in Society also offered him many comforts, and he was too often smug about accepting those as though it were his due.

For every door open to him, Adela had met with a similar door shut in her face. But it did not deter her. He marveled at her enthusiasm and spirit, her persistence when others would have given up hope.

Later that night, as they lay in bed and made plans for the following day, he wrapped her in his arms. "I thought you would be exhausted and only think of sleep. But your eyes are shimmering starlight and I think you will chatter for hours."

She nestled against him. "I shall spare you my prattling, but I am thrilled to pieces. Aren't you? I was afraid Devonshire would never match up to Greece or Italy in your mind. But I think we did all right for the start of our honeymoon, don't you?"

"More than all right, love." He kissed her on the forehead, a little distracted by his own thoughts.

She lifted onto one elbow to study his expression. "Are you worried we have already reached the high point in our marriage and it will be dull from here on out?"

He kissed her again. "The thought never crossed my mind. If you must know, I was thinking about how every day will bring something new and interesting because of you. I never looked at life the way you do. You see importance in the smallest things and they suddenly shine brightly because of you."

She rested her hand atop his chest and gently played with the sprinkle of hair across it. "That is a very nice thing to say."

"You are good for me, Adela. Until you came along, I looked at everything from my high perch. It is a lofty view and one can miss a lot from that height."

"And I pulled you down to plant your two feet firmly on the ground," she teased.

He laughed. "What you did was make me open my eyes and see what others saw. We are a good fit, you and I. Not only in the bedchamber."

He shifted in order to roll her under him. "However, I would not like to overlook our explorations in the bedchamber."

"What about you? Are *you* not exhausted and achy from all that digging you did today?" She was smiling and the warm glow in her eyes was inviting.

"Thoroughly, love. But you are impossible to resist." He began to kiss his way along her lithe, little body and her full breasts that utterly beguiled and fascinated him. He loved how sweetly she received his advances.

They coupled only the once because they were to rise early on the morrow to continue their dig, but their love-making was most satisfying.

Adela fell asleep with a smile on her face.

Being with Adela was indescribably good.

There was something precious in the way they were getting to know each other, in the way they were growing together as a couple, and at the same time, keeping true to themselves.

This bond forming between them was a palpable thing that one could almost reach out and touch. They were two very different people, but would now move together as one through life, like a moon and planet forever connected in their orbit. Separate, and yet always bound.

Yes, Adela would like that description.

She would also be thrilled when she and her fellow explorers came up with a name for the creature whose giant bone they had found.

Adelus dragonus?

Adelasaurus?

He kissed her softly on her smiling lips and then fell asleep holding her in his arms.

What treasures would they find tomorrow?

Not that it mattered to him anymore.

He had found his treasure and she was sleeping right beside him.

A duke for Adela, her father had once said.

But it should be the other way around.

An Adela for the duke, for wasn't she the real prize?

EPILOGUE

Devonshire, England
June 1824

ADELA AND HER friends had stumbled upon an entire trove of bones that Ambrose quickly realized would require them to extend their honeymoon. This extended stay is what they had spent the past few days organizing. First by arranging to secure the cave site to keep unscrupulous relic hunters away, and next to bring in experts on staff at the Huntsford Academy to catalogue and properly wrap each bone for carting to London.

"Ambrose, you look worried," Adela said, coming up to him later that morning as he stood pensively outside the cave.

"No, love. Just thinking. This project is bigger than I ever expected, but I cannot stay here the entire time it will take us to properly secure the site and remove everything to be found. It could take years to fully explore this cave and the ones around it. I'll have to return to London at some point soon and resume my duties there."

She brushed back a few wayward curls that had escaped their pins on this windy day and smiled at him. "What do you propose?"

"That we spend two months here and then two months in London, keeping to that schedule as much as we can. It is a bit of a trip, but I can ride back and forth alone if it becomes too much for you. Hopefully, it won't. I think this can work. I have good people in place to manage the Huntsford holdings during my short absences, and Julius can attend to whatever else needs to be done. Octavian will help whenever he can, but his Admiralty duties will take up most of his time."

He sighed and shook his head as he continued to discuss his thoughts. "Thank goodness Syd stayed true to her word and remained in London. Octavian would have gone after her and it could have destroyed his career."

"Syd thinks too highly of Octavian ever to let it happen. Gory wrote to me and told me what she thinks happened that night before our wedding. Seems Syd's father was trying to marry her off to a business partner of his he had swindled."

"Dear heaven," Ambrose muttered.

"When Octavian foiled that, her father handed over Syd's cousin who was the father's ward. But the cousin fell in love with the business partner and he with her. Can you believe it? What a relief for all concerned."

"Until her fool of a father swindles another partner."

Adela sighed. "Let's hope he's learned his lesson."

"A man like that? Who would attempt to sell his own daughter to save his hide?" Ambrose caressed her cheek. "Love, people don't change. They never do."

She nodded. "Well, I hope she will give Octavian or Gory some warning if it happens again."

She nestled in his arms, not caring they were at the dig site and all her friends were looking on. "As for us, I don't mind traveling back and forth with you. Nothing matters more to me than being with you. Isn't this discovery the most exciting thing ever to happen in your life?"

He laughed as he put his arms around her. "No, you are. I was beginning to despair of ever making a love match until you came along. These finds are extraordinary, but I would never choose them over you...and you can put that in a starred page in your diary."

"My diary is filled with stars on the pages I have written about you, as if you didn't know. Have you been reading it?"

He grinned at her. "No, love."

"Not that it matters. I have no secrets from you. You are the best thing ever to happen to me. Oh, I will cry if we keep up this conversation. I never dreamed I could be this happy or that anyone could love me so deeply...oh, dear. I must stop talking now or I shall turn into a watering pot. Besides, we have work to do."

She squirmed out of his arms and grabbed her journal, then sat on a nearby bench.

Ambrose sat down beside her. "What are you writing?"

"Making a list of things we have yet to do."

He cast her a rakishly hot look. "Top of the list...make love in a carriage."

She gasped and then broke into mirthful trills of laughter. "Behave yourself, Your Grace."

He arched an eyebrow. "Must I?"

She set down her journal. "Yes, my naughty husband. We will get nothing done if all we do is think about bedding each other all day long."

He gave a mock sigh. "Very well, I'll do my best to behave...during the day. All bets are off at night."

She kissed him. "We'll need a place to stay for the duration of the dig. I thought of letting a house, but I think the Blue Rose Inn is quite nice and will serve us better. It would save us the need to hire a staff since they already have a cook to prepare our meals and maids to clean our rooms and tend to our garments. Also, we would not need to concern ourselves with keeping a house in good repair or tending a garden."

"I'm sure the innkeeper will be pleased to have us remain. What's next on your list that you are furiously scribbling down?"

"Who are we to bring in to assist us? Only your Huntsford staff? Can they be spared from the Huntsford Academy for that long?"

"Yes, some of them can be taken off other museum projects. But we ought to bring in an expert or two from the British Museum to add authority to our discoveries."

Adela pursed her lips. "Do you really think it is necessary?

Having your name behind these finds ought to be enough. There is no one with a finer reputation than yours."

He caressed her cheek. "Says my obviously adoring wife. We will remain in charge, but having the British Museum behind us is important."

"All right, but I will not have the Royal Society involved. Of course, the Duke of Lotheil is always welcome, but I will not allow any of their other members to set foot here."

"You'll have no argument from me." He frowned, for he was still quite angry over the way Adela and her friends had been shunned and ignored by their Fellows. "What's next on your list?"

"I'd like to invite Syd and Gory to join us. Marigold, too. I don't know if the Farthingales will allow her to come because she's still a little young to be trusted on her own. In truth, I think she is wiser than me or my friends and will likely be a better influence on us than we are on her. But there is no harm in asking John and Sophie if she might join us. Would you mind?"

"Not at all. I'll reserve rooms for all of them at the inn should they accept. Invite John and Sophie, too, if you wish."

Adela nodded. "I may do just that. Gory will leap at the chance to participate in the dig. She will be quite helpful because of her knowledge of anatomy. As for Syd...her knowledge of skeletal composition will be helpful, too. But I want her here mostly because I am afraid of what might happen to her if she remains in London without us. Even if things appear to be resolved, I'd still like to get her away from her family and this seems a very good excuse."

Ambrose nodded in agreement.

The sun was bright and breeze cool as they continued to set their plans. Ambrose had never felt so at peace as he did in this moment. "My brothers will take up much of the slack when dealing with Huntsford business affairs, but I would like them to join us, as well. We often explored the countryside around our summer estate near Thurlestone with our father. It isn't very far from here. I think they will be eager to join us for as long as they can manage. Perhaps we'll even take a few days and visit Thurlestone once they arrive."

"Do you have any caves on your property?"

"Yes, but we never found anything close to this extraordinary site. No cave art. No artifacts. Although it might be worth another look now that you've found these. I know it will mean a lot to my brothers to be a part of our dig. Not to mention, Octavian's brawn will be quite useful. He always enjoyed physical labor."

"Let's write our letters as soon as we return to the inn tonight."

"All right, love. But I will add two others to our list. My valet, Saunders, who has always had a love of archeology."

"Yes, he told me. I think it is an excellent idea. He will be thrilled."

"And we must invite Mr. Hawkins to join us."

Adela's eyes widened in surprise. "The young reporter from The Tattler?"

"Yes, we know he is also a lover of archeology. And what better way for our work to gain popular recognition? That gossip rag reaches people from all walks of life whereas the scholarly journals, while important, reach only the scientifically-minded elite."

"Oh, I see your point. But we had better set down rules if he is to join us. His articles are only to be about archeology."

"Agreed."

As the weeks passed and their plans began to firm, Ambrose watched Adela blossom. He had always thought her beautiful. But she flowered a little more with each passing day. He had expected them to tire of each other a little, for they spent day and night in each other's company.

His concerns were unfounded.

If anything, he craved her company more each day and missed her every minute they were apart.

Gad, was this how it felt to be in love?

His valet, Saunders, and an excited Mr. Hawkins were first to arrive in mid-July. The young reporter hopped down from the coach and rushed forward to greet them with a gap-toothed smile and a cowlick poking up from his sandy hair. "I was about to quit that awful rag when the owner called me into his office and handed me this assignment. I cannot thank you both enough, and wish to assure you my reporting will only extend to the cave site. No gossip will take place. I shall only report on dead things."

Ambrose grinned. "You and I will have no quarrel so long as you stick to this arrangement, Mr. Hawkins."

"I give you my word of honor, Your Grace."

It was not long before Adela's findings caught the imagination of the entire country. The Tattler, diverging from its usual gossip, printed the weekly reports sent by their young reporter. To his credit, his stories were extremely well written, factually accurate concerning every new find, and yet inspirational to all who held dreams of discovery and adventure.

Miss Appleby's artistic talents were put to use as Ambrose hired her to draw the caves, the surrounding countryside, and their actual dig site. Those drawings would form part of their Huntsford Academy exhibit. The Tattler also hired her, at Mr. Hawkins' urging, to draw scenes for them to put in their weekly special editions.

Miss Appleby was also working with Adela to document the cave wall drawings, sketching them with precision in order to detail the dots and other markings surrounding the various scenes depicted by the ancient artists.

Ambrose could not have been more pleased with how smoothly everything was going until one day he noticed Adela suddenly run out of the cave and into the nearby copse of trees. "Adela!"

He ran after her.

What was wrong?

He knew her parents were supposed to come by today, but had sent their apologies and assured her they would make it another day soon. This was the third time they had done this to her and he knew she had to be overset by it. "Love, what's the matter?"

She turned away and cast up her accounts.

Ambrose did not know what to do beyond holding back her hair and putting an arm around her waist while she struggled.

Her eyes were watery and she looked quite miserable by the time she finally straightened and gazed up at him. "Must have been something I ate. My stomach has been queasy these past few days."

He put a hand to her forehead. "You're not running a fever. Perhaps it is eating at you that your parents–"

"No, it is just my stomach. My parents have been disappointing me for years. This is nothing new for me. Nor does it hurt nearly so much as it used to now that I have you. You are wonderful, you know."

"So are you, love." He brushed a few damp curls off her face, for she looked flushed and little beads of perspiration had formed across her brow.

He took out his handkerchief and left her a moment to moisten it in a nearby stream, then returned to her side and gently dabbed it on her brow and along her neck. "Does this help at all?"

She nodded. "My nausea seems to come on in the morning and then I am better by the afternoon. Perhaps I am eating too much. My clothes are getting tighter, too. Have you noticed? How about you? Are you putting on a little weight, too? The inn's cook does serve hearty meals."

"No, I work it off with all the physical labor I do. I'm–" He sucked in a breath.

Lord, he was dense not to have noticed sooner. "Adela, love..."

She leaned against him as another wave of nausea washed over her. "I'm so sorry, Ambrose. This time seems to be a little more difficult than usual. I'm not doing very well. I think I need to return to the inn."

"I'll take you there, but I am also going to summon a doctor."

"Nonsense, this will pass."

"Yes, in about nine months' time. Well, probably less depending on how far along you are."

"What?"

"Adela, it is quite possible you are not ill. I think you are carrying my child."

It took a moment for his words to sink in, but she gasped and then her smile turned radiant. "Do you think so, Ambrose?"

"Yes, my beautiful love." He lifted her in his arms with exquisite care and hugged her to him. "Our little duke-in-waiting. It is very possible and makes perfect sense. But this changes what you can do around here. No more lifting or heavy work for you. The most strenuous thing you are to do is write letters or jot notes in your journal."

"But I am not an invalid."

"No, however you are in a delicate way. I couldn't bear it if you were hurt. You are the most precious thing to me. I know I will be a protective ape over you, but don't deny me. I need you to be safe. My heart will never recover if I lose you."

"You won't, Ambrose."

He emitted a ragged breath. "Promise me, love."

"I promise." She hugged him fiercely. "My friends and your brothers are coming next week. Let's keep it quiet until then."

He laughed. "If we can. I'm sure the ladies in your club suspect something already. Women are usually quick to pick up on such things," he said now sobering as he gave her another gentle hug. "I want you to know that you fill my heart with unfathomable joy. But there will always be room for our children. I will never ignore them as your parents have ignored you."

"Nor will I. If there is one thing I've learned from my years growing up, it is the importance of letting your loved ones know how much you care for them. I love you more than anything in existence, Ambrose. I will love you and our children so deeply and always let you know it. None of you will ever be an afterthought and nothing in my life will ever be more important than you and them."

And this is how it was to be.

Their little duke-to-be arrived squawking precisely nine months from his date of conception, his arrival coinciding with the grand opening of the Hall of Dragons at the Huntsford Academy. Ambrose had insisted on their remaining in London the last three months of Adela's confinement because he trusted no one other than Dr. George Farthingale to supervise the delivery.

Marigold had accompanied George and now rushed in to congratulate the proud parents on their precious delivery. "Isn't this the most wonderful news, Your Grace? A son! And now we shall have two dukes for Adela."

He smiled down at his exhausted but beautiful wife. "Indeed, two dukes for Adela. I cannot speak for that noisy little fellow, although I expect he will love his mother fiercely. As for this duke, I lost my heart to her long ago and she will always possess it."

He leaned over and kissed her forehead. "I love you, Adela...mother of little dukes and ancient dragons."

THE END

Dear Reader

Thank you for reading *A Duke For Adela*. When Adela knocked Ambrose over in his own museum, neither one of them expected this inauspicious start to lead to love. But they were meant to be together, for who could better appreciate all of Ambrose's work than bluestocking Adela? I hope you enjoyed these latest in the Farthingale series, including *The Viscount And The Vicar's Daughter* where we first introduced Adela. Coming up next are the romances for Marigold Farthingale, and Ambrose's brothers, Octavian Thorne (that big, hunky ox), and Julius Thorne, their very capable and confident younger brother.

I welcome you to all the stories (including several novellas) in the FARTHINGALE SERIES, and if you are in need of even more Farthingales, then please try my Book of Love series where you will meet a host of Farthingale cousins, all of them sweet and innocent young ladies who cannot seem to keep out of trouble. In fact, they attract trouble wherever they turn, especially when it involves some very steamy, alpha heroes and that mysterious, red-leather bound Book of Love. The next release in the Farthingale Series is *Marigold and the Marquess*, where Marigold meets her handsome neighbor, a grumpy marquess who has just moved in across the street at Number 2 Chipping Way. That story will be followed by *The Make-Believe Marriage* because Lady Sydney Harcourt and the Duke of Huntsford's brother, Octavian Thorne, are going to have to do some quick thinking to keep her conniving father from selling her off in marriage to one of his creditors in settlement of a large debt. What are the chances Syd will fall in love with that big ox of a Thorne? Hint: I'd say they were pretty good. As for Julius and Gory? Our Regency goth debutante is going to turn to Julius for help when someone murders her odious uncle and she is worried that she might be accused, or worse, that she might be the next victim on the list.

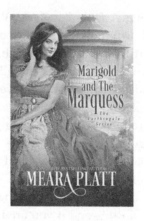

Keep reading to enjoy the first chapter of *Marigold and the Marquess*, and don't forget to grab your free Farthingale novella after the sneak peek.

SNEAK PEEK:
MARIGOLD AND THE
MARQUESS
CHAPTER 1

Chipping Way, London
April 1825

LEONIDES POOLE, MARQUESS of Muir, had been warned about moving onto Chipping Way, one of the loveliest streets in Mayfair, for it had become known as a parson's trap for the unwary bachelor. He had dismissed the notion as preposterous until this very moment when a breathless and utterly stunning young lady ran into the garden of his townhouse at Number 2 Chipping Way on what was a crisp and pleasant spring day.

He watched from his study window as the little whirlwind in blue muslin lunged and leaped amid his shrubbery attempting to catch a swiftly moving...was that a skull she was chasing? "Sterling, who is that odd young lady?"

His usually staid butler peered out the window and immediately chuckled. "That would be Miss Marigold Farthingale, my lord. I believe her father is cousin to your neighbor at Number 3, Mr. John Farthingale. He and his wife are sponsoring her come-out."

"Well, she is certainly *out there,* isn't she? What in heaven's name is she doing?"

A twinkle sprang into his stoic butler's eyes. "I have no idea. Shall I assist her?"

"No, I'll go to her." Leo buttoned his waistcoat in order to make himself moderately presentable, and then walked out of his study. He had purchased the townhouse only a month ago and the house was still sparsely furnished, although the rooms he had attended to were handsomely decorated, but not overly elegant since he had no wish to live in a museum.

A man ought to be comfortable in his own home.

Was he not desperate for that elusive comfort?

There were no dark curtains shutting off light to his rooms and no windowless rooms to remind him of a prison cell.

He strode through his parlor and out the matching glass doors leading onto his terrace, scanning the professionally landscaped garden in search of Miss Farthingale. A moment's disappointment washed over him when he did not see her, nor did he catch sight of her when he stepped onto the grass and began to peer through the flower beds.

Had she run back home?

Suddenly, the skull tore past him.

Chasing after it was the angel in blue who was so intent on her mission, she did not watch where she was going and ran straight into Leo. "*Oof!* Goodness, where did you come from? I did not see you there."

How could she miss him? He was built like a block of stone.

Blue eyes the color of a tropical sea and framed by velvet-black lashes stared up at him as he wrapped his arms around her to keep her from losing her balance and tumbling into one of those flower beds. "What are you—"

"I shall explain later," she said, pushing out of his grasp and now attempting to dive into a nearby patch of rhododendron.

"Oh, no, you don't. You'll tell me now." He caught her by the waist before she disappeared within the greenery.

He turned her to face him, now managing a good look at the girl.

Blessed saints.

He suddenly forgot to breathe.

Gad, she was exquisite.

Not a sophisticated, *ton* beauty at all, but beautiful in an ethereal, faeries-dancing-amid-the-bluebells way.

He smothered the urge to grin, for her features could only be described as part angel and part imp.

Mostly imp because of her big eyes and slightly pointy ears.

"Who are you, and why is your skull running circles around my garden?" In his entire life, he did not think to ever ask anyone this question. It was absurd but also wonderful because he was in desperate need of just this ridiculous intrusion in his life to make him feel alive again.

"Sir, I do apologize," she said, with a lick of her cherry lips, the gesture immediately putting his heart in palpitations. A light breeze blew a few dark curls across her brow, but she merely shook them off while he still held her. "I am your neighbor at Number 3, Miss Marigold Farthingale. A pleasure to meet you…er, may we dispense with the introductions for the moment? Please let me go. I must stop Mallow before he buries my treasure."

"Treasure?" Since when were skulls prized as such by anyone other than ghouls who crept into cemeteries at night to steal them?

The skull darted out of the rhododendron and leaped into his forsythia.

The lovely Miss Farthingale moaned, squirmed out of his grasp again, and was about to plunge head first into his forsythia when he stopped her by wrapping an arm around her waist and drawing her solidly up against him. "I forbid you to destroy my flower beds."

She turned to face him, frowning up at him. "Sir, I shall never catch him if you insist on holding me back."

He was no coxcomb, but women usually enjoyed being in his arms. This young woman was paying absolutely no attention to this fact, nor did she seem to care he was a marquess. Instead, she cast him a look of irritation before peering over his shoulder to shout at the now barking skull. "Bad dog! Oh, you are a very bad dog, Mallow!"

Leo sighed and waited for her dog – a little fellow who could be no bigger than the size of a squirrel – to dart past them again. "Mallow, sit!" he commanded in his most authoritative voice.

The skull immediately came to a halt on the grass beside them.

"Well done," Marigold said, now casting him the softest smile before kneeling beside this *thing* that appeared to be a head but not of any creature Leo could recognize. She popped it off Mallow and then sank down on the lawn and tucked her legs beneath her shapely bottom.

She took both her dog and that bizarre oddity onto her lap.

Mallow turned out to be a little spaniel with a big attitude.

He growled as Leo knelt beside him and his mistress.

Leo shot him a look of caution to establish that he was the dominant male in this relation. Fortunately, the dog quickly acquiesced. "We shall become good friends, you little knave," he said, giving Mallow a gentle rub to his belly before turning his attention to the exquisite girl. "Would you mind explaining what that was all about?"

She graced him with another soft smile. "Have you heard of the Huntsford Academy?"

"Yes, Huntsford is a friend of mine."

"His wife, Duchess Adela, is a very good friend of mine, and this is one of the relics from her Devonshire dig. I helped unearth it. In fact, I just returned from there this morning with a crateful of bones I must deliver to the academy as soon as my aunt and uncle return from visiting their daughter, Dillie. Thursdays are her 'at home' days. Well, she is Duchess Dillie, the Duke of Edgeware's wife. Do you know them?"

He nodded. "Edgeware and I are quite well acquainted."

"Is it not odd?" She absently petted Mallow who was now licking himself obscenely while sprawled on her lap.

Leo stifled a grin. "What do you mean?"

The sun shone down upon both of them and a light breeze carried the scent of lilac in the air. The girl cast him another smile, and he realized this was her naturally cheerful repose when she was not chattering or thinking of pressing thoughts.

It did not surprise him that Marigold was a happy soul. Yet, she did not appear to be the empty-headed sort to prattle incessantly.

That was a point in her favor.

Leo could not abide people who would not stop talking simply because they liked to hear the sound of their voice. Hers was quite pleasant, not that it should matter to him.

So was the lovely shape of her lips, not that this should matter, either.

Mallow paused in his preening to growl at him again.

Oh, that little hound knew what he was thinking.

Marigold was obviously too innocent to understand the surprising need she stirred in him, and had not a clue how tempting she looked.

Her hair was dark, the color of black satin.

And those eyes, that deep azure of the sea.

She smiled up at him yet again. "We know several people in common but have never met until this very moment. Do you not find it curious?"

"No, I have not been in London for a while."

"Are you back now to stay? Since you mentioned this was your home, I assume you are the Marquess of Muir, Leonides Poole."

He nodded. "That I am."

"A pleasure to meet you, Lord Muir. Forgive my intrusion."

"No harm done." It was early afternoon and Leo was ready to take a break from his work, anyway. "Would you care to join me? I was about to have refreshments on the terrace."

"I should like that very much, but I had better not. I hope you will invite me again soon, however."

"Yes, I will." One in his position could not afford to let a ray of sunshine like Marigold slip away.

She glanced at Mallow. "He is restless and will not behave for long. He can be a very naughty fellow, at times."

Leo smothered another grin, for so could he be naughty.

Men were men, no matter what breed, and this girl was lovely.

He would never misbehave with Marigold, of course.

The girl was luscious, but far too innocent.

He lifted the skull from her lap and reached out a hand. "Let me help you up, Miss Farthingale."

She plunked Mallow in his outstretched hand instead and gracefully rose on her own.

"Behave," she warned the tiny spaniel when he barked as she took him back in her arms. She was trying to come across as stern, but her voice was too soft and lilting to scare that impudent beast.

Since she had her hands full with the squirming spaniel, Leo offered to carry the skull for her as he escorted her across the street. "You are frowning, Miss Farthingale."

She shook her satin mane of hair. "The hour is growing late and I must get that crate of bones to the Huntsford Academy before it closes. But Aunt Sophie and Uncle John are not back yet. Well, they are not truly my aunt and uncle but it seems quite cumbersome to constantly refer to John as my first cousin once removed. He and my father are cousins."

He merely nodded, for Sterling had confirmed this to him earlier. "I will take you to Huntsford's museum. Most of my work is done for the day and it will do me good to get out. Bring your maid along for the sake of propriety."

Her eyes sparkled as they widened in surprise. "Are you certain you don't mind?"

"It will be my pleasure." He opened the gate to the Farthingale townhouse and escorted her up the walk. "Give me a few minutes to have my carriage readied and I shall come by to collect you shortly."

She cast him a radiant smile. "I shall be waiting with the crate, but without Mallow. He may be little, but he can cause big mischief. It would not do to bring him with us only to have him chew the prized exhibits. However, I had better ask my cousin Violet to join us. She is more appropriate a chaperone than a maid. She and her husband reside at Number 1. Do you know Captain Brayden?"

"Yes, Romulus? I also know his brother, James, Earl of Exmoor."

She shook her head. "You really know everyone, don't you?"

He shrugged. "Our elite circles are small. We go to the same schools, fight the same wars, belong to the same clubs, go to the same parties. I've been away from England for a while and haven't seen any of them in several years."

"And now you are rekindling your acquaintances?"

"You might say that."

"Then shall I see you at the round of balls, soirees, and teas? This is my first year on the marriage mart, however I have been in London for quite a few months now...well, traveling back and forth to Devonshire and those ancient caves. Thank goodness for my friends and family, for I would otherwise find this matchmaking marketplace quite daunting."

"You won't be in it for long, I'm sure. Some gentleman will come along and quickly claim you."

She laughed. "I hope not. I am in no hurry to wed. Eighteen years is a little too young to be married, don't you think? Twenty is a much better age. I wish I were twenty, already. Most of my friends are, but they think of me as a child and do not take me very seriously."

"Because you are charmingly innocent and obviously have little experience in the world. That is a good thing. The world can be harsh."

He had walked her to the door and now waited for Pruitt, the Farthingale butler, to open it and allow her in before he left Marigold's side to call for his carriage.

"My time in the Devonshire caves with the duke and duchess, and the Huntsford archeological staff was a marvelous experience. But you are right. Other than that, I've done nothing of note."

"I was not criticizing your inexperience, Miss Farthingale. All I meant is that you have time to achieve your dreams. There is no need for you to rush through life." He caressed her cheek, annoyed with himself for doing so. But she was such a bright, little thing and he had been in a dark pit far too long.

A literal dark pit, imprisoned overseas as he was for years until the Crown negotiated his recent release.

Perhaps this is why Marigold and her sunshine disposition fascinated him.

This girl was the *elysian fields* to him, the paradise where heroes went upon their death. He was still living and breathing, of course. But his soul had died while he was locked away in that enemy dungeon without hope of ever finding freedom again.

Perhaps this is why he felt a sudden ache to kiss her.

Why had he warned her against rushing her life experiences?

Was his own life not a perfect example of why one must seize every moment offered? Four years lost in that purgatory and never to be reclaimed.

He felt the loss acutely.

Pruitt opened the door, bringing an end to their conversation.

Marigold cast him that soft look again. "I shall see you in a few minutes."

He nodded, surprised by how much he was looking forward to it.

Whether the Chipping Way curse held true and he would inevitably marry this girl was another matter entirely, for he was not fit yet to undertake a serious courtship.

Perhaps he would be ready by the time Marigold turned twenty.

He dismissed the notion as he strode across the street to return to his home. The girl was a diamond of the first water and would be taken well before the end of this Season.

The possibility hit him like a punch in the gut.

To his dismay, he wanted her.

His idiotically possessive instincts were taking over and he could not see himself with anyone but this girl.

By all that was sainted.

Had he lost his mind?

It was too soon for him to think seriously about commitment when he could not even trust himself with as simple a chore as getting back into circulation among the *ton* elite.

Besides, he had unfinished business here in London and he dared not drag that innocent girl into his life should matters turn ugly.

No, he was not under any circumstances going to court that ebullient bit of froth by the name of Marigold Farthingale.

But would his heart listen?

GET MARIGOLD AND THE MARQUESS NOW!

Interested in learning more about the Farthingale series? Join me on Facebook! Additionally, we'll be giving away lots of Farthingale swag and prizes during the launches. If you would like to join the fun, you can subscribe to my newsletter and also connect with me on Twitter. You can find links to do all of this at my website: mearaplatt.com.

If you enjoyed this book, I would really appreciate it if you could post a review on the site where you purchased it. Also feel free to write one on Goodreads or other reader sites that you peruse. Even a few sentences on what you thought about the book would be most helpful! If you do leave a review, send me a message on Facebook because I would love to thank you personally. Please also consider telling your friends about the FARTHINGALE SERIES and recommending it to your book clubs.

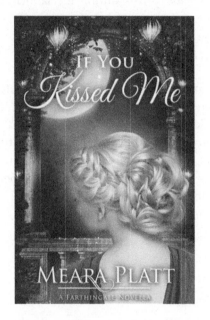

Sign up for Meara Platt's newsletter
and you'll receive a free, exclusive copy
of her Farthingale novella,
If You Kissed Me.

Visit her website
to grab your free copy:
mearaplatt.com

ALSO BY MEARA PLATT

FARTHINGALE SERIES
My Fair Lily
The Duke I'm Going To Marry
Rules For Reforming A Rake
A Midsummer's Kiss
The Viscount's Rose
Earl Of Hearts
The Viscount and the Vicar's Daughter
A Duke for Adela
Marigold and the Marquess
If You Wished For Me
Never Dare A Duke
Capturing The Heart Of A Cameron

MOONSTONE LANDING SERIES
Moonstone Landing (novella)
Moonstone Angel (novella)
The Moonstone Duke
The Moonstone Marquess
The Moonstone Major

THE BOOK OF LOVE SERIES
The Look of Love
The Touch of Love
The Taste of Love
The Song of Love
The Scent of Love

The Kiss of Love
The Chance of Love
The Gift of Love
The Heart of Love
The Promise of Love
The Wonder of Love
The Journey of Love
The Treasure of Love
The Dance of Love
The Miracle of Love
The Hope of Love (novella)
The Dream of Love (novella)
The Remembrance of Love (novella)
All I Want For Christmas (novella)
Tempting Taffy (novella)

DARK GARDENS SERIES
Garden of Shadows
Garden of Light
Garden of Dragons
Garden of Destiny
Garden of Angels

THE BRAYDENS
A Match Made In Duty
Earl of Westcliff
Fortune's Dragon
Earl of Kinross
Aislin
Genalynn
A Rescued Heart
Earl of Alnwick

ABOUT THE AUTHOR

Meara Platt is an award winning, USA TODAY bestselling author and an Amazon UK All-Star. Her favorite place in all the world is England's Lake District, which may not come as a surprise since many of her stories are set in that idyllic landscape, including her paranormal romance Dark Gardens series. Learn more about the Dark Gardens and Meara's lighthearted and humorous Regency romances in her Farthingale series and Book of Love series, or her warmhearted Regency romances in her Braydens series or Moonstone Landing series by visiting her website at www.meara platt.com.